SOLITAIRE

"Gripping... the reader is snared from the beginning. Ashley never disappoints."

Carousel

"A very thought-provoking and crafted work that deserves a wide audience."

Books for Keeps

"A brilliant thriller with an ingenious and completely unexpected early twist, which is bound to keep the reader hooked until the end of the story... complex and exciting."

School Librarian Journal

SOLITAIRE

Bernard Ashley

USBORNE

For Iris, in our special year

Acknowledgements:
I should like to thank Iris Ashley, Marlene Ashley,
Edgar Francis, George Hore, Terry Mott, Jason Warren –
and the Usborne editorial team – for their invaluable help
with *Solitaire*, my twentieth novel.

B.A.

First published in the UK in 2008 by Usborne Publishing Ltd., Usborne
House, 83–85 Saffron Hill, London EC1N 8RT, England. www.usborne.com

First published in 2008. Text copyright © Bernard Ashley, 2008

Cover photography: Helicopter © epa/Corbis. Boat © Gunter Marx
Photography/Corbis. Beach © Sergio Pitamitz/Getty Images.

The name Usborne and the devices ♛ ⊕ are Trade Marks of Usborne
Publishing Ltd.

A CIP catalogue record for this book is available from the British Library.

FMAMJJASOND/10 96185 ISBN 9780746081372

Printed in Yeovil, Somerset, UK.

Part One

AUTHOR'S NOTE

I have invented the African country of Gambellia –
'a mosquito bite out of Tanzania'.
B.A.

Chapter One

'Poor devils! Look at them! That's so *terrible*!' Joseph Lewis jostled against the restaurant window of the cruise ship – staring at the harbour below where sick and injured war victims spread like a wound across the quay. The ship's double glazing cut out the sounds of the suffering, but the sight was grievous. There was no running and shouting like at a car-bomb scene – first aid had been given somewhere beforehand – but women, children and old men crowded pathetically towards the ship: the leaning, the stretchered, and the crutched; a distressing clamour to get to the gangplanks.

The stewards had tried to carry on serving dinner as if the *St. George* was in some sort of parallel universe; but diners with a harbour view had set the general tone.

'I wish I'd started at medical school, I could go down and help.' This voice was Rachel's – Joseph's older sister – who got a frown from her father.

'Best not to get involved. They know what they're doing. We keep out of their way, leave them to it,' Rex Lewis said. 'It's best for them…'

Like watching dramatic news on television, the Neptune Restaurant eyes were riveted on the shuffling war victims. All the wounded were black, but there were white, black and Asian workers among them, presumably medics, one of whom was carrying a legless boy on his shoulders.

'Poor kid!' Joseph said.

A woman leaning over him at the window vigorously shook her head. 'It's their war, you know – their war!'

The *St. George* was berthed in Moebane harbour, on the coast of Gambellia, the East African country – like a mosquito bite out of Tanzania – that had been war-torn for the past year. The stop was not on the ship's schedule, but its small size had allowed it into the harbour. That morning the captain had announced that they were putting-in to respond to an emergency request received from *Médicins Sans Frontières* to take off sick and wounded women and children – victims of the Gambellian civil war – and ferry them to a hospital in Madagascar, a port of call that *was* on the Indian Ocean cruise itinerary. This news had been greeted like the Marylebone Cricket Club announcing that the Second Test had been cancelled at Lord's in order to host a gypsy wedding. Why should a British cruise ship get involved in someone else's war? These Africans were at each other's throats the whole time, why should their tribal conflicts alter civilized people's plans? No one was racist, of course, but what right had this war to spoil someone's holiday? Would people *ever* be able to do anything on the leisure front if a war always had to be accommodated?

But the protests were ignored and the ship's course had been set for Moebane, and in his heart Joseph was looking forward to telling his friends that he'd been to a war zone in the summer holiday – until the reality of those injuries had just hit him. But everything went out of his head when a sudden shattering sound stopped his heart – a devilish screech and a huge explosion.

'Help! They're being bombed!'

'It's a rocket – hit the quay!'

'Get away from the window!'

The shock wave rocked the ship and set it tugging

violently against its moorings. On board there were screams and shouts, plates clattering to the floor, wine spilling, napkins scattering – and people making for the door. The missile had landed in the middle of a line of warehouse sheds, demolishing the corrugated structures in a great flash, shooting debris high into the sky to fall and randomly maim. The quayside lights cut off as war victims and their helpers scattered for cover – running, crawling, limping, carrying and being carried – some waving for help, others lying still and bleeding and vulnerable on the planking of the dock. Fire licked and black smoke billowed as a second explosion rocked the ship and sent a spout of harbour water into the air.

'Help!'

'Get back, get down!' Joseph's father shouted.

'Get *out*!' shrieked Joseph's mother as her husband ran them, doubled over, for the restaurant doors and the further side of the ship. Now stewards ran, too, and the restaurant emptied except for one thin-faced old man in an immaculate dinner jacket who sat shakily lighting a cigarette. The ship's hooter suddenly jumped everyone, and the gangplanks were quickly winched up.

'Don't go below!' Joseph's father shouted. He ran his family to the starboard side of the promenade deck and made them lie flat on the deck in the lee of the ship's superstructure. Beneath them the vessel shuddered and the screws churned astern – as a third rocket screamed in to explode on the dock they were leaving; the ringing in Joseph's ears muting the screaming and the shouting of the war victims – those already on board, and those left in tatters behind.

The *St. George* made good speed out of the small harbour, zigzagging to port, to starboard, to port, to starboard, as two more explosions – one on the dock again and the other in the sea behind – seemed to show the limit of the rockets' range. Cold-faced and staring at each other, the Lewises got to their feet, Rex puffing out his cheeks and trying to hold his family in his arms. Around them passengers called, swore, blamed, and wept.

'I'm sorry...you've seen it...up so close.' Joseph's father sounded very emotional himself. 'But that...is war!' Safe and out of range of the shelling now, he led his family to their suite on the deck below: a superior cabin for himself and his wife, Penny, and two smaller cabins off it – one on either side – for Joseph and Rachel. But the girl hardly got in through the cabin door before she clutched, shaking, at her mother.

'I saw dead people!' she shrieked. '*Dead people! And...a...head!*'

Penny Lewis patted her, tried to calm, poured water – but Rachel was inconsolable, and becoming hysterical. For Joseph, his sister's reaction was his own, acted out. He was shocked, stunned, grasping unbelievingly at what he'd seen. He had seen that head, too – it had rolled, like a coconut on a beach – and he stood there shaking at the memory of another victim lying gory and pulped like a hedgehog on a busy road – which suddenly made him vomit, a quivering victim of war himself.

'I'm sorry, I'm sorry, I'm sorry!' Rex Lewis tried to comfort his family. 'The intelligence must have been so poor – not to know we'd be in rocket range, going in...' He ran Joseph into the big bathroom and switched on the shower, stripping him of his messy shirt. Penny took Rachel into her cabin and tried to persuade her to lie down on her bed. While unbelievably – and very audibly because the cabin doors to the corridor were still open – drifting down from the saloon on the deck above came the sounds of the dance band playing the curtain-up music of *Cabaret Night*. Which told Joseph that the ringing in his ears had ceased – and that the entertainments officer thought the sights and sounds of Moebane should be put behind them.

The sun deck under a starry, tropical night was usually a place for leaning on the ship's rail and clinking glasses carried from the Sundowner Bar. But not tonight. Tonight, the bar was where ice and clean water were available, its fridges quickly stocked with basic medical supplies brought up from the ship's infirmary. And with the creams and antiseptics and antibiotics had come the ship's 'surgeon', Dr. Attlee, and Chris, the male nurse – because the sun deck was now an emergency ward, lit by the moon and arc lamps. All the passenger cabins on the *St. George* were filled, and with crew space overcrowded already, the sun deck was all there was to serve the Gambellian victims – rows of them on sunloungers, lilos, emergency mattresses, ship inspection dinghies, on the planking itself – over which ship's hands were now erecting the awnings they'd taken down in the late afternoon. Two passengers happened to be doctors, another was a retired midwife – otherwise a member of the ship's company on either side of the deck kept the cruise clients away.

The sounds were distressing: a mother whose children had been torn from her on the quayside wailed louder than the excruciation of any war wound; victims screamed as burns were dressed without anaesthetic; people wept, calling names of the missing; and death rattled in a throat on a chaise longue. While in the Starlight Room below, the Flotsam Four feverishly sang and danced to a small audience who must have hoped that the flashing of those long legs would shut out the sight of missing limbs back in Moebane.

Evening became night, the moon dipped away over the horizon, and the *St. George* throbbed its fluorescent wake south-eastwards towards Madagascar. Joseph lay on his bed in his cabin, seeing the scenes again – the flash of that first rocket, the rolling of that cut-off head, the awfulness of the terror when those wounded people were blown apart, hobbling for the ship. The ringing sounded in his ears again as he smelled the pungency of the explosives, and the taste of vomit came back into his mouth. And no matter how hard he tried to find a comfortable position, whatever thoughts he desperately conjured of happier, normal things, his head and his senses failed even for a second to rid him of the shock-horror of that quayside.

So he got up. In his grey boxers and his Marlow Rugby Club shirt and shorts, he slid his feet into his moccasins and quietly went for the door into the corridor. That awful music had stopped, and all he could hear was the sound of the ship's engines. By the night-lighting along the corridor, he made his way cautiously towards the companionway that would take him up to the promenade deck and round to the steps to the sun deck. He belonged to the school Air Cadets, and part of his training was in first aid. He knew how to cleanse and bandage wounds, how to splint a broken limb, and how to take a person's blood pressure – so couldn't he be useful, helping with the war victims? He thought so. But when he finally reached the sun deck his way was barred by a ship's officer.

'I'm sorry, sir, the sun deck's closed to passengers tonight.'

'I'm not a passenger. Well, I am a passenger – but I'm in the Air Cadets and I'm trained in first aid. I thought—'

'That's very kind, sir.' The officer sounded Scottish. 'But we're assured everything fo'rard is under control.' His arms weren't extended, but they looked ready to grab Joseph if he tried to dodge past.

Joseph peered beyond the man, but he could see nothing, just the dispersed glow of the emergency arc lights under the awnings. And there was nothing to be heard from here, only the sound of the *St. George* cutting through a placid sea. And something else. *Was that something else?* As Joseph turned to go back down the companionway he distinctly heard a sound in the sky. The officer must have heard it, too, because his attention wasn't on Joseph any more. Both of them turned to stare up into the night – where they could see nothing, but could clearly hear the sound of a helicopter. It was showing no lights, its approach signalled only by the clacking of its engines and the fanning of its blades.

'Who the deuce is that?'

But someone monitoring the radar on the bridge must have picked up this aircraft and suspected danger – because the ship suddenly veered to starboard.

'Unfriendly!' The officer cursed – and abandoned his post to run for the companionway, skidding down the handrail.

The helicopter was getting closer. Its clatter was frightening. People on the sun deck started shouting and screaming, and now, in the first rays of dawn, Joseph could see the craft: painted in military camouflage, heeling to come alongside the *St. George* about fifty metres out. It jerked to starboard itself, and suddenly the air was filled with the spit of rapid fire from machine guns. Bullets hit all around him, glanced pinging off the thick superstructure, pierced the deck – he saw the spreading splinters. Help – this was real! He threw himself down and curled into a tight ball beneath a lifeboat – and suddenly a blinding flame spurted from the helicopter gunship with a world-ending whoosh, a sheering shriek, and a hell-deep explosion somewhere below the *St. George*'s waterline.

The ship shuddered, rattled in every bolt, its decks leaped, bodies were thrown and skittled, and Joseph was spun aside in the blast; the last thing he saw, a flying spar from the Sundowner Bar.

*

Down in their pitch-black suite, Rex and Penny Lewis were tipped from their bed as if a tidal wave had struck. The cabin tilted violently one way, then the other – before the ship groaned and settled to a forward slope, the place rattling with falling brushes, shoes and toiletries. Rex grabbed at the torch he had hanging by the bed.

Penny shouted for her children; groping at the door to Rachel's cabin, while Rex went for Joseph's. With another lurch, the *St. George* – flooding through the huge hole in its port side – sank forward to an angle which knocked them off their feet and sent them cut and bleeding into Rachel's cabin.

'Joseph! Where's Joe?'

Which were the last bewildered words uttered by any of them. A surge of seawater raced up the slope of the corridor where floor was now wall, bursting through cabin doors as the ship filled with ocean in every cubic millimetre, sending its five-and-a-half-thousand tons down to the ocean floor, two thousand metres below the flotsam of the victims who had been up on its sun deck.

A final berth for cruise luxury.

Chapter Two

The storm tossed him ashore. Without the rage of the sea he might have drifted further on the ocean current – and died of dehydration, or sunstroke, or the sucked belly of starvation. In the bay where the palms danced, devil-frenzied, and the sand was pitted with heavy hits of rain, the sea swung his legs around higher than his head and left him there on the beach, slumped between life and death in that fragile state where things can go this way or that between waves – lying so still that the hole-digging ghost crabs higher up the beach went on with their toil.

Plovers trotted forward and back, pecking on the tide, and flies investigated his moist eyes before leaving him for open mussels. And in and out ran the sea, quietening now, almost timid – while he lay, an exclamation on the beach; or, rather, in the fall of his limbs, a question mark.

A question that was answered by a groan, and a spasm, and a sudden vomit of seawater and bile. The crabs shot to cover as he shaped himself another way on a jigsaw of granite outcrop, like a drunk in a bus station nuzzling hard pillows. Lightning flashed the sky to the sound of distant thunder, but nothing would move him until his body had recovered enough to let consciousness in.

He came-to somewhere else. Sand granules still stuck to his limbs but he was off the beach and lying on squat-leaved grass beneath the shade of a broad tree. His head throbbed to the sea's rhythm, and when he tried to stand it was if he had stepped aboard a bucking raft. The pit of his stomach took a three-sixty degree churn, and he had to grab at the trunk of a tree to stay balanced on the sides of his feet. 'No-ooo-oo!' he croaked out, the world twisting as he gripped. But he clung to his mast until the sea calmed and the raft beneath him stilled – and he could crouch on the ground and clutch his head; while slowly, slowly, slowly, nothing went around any more.

He had a raging thirst. His tongue was swollen and his mouth felt cracked with dryness. He needed water – but where was he? No shirt! What state was he in? He looked down and groaned with the headache of dehydration. There was rough sand down the front of him, grey boxers, bare feet, nothing in his sucked belly – and nothing in his head. Again, *where was he?* And wherever he was, what was he doing there? How had he got to this place? He stood and looked down at himself again, saw every crease, mole and sprigging hair – with no idea in the world where he'd come from.

He had stood to a headache, now he crouched again as it throbbed on. But did any change of position clear his befuddled head? Did it hell! Not that he needed answers right now – there was no one around to explain himself to: this way were trees, bushes and the sound of a bird; that way the roar of the sea. Unsteadily, like learning to walk, he made for the beach: to see there on the sand, wedged between flush patterns of dark rock above the line of the tide, something he seemed to know, something he'd recently known very closely – a small, black, covered dinghy, ripped open on the rock and gasped out. So was that anything to do with him being here?

And where was here, anyway? Was there a village nearby, a town, somewhere to get food and clothes?

He walked up the beach again and came to a small, natural bowl in the granite outcrop, filled with clear water. He dipped in a finger and tasted it. Not salty: it was rain, not sea. Cupping his hands, painfully he drank from it, those first sips like acid as they trickled round his swollen tongue and opened up his throat. The second handful was better, and the third refreshing – but he wouldn't overdo it. Instead, he found some shade and rested until he felt just about good enough to set off along this coast and find some people.

So, which way to go, left or right? From facing the sea he set off to his right. He could see that this part of the coast was a bay, about eighty metres across, with large smooth granite boulders at either end. In this direction there was an obvious passage between two of the boulders, so he headed for it – through there could be a pathway to people. But once he was beyond the boulders the beach disappeared, leaving only smooth rock with waves breaking, and clumps of tall, overhanging trees, fronds of palms with green coconut clusters, and the sudden sight of a nut bobbing in the water like a black head. There was no path, but there was a way. Moving from the sea but keeping it to his left-hand side, he walked between trunks, through clumps, over rotting logs and round steaming, mossy boulders. Ferns were everywhere, though his feet made no complaint at what they trod upon. His soles were as tough as rope.

On he went, pushing through the next spiderweb and round the next rock, certain that the next time he looked up he would see signs of people. But, nothing. Along the coastal way, push was often clamber, and soon he was sheened with sweat. To his left, there was always the sound of the sea, sometimes near, sometimes distant; to his right, trees, flowers, bushes, fruits, with leaf-rot beneath his feet – and rising up way above him an incline of granite boulders and tropical growth.

His eyes smarted with sweat as they strained to focus on the way ahead along the coast. And it was a pleasure when rain began to fall, nothing heavy, but refreshing and short. Still thirsty, he licked the fresh wet off a curve of palm fronds and trekked on, with no idea where he was heading, or towards whom.

The next beach was different from the one he'd left behind. This was shaled in small coral at the nearer end, but as he walked across the sand to cool his feet in the water, the surface was smoother than before; and what came into his head was 'talcum powder'. He pushed on. He didn't know the time, it was just hanging over him – a flat, whitish daylight, but somehow with more the feel of afternoon than morning. This beach was longer than the first one, with a spread of rock-free sand bordered by a line of palm trees curving out seaward for light. It was more open than the first, and he searched the wideness of the sea for signs of boats – but there was nothing to be seen; nothing but sea. Waves broke on a reef a hundred metres out, and closer-by the shallows were patched dark with weed and spiny sea urchins. Paddling was nowhere in his mind, though; what was driving him was *help* – someone to tell him where he was.

He left the beach and searched on beyond. However big this country was, somewhere it had to have a town, a community, and – come on! – some *people*. So it was push onward. His way led him inland again, and uphill – hands and feet time, pulling himself up by tree trunks, clambering over greened rocks, slipping on wet leaves – taking him through a rainforest, just the odd bird calling, and silken webs where rainwater dripping off the leaves alerted small spiders. At first he'd stopped to clear them with a chop, but now he crashed on, regardless.

And a new, terrifying thought suddenly churned him. Here he was, trekking noisily on – but what if this was hostile territory? What if right now he was being tracked and lined up for an attack? Which was crazy thinking! Why should anyone want to hunt him down? He wasn't much of a threat in his boxers. And, anyhow, wouldn't they have done it by now? He went on, still climbing the only way to go, up and from the sea, until the net of light at the tops of the trees told him he was coming to some sort of summit – with a great hope of a good view. From the peak he might see dwellings, and roads, a way to go for help. *Please!*

But the summit was more than a kilometre off through difficult terrain – and when he got there, step by slippery step, the view was totally hemmed in by cloud, clinging around his shoulders like a wet sheet. He could still hear the sea somewhere below him, nearer again now, but going down would be trickier than the climb up. A slip on sodden ground and a twisted ankle would leave him helpless up here. He needed a walking stave, but he could see nothing promising: the fallen boughs were rotten and the bamboo was hollow. Yet after a good search into denser growth he came across a tree with a likely branch the thickness of a walking stick. He set to and bent the green wood over, twisting it backwards, forwards, sideways – until finally he broke it free and snapped off the leafy end, gripping the stave firmly as a third leg to help him down through the rotting leaves to where the sea sounded close again.

Was he still going in the same direction? Well, how was he to know? The sun was hiding away, but by going for the light and the louder sea, he came through the final fringe of forest to open land. Civilized, purposefully cleared, open land. 'Great!' he shouted, and shocked himself with the sound of his voice. In front of him was a concreted area about the size of a tennis court, except that it was square, not rectangular. This was different from the surface so far, this was man-made, the sort of place where people lived. And on the further side of the concrete oblong, set off some way along a narrow path, was a lowish building with a corrugated iron roof. He ran to it, but cautiously, a run that could suddenly swing him back the way he'd come and take him legging for the cover of the trees. 'Hi!' he shouted. 'Anyone about?'

Too low for living in, this building had a wooden door but no windows. He put his head inside like a cautious cat. What would he see – signs of people, or of an animal? But it was empty, apart from a tall drum smelling of fuel. Outside again, now he saw where a branch of the concrete path led to a wire-fenced garden with a gate about fifty metres away. But the gate had a lock on it, and it wasn't a garden, nothing grew in it, there was just a slatted wooden sort of kennel in the middle, with a sloping roof and a small padlocked door. What on earth was this? And then his eye went to a wire running from the compound to a tall pole, on the top of which was – nothing! He took a close look at the rusty lock and the spiderwebs that bound the gate to the rest of the fence; and he puffed out his cheeks in disappointment. This wasn't a place anyone visited every day. Nor every week. Nor... And there by the gate to the compound he hunkered down and held his head in his hands. This was not good! This was so heavily *not good*. Because this place needn't even be visited every month, or every year!

So what could he do except press on? He walked beyond the concrete compound and into the soft scrub again, still keeping the sound of the sea to his left, still going in the same forward direction. But this scrub was all that there was: there were smaller shrubs and it was more grassed, so less strenuous to push through, with sweet smells and – *thud!*

What was that? He was being followed! Had someone jumped down from out of a tree! Had a wild animal landed? He swung about him in panic – to see a shining yellowy-brown coconut rolling down a slight slope towards him. *Coconut* – not a man, not a hunter; but a lesson that in terrain like this, as well as your stare ahead you needed eyes for your footing and eyes above you for the monster of all nuts that could drop down and fracture your skull.

What seemed to be the natural way ahead now moved him nearer to sea level again, where he could see more of the hard rock that formed this land. *Granite?* He was coming to another beach. Well, who knew? This beach might have people on it...

Or not!

He rounded a high, rough outcrop, ten times taller than he was, and squeezed down through a crack to more boulders, worked smooth at their lower levels where the sea had changed them. Now he was on the beach. But what was that? There ahead on the sand and flat granite lay a washed-up creature – which could be a large seal, black and shiny. Cautiously he went towards it – it could still have attack left in it, a goring or a tusking for a nosy land kid – when it suddenly flapped. He jumped. A fin? A limb? No, a small gust up the beach had just puffed up what it was, what it had been: a black, punctured, rubber dinghy.

He had been here before.

'*What?*' He was on the beach he'd started from. He'd kept the sea to his left throughout his trek for help – but he'd not been travelling consistently either to the north or to the south, but to west and east as well. He had trekked full circle, like a lost soul in the Sahara. Which, by never losing the sound of the sea, told him only one thing: he was on an island. An island which seemed uninhabited.

So was this island the place where he belonged?

Chapter Three

Michael Symonds OBE sat in the back of his company Jaguar XK while his driver negotiated the right turn into Church Road, Little Fletching, in Buckinghamshire. Just short of five hundred metres along the road they came to the grassy churchyard of St. John the Baptist – where the car made a five-point turn, while Michael Symonds, broad-shouldered with cropped grey hair, marched around the flinted church towards the newer gravestones. But as soon as he was out of sight of his car he slowed. Everyone in his company knew his grief, but no one was allowed to talk about it, and no one was ever allowed to see him in distress. Which, with his good-natured humour, he never made difficult for them.

He passed the grave of his wife – *Margaret Symonds, née Evans, aged 57: too soon* – and tipped her a little salute before walking on to the newly chiselled gravestone which stood erect in the turf. He stood parade-still as he read it.

Penelope Lewis (42)
Rex Lewis (45)
Rachel Lewis (16)

Mourned by a loving father
and grandfather

He took in a huge breath that caught in his throat. He hadn't brought flowers. *He* was there – and he knew he was there, and his belief meant that those he mourned also knew he was there.

The Reverend Felicity Bennett gave him time to pay his respects. She had watched him from the vestry and timed her solace carefully. Just as the man turned away from the tombstone, she arrived at his side.

'Mike...'

'Fliss...'

'How are you?'

'Not so bad, considering...' He smiled. 'You all right?' He waved an arm around the churchyard. 'Keeping this lot in order?'

The Reverend Bennett laughed. 'I leave that to a higher authority!' They started walking back towards the church. 'I just happen to have made a pot of tea, too big for one, really...'

'Tea bags, Fliss, cut out the waste. Look at the specification and trim the margins. But if you've got a spare cup...' She had been a great strength to him over the past five years: helping him through the death of his wife, and now the deaths of his daughter and granddaughter. They had shared many cups of tea, and a good few confidences.

A few minutes later they were sitting on either side of her desk in the vestry, each with that look on their face that said drinking tea wasn't the real purpose of this tête-à-tête.

'I'm thinking of *closure*,' Fliss said.

'What, the east door, the church, the grounds? Shut down and put it all up for development?'

She laughed, then went serious again. '*Your* closure, Mike.'

'How, my closure?' But he sipped at his cooling tea as if it were scalding his lips.

'The empty space on the tombstone. Isn't it time to fill it in, don't you think? Give Joseph his rest? The others aren't actually there, the parish records show that; Joseph doesn't have to be there, either...'

Mike Symonds put down his cup and placed his hands in his lap. Now his eyes welled with tears, because Fliss was a vicar and people could show grief before her; but he drew in a deep breath as if to keep his voice from cracking up. 'Fliss, they found the others; they couldn't get at them, but they used the most sophisticated equipment to identify three bodies in that cabin, and only three. One of the survivors, a ship's officer, said that a boy had gone up to the sun deck and told him he was an Air Cadet. That boy was my Joseph.' He nodded, confirmation for the vicar, reaffirmation for himself. 'Some of the survivors from the sun deck were picked up miles away on the current. Some inflatables and wooden loungers fetched up on the African coast. And Africa's a very big place.'

'But what are the chances – so long after...?'

Mike Symonds stood up. 'Every chance. He could be wandering, or taken into a community, or trying to make his way back – he's a spirited lad. They came to the house and took his DNA, and until I know, I'm not having Joseph recorded as dead – I won't have his name inscribed until I have proof of his death.' He suddenly laughed. 'Why now? You're not paid by the word, are you?'

Fliss shrieked – shocked and amused. Mike Symonds was an extraordinary man. 'I am *not* – although the stonemason is! It's for you. Mike…closure means closing a chapter and moving on.'

Mike smiled. 'But I happen to like long chapters, and trilogies, and I especially like sequels.' He opened his arms. 'And where do I move on to? What's next for me? I had a good career in the army and now I'm a very successful businessman. I don't have any dragons to slay…'

'You have one soul to put to rest.'

Mike Symonds coughed. 'Which is where we part company. Because we shan't be filling in that space on my daughter's and my granddaughter's headstone until I am satisfied that it's cast-iron right to do so.'

Fliss Bennett had stood, too. Now she took Mike Symonds's hand and patted the back of it. She was going to say something else, but he interrupted her.

'But I'll put the request in my will. I promise. I'll call in my solicitor and do it today. When I go to my rest, if Joseph hasn't been found by then, his name can be inscribed.' Now, somehow, he twinkled: 'But I've got a feeling, a strong feeling, Fliss, that the rest of the chapter has yet to be written...'

And with the straight face of a soldier denying emotion, he squared his shoulders and walked briskly back to his waiting car.

Man needs food, shelter, and deep sleep to survive; and with food goes water. The boy was both hungry and thirsty; but first he wanted to sort out where he'd sleep. He needed shelter; not so much from the weather as from the animal world. Large bats were beginning to circle, and the hunters of the night would soon be coming out. The trees, shrubs and long grasses, the cracks and holes, the leaf mould and the canopy – the whole island harboured the things that could come out to harm him: the whistles and croaks and the squeals told him so.

Which included humans! He'd seen no footprints in the sand, no signs of trails or paths; but there could easily be humans on this island, and not the sort he'd first looked for. They could be living somewhere in the dense interior – watching him. Watching him right now! He suddenly crouched low on the sand and looked all around in two urgent sweeps. The trees were still, most of the cloud had cleared, and somewhere on the other side of the island there was a sunset, the seep of it was in the sky like blood on a bandage. He shivered.

The hut! That would be the place. He could tip over that fuel drum and roll it against the door to keep it shut against everything bigger than a mouse. The thought – and the action. He jumped to his feet and headed off before he lost the light, because he'd get nowhere in pitch darkness. He left the beach and went back the way he thought he'd come – looking for signs that he was on the right track. Had he passed this clump, had he seen that mossy boulder before? Until, there it was: the garden that wasn't a garden and the small hut with the whiff of fuel coming from it – and still enough light in the sky for him to see the interior. It was a big drum, and when he rapped its side it sounded full. It would take a huge push to tip it over, and what if it rolled and trapped his leg or his arm beneath it? And what if he got the drum across the door and couldn't pull it away? He could be trapped in here until someone eventually came and found his skeleton. Or didn't! Ever! So he left the drum where it was. In any case, the door to the hut fitted quite well, so he wedged it tight with the end of his stave and went to the furthest corner of the small space where he hunched himself down, chafing his back on the grey block wall. Like that he sat listening to the sway of trees, the thud of a falling coconut, the squeaking of bats and the squeal of something being killed – until finally his head dropped on his chest, and, knocked out as if he had been darted with a tranquillizer, he slipped sideways, and slept.

A first crack of daylight slid a few centimetres under the wedged door; otherwise the hut was so dark that he slept on, curled up with his head resting on an arm. But after hours of cloudless sunshine the wet heat of the day made an oven of the hut and he woke up sweating – back to the concrete reality of where he was.

Which was *where*? He prised his stave from the door and opened it to the scorch of the high sun – suddenly knowing how he had come to be where he was right now, remembering everything of yesterday's trek around the island. But he still had nothing in his head from before he'd found himself near that beach with the rubber dinghy. But, like the previous night, urgent needs made him think forwards. And this instant he urgently needed to pee, after which he needed food – his stomach was growling at him like an angry animal. He made for the door, but some basic human instinct turned him back to check on the place he was leaving. And a shudder shot through him as he saw what was on the concrete floor, there in the corner where he'd slept – a giant centipede about twenty centimetres long, lying with its front end flattened where he'd rolled on it in the night, its scarlet legs working slowly in its death throes. He shot into the open, jigging frantically, checking his boxers and the backs of his legs. But he'd been lucky – he hadn't been bitten. One thing was for sure, though…he wouldn't sleep in that hut again; he'd find some place nearer the sea, below the vegetation line.

Now he was nearly wetting himself. In a civilized way he faced away from the compound and peed against a tree, before setting off in search of food and drink. But there was no easy water; the sun had dried all the leaves, which meant the granite puddle down near the beach would be dried out, too – and at the frightening thought of dying of thirst, a sudden shiver gripped his body and sent his heart racing, his breathing shallow and difficult, perspiration suddenly springing all over his skin. His brain spun round in his skull – so he crouched before he fell; hunkering there till the dizziness slowly cleared, and the vertigo feelings in his stomach went away. He *wouldn't* die of thirst and he wouldn't starve – he would crack a coconut on a rock for food and he would drink from it. The inside of a coconut was liquid – although, could people live long without water? What if it didn't rain again for six months?

He was suddenly on his feet. *Six months?* What stupid thinking was that? Of course it would rain again soon, look at this lush vegetation. Meanwhile, he knew what he had to do. He had to investigate the interior. He'd trekked around the outside of the island, now he had to search across it. He had to find food and water. He looked up at the sun. It was overhead, which was a good marker, because he could reckon it was midday. The night before, when he'd seen the sunset sky, it had been over there to his right – which had to be west – so facing the interior of the island right now he was facing north-west. Which meant that coming back to this point meant heading east, the sun to his left; although how was he ever going to get lost? He only had to head for the sounds of the sea and follow the coast to get around to where he'd want to be by nightfall – the granite boulder beach.

He took his stave, the nearest thing he had to a friend, and set off inland, to the south. It was dense terrain, all leaf mould and reddish earth underfoot, still wet from yesterday's storm, scattered with granite rocks of all sizes. In places, a wild network of dead foliage spread itself, with fallen fronds of bamboo interwoven in it: and sudden flashes of scarlet took his eye – bright little birds flying in like handfuls of flame to land on a tree hung with purplish fruits. He watched one as it pecked at the dropped fruit on the rainforest floor, and his stomach growled at him again. If the fruit didn't kill a bird, might it kill him? Well, he wouldn't take a chance – not so soon. He'd hardly started his trek inland, there might be other food; and he always had coconut to fall back on. But, what was this? Climbing further – it was mostly uphill with a thickish canopy of branch and leaf overhead, foliage all around – he came through a clump of undergrowth to the foot of a stark granite crag that rose high above him, and there was a small pool spread beneath, about three metres by four. Its surface was covered in weed, and he might have stepped into the green of it but for a sudden movement and a *plip* as something dived for cover.

He crouched at the edge. This couldn't just be rainwater from the storm, the weed wouldn't have grown over it since yesterday. And it couldn't be seawater, either, not up here. So, what was it? It didn't smell stagnant, so could it be a run-out from the crag above? Carefully, he scooped the weed aside to reveal clear water beneath; and with his other hand he cupped up a mouthful: studied it, sniffed at it, and very, very, cautiously he dipped the tip of his tongue into it. And it tasted of…water! Fresh cool water: his hand going into the pool had felt a drop in temperature from the humid rainforest around him. And when he looked to the far side of it he saw a clear channel where water was trickling out – no tropical waterfall, but a small, steady flow. He'd come across a spring – and there should easily be enough in here to last one person between rains. Now, clearing more weed, his first thought was to step into it and wash all over, get rid of the concrete dust, the mud, and the dried sweat. But he stopped himself. You didn't wash where you drank. The sea – useless for drinking – would be the place for washing. So he cupped again, and scooped, and drank his fill, standing up with the satisfaction of feeling satisfaction.

He looked back to the way he'd come. Would he remember the directions to this place? Was there a tree or a boulder with any sort of memorable mark that would point him here? There wasn't – but the island wasn't big. He'd definitely be able to track down the pool before he died of thirst. He looked all around him – and suddenly shouted, 'Yes!' He was going to live! This spring was a real find. He had coconuts and water to keep him alive: he was going to be all right. And in that moment he suddenly realized something else. He didn't feel afraid. Visions of hunters hadn't come into his head; nor had any dark fears of animal attack; that had all been night-time stuff. Rats, scorpions, giant centipedes, spiteful insects, yes – he'd got to be very careful; but even with those dangers, here in the calm of his island, even away from the sound of the sea, he had the very strong feeling of being at home.

He headed on, going gradually south-west, downhill now, relying more on his stave. This course should bring him out somewhere near the second beach he'd come to yesterday. And if it did, he would backtrack for another drink at the spring, and head the other way, north for the boulder beach – because he had something he wanted to check out there; no, something he *must* check out before dusk.

And he was right about his directions. Descending towards the gentle sounds of the sea, he pushed through fresh undergrowth, old and new bamboo, hardwood, and more of those purplish fruit trees the scarlet birds liked. And to the side, in front of him, was a mossy rock with a rough scuff of clear granite showing through, definitely a handhold; and he reckoned it had been his. He turned onto the same trail but eastwards, and pushed on down to that beach where the sand was coral at one end and fine at the other, like talcum.

Which was when he realized that he was talking to himself. 'So here we are at Talcum Bay,' he was saying. 'Right! I was right, my friend!'

'My friend'! He snorted. That would be his stave, there was no one else; and straight off, he turned and went searching for a fallen coconut. Food, to keep him alive before he sorted any other basic need.

Chapter Four

The Lewis family house in Marlow was a short walk from the station, which had always been handy for Joseph's father on his journey to the Ministry of Defence each day. It had been handy for Joseph's mother, too, just a short distance from the M40 and the M25, which made driving to her gift-shop chain fairly easy. While Rachel and Joseph had cycled to King Henry High without breaking sweat.

But today, like every day, The Beeches was empty of life. The CCTV cameras still swivelled, the exterior lights would come on if a fox sniffed through, and the buzzer at the front gate still had a small yellow light glowing behind the touch pad. The house hadn't changed since the family had left for their Indian Ocean cruise on the *St. George*.

Today Mike Symonds was alone in his blaze-red Chrysler Crossfire Roadster. He stopped on the concrete run-in to the gate and pointed his remote control at the sensor in the brickwork. As if moved by ghostly hands, the gate swung open and he drove to the front door, and with a look up at the sky, left the car's soft top down. He pulled the house keys from his pocket, looked at them, and suddenly ripped off the cheap cardboard tag that read *Penny*. It looked too much like the ID an undertaker would tie to a toe.

The place was kept clean, he saw to that. A local couple went in to attend to the house and garden, ensuring that everything was as it had been when the family left to go to Heathrow; internal doors open, window curtains apart but not fully, blinds half down – what his daughter used to call 'in-but-out'. As he opened the door the alarm buzzed, sending him to the concealed panel to tap in the entry code.

It was as if the family had gone to the pictures; the doors on the stereo cabinet were open, and a *Radio Times* was slung on a sofa, always that week's edition. Dust sheets resembled shrouds, and when Joseph came back, the house – *his* house now – was going to look up-and-running. Joseph wouldn't live here alone – he'd move in with Mike – but the Lewis family home was always going to be the Lewis family home; because Mike was not going to accept that his grandson was dead.

After the attack on the *St. George* and a catastrophic explosion in the ship's hold, the vessel had sunk in minutes. But using shipyard diagrams and the cruise line's copy of cabin allocations, the most modern search-and-rescue diving techniques had satisfied him beyond all reasonable doubt that the three bodies seen through the portholes in the Churchill Suite were Penny, Rex and Rachel Lewis. But not Joseph. Joseph wasn't with them. Night-vision equipment showed that he wasn't anywhere in the suite – and there was the inquest evidence of the ship's officer who described a boy like Joseph up on the sun deck just before the gunship attack. And others on that deck had been found alive – casualties of the Gambellian civil war picked up from the sea, clinging to floating debris and inflatables, with two Africans on a life raft beaching on Platte, an outer island of the Seychelles. Plus, a *Médicins Sans Frontières* doctor and an injured refugee had made it back to Gambellia in a ship's dinghy, speaking of others in the water drifting away on planking and loungers and in the maintenance dinghies used as emergency beds.

Meanwhile, the identified white bodies did not include Joseph Lewis: he wasn't found inside the ship and his body wasn't floating in the water; so shutting his mind to sharks, Mike Symonds reckoned there was every chance that his grandson was alive somewhere. The world is a big place, and the Indian Ocean is a big part of it. He still kept hope alive that Joseph was living some kind of life with a remote people somewhere, or was avoiding wars and tribal conflicts to make his way back to civilization. And one thing was certain – with the slightest glimmer of a sighting, Mike would move heaven and earth to reach out to him.

He shouldn't do it, but he could never not. He walked up the broad staircase to Joseph's room and went inside. He drew in a deep breath and looked around. This was Joseph's room on a good day – no socks on the floor, no console games scattered, no hair-gelled dents in the pillow, no clothes over backs of chairs, no standby light glowing from the computer with its flight simulator joystick, no puffy canvas laundry bag with yesterday's clothes in it. Folded on his pillow were Joseph's Marlow Rugby Club shorts and shirt, the swan badge prominent against its deep blue background; the nearest he ever got to wearing pyjamas. The summer sunshine shone in through the window and showed up the dust falling onto the recently steam-cleaned carpet. He came out again, and went along to Rachel's room. Here her death had been acknowledged; her room had been cleared, now looking like a guest room in a good hotel. The only personal item was a chalk and charcoal portrait of her done when she was fourteen. Now Mike wept. There was a presence in Joseph's room; there was only a memory in here – of a loving granddaughter who'd laughed at his choice of clothes and at the shape of his ears. *Bat*, she'd called him – and she'd told her friends he found his way by radar.

Choked, Mike went downstairs. He had never gone into the master bedroom, and he never would – that had been *theirs*, Penny's and Rex's; Mike's assistant, Diana Lucky, had come one afternoon to clear it, quietly leaving watches and jewellery from the bedside drawers in a briefcase on Mike's desk. Now he checked the fridge, humming as it kept a pack of Coke cans cold for a thirsty kid coming in one day. And having done that, he left hurriedly, just remembering to set the burglar alarm – whose code was based on Joseph's birthday.

The date of birthdays past, and, Mike was adamant, the date of birthdays to come.

Hunger came first. A wash in the sea would be good – sweat and concrete dust had made him itchy – but his stomach was angrily rolling its emptiness. Coconuts take some splitting, though. What he needed was something sharp for piercing one of the 'eyes' so as to drain out the water, then something heavy to hit it with – or a hard rock to thump it on. Well, a hard rock was no problem, the island was strewn with them. And the coconut he'd got seemed about right; it didn't look a recent fall and the outer husk was easy to pull off. But, something sharp? What was there around that could poke and pierce?

He walked along the shoreline and looked for long thin stones; but there was nothing. He went up into the vegetation and searched for anything else that might do; but not even hardwood would be strong enough, even if he could find a spiky piece; pretty much anything growing would snap before it could pierce a coconut eye. So, do the other thing – go without! Okay, emptying the water would have made the coconut hollow and easier to smash, but a bit of muscle could crack it with a mighty blow, couldn't it?

His anvil was there to the side of the beach – a flattish rock with a dip in the top. These rock cavities were all over, as if the whole place had been hit at some time by a meteorite shower. He laid the coconut in this small granite basin and went looking for something to hit it with. But finding the right hammer wasn't so easy after all.

The granite on the beach 'grew' there, it wasn't loose, which took him up into the scrub again. But when he tugged at likely pieces of rock, they were rooted just as fast. He scraped, he uncovered, he pushed and pulled – and then, poking around, what was that over there?

In a small clearing he found something that stood him up straight, had him twisting over his shoulder as if there might be ghosts about. It was a half-buried wall, a greened-over, shrub-entangled ruin of a building, about four metres by five, a hundred years disused by the looks of it. The wall was built of granite rock, and held together – where it *was* still held together – by cracked, dried mud. And on an earthy patch in the middle of it he saw fresh droppings. He bent to them. They were greyish, dry but not mildewed, clinging together in small piles. Sheep! Or goats! Please God, they weren't boar – although he guessed boar droppings would be bigger, like pig.

So! *People – once upon a time!* The first signs of living – apart from that concrete place where he'd slept – an olden-time shack with fresh droppings. '*Goats' milk!*' he said to himself; if he was lucky... And 'milk' brought him back to his search for a rock to smash a coconut. Well, that was easy now; he had a ready-made supply right here in the wall. He chose a smallish piece that fitted the contours of his palm, felt as if it belonged; and clutching it he reckoned he'd got another friend to go with his stave. A tool.

And friend it was. With the coconut sitting snug and ready in the basin, he lifted the rock high over his head and brought it down with everything he'd got. Smash! The coconut shell split into a dozen pieces, clung all over with white 'meat', its water spurting and spilling. 'Yesss!' he yelled, and tooth and nail he set about the food. Never mind the shell scratching his face, the gorging of the 'meat' silenced his empty belly. And, as if he had conquered the world and not just a coconut, he yelped and danced on the sand like a toddler, gave the island the present of an almighty burp, and ran splashing into the sea – for a wash, and a cooling swim.

He found goat; but not till after he'd found his bed for the night, his main reason for coming to this beach. His sleep might not be deep, but he reckoned he could do without an unwelcome bite in the boxers. Near the top of the beach there were two five-metre-high granite boulders set very close to one another, above the tidal mark but below the vegetation line; and – thank you very much! – in the dark crevice where they almost touched ran a ledge like a bunk, carved into one boulder and overhung by the other, dry and sheltered. It would take some climbing on to –

a few of the bigger rocks from the wall would need to come down here for steps – but what a great place to sleep! No crab could climb to it, and the chances of a scorpion down here were zero. All it needed was something to soften it for comfort.

His boxers still drying on him, he went searching along the shore for bedding, gathering handfuls of the softest ferns and rushes and washing them in the sea to free them of insects and larvae, spreading them to dry on a hot rock. Only now, pleased with his bit of home-building, did he set off to find those goats. At any rate, he thought they'd be goats, not sheep, because as milking animals goats were more likely to have been kept.

Listening did the trick. All the signs the day before said there'd been a recent storm, so maybe he hadn't heard the goats because they'd been sheltering. But today, with the sea very quiet and hardly a riffle in the trees, with the sun poking hot fingers through the foliage, the island seemed to have the calm of a normal, natural life. If there were goats, he'd hear them today. He had explored the island going right all the time yesterday; now he set off to the left, across a corner that would eventually take him back to the sea again. And with basic needs just satisfied, instead of looking for water or food, he used his ears, listened to birds calling – the *'chirrup'* of one of those red flashes, the *'kraa'* and the *'whoop'* of other species he couldn't see – picking his way over boulders, through dense bamboo, stepping over a burdened trail of black ants, making a deviation round the web of a large black and yellow spider, till, stopping to wipe an arm across his brow, his ears still pricked, suddenly he heard it. The sound of a bleating goat: definitely the sound of a goat, coming from his right, on the seaward side. He crept slowly on, choosing each footstep so as not to crack a twig, skinning past every bush so as not to swish the leaves. And pushing through a dense thicket of palms, he was brought up short by the sight of the creature he had heard. Which was no nanny! Standing in front of him was a huge male goat, a metre tall, with two wicked-looking horns that curled and pointed forwards – lethal if it charged. It raised its head at the movement in the thicket. It was eating the fallen fruits from one of those trees the red birds liked, which it left to stare towards him, hostile, ears cocked beneath its sharp horns. He caught his breath, stood as still as he could, off balance. The buck went on staring at him, prehistorically fierce in its long, straggly black coat, taking an age before it shook its head wildly – *was it going to charge?* – and finally went back to its fruits.

There was only one thing to do – back off. If there were milking goats around, they weren't anywhere near this solitary male, eating beneath the tree as if this was *its* island – pawing its determination to defend its territory. Milk would be good to have, squirted fresh from a teat direct into his mouth – but not any more, not if this creature wasn't going to let it happen.

...Thoughts which brought on a fresh thirst. Sliding away from the buck, he tracked back to the ruins of the old shack and went off in the general direction of the spring. It had to be trial and error, there were no trails on the island, but he knew he had to go mainly uphill – the spring had been on higher ground – and he had to look carefully at the boulders and the trees. He needed to tell this tree from that similar tree, this rounded rock from that lookalike. And after a few false trails, by calling up what he'd seen yesterday and this morning, he eventually climbed to find his fresh water, the weed-covered spring that was going to help to keep him alive.

He cleared just enough of its surface to drink, and he drank, and drank. And he started to plan. It was crazy to trek up here every time he wanted a drink. What he needed was something for carrying fresh water back to the place where he would sleep – the space between those huge boulders on the beach. So, what could he use to do that? Well, all he could think of was coconut again. If next time he could split a shell in two instead of twelve he'd have a pretty handy vessel, wouldn't he?

He headed back for Talcum Bay. The track he took was familiar now, swinging back down the hill with his stave. Okay, he'd give that buck its space, but otherwise this place felt like his, where he belonged. He'd survived yesterday, and he'd survived a morning today; he'd eaten, and drunk, and explored; and already he was thinking of improvements to his situation. So he was at home. And in that contented frame of mind, something that he skirted on the downward path threw an idea up at him, and with it a sudden new excitement. It was a mud-filled hollow, still moist with the rain from the day before, which he could jump or go around; but, instead, he bent to the heavy red soil and dug his fingers into it, dredging up a handful. It was soft and smooth, and so satisfying to feel, that instead of throwing it back he began moulding it. A few handfuls of this, and he could make himself a mug! A few handfuls more, and he'd have a pot – a clay pot, to fire on a rock in the heat of the sun...

'That's what we'll do!' he said to the island. He nodded, and smiled. Now he had his stave, and his tool, and next would be – a pot. 'Yes!' he yelled – his sudden shout sending a pair of pigeons flapping from the bush. He scooped up as much mud as he could carry and took it to his beach – the start of an afternoon spent making journeys to the mud and fetching enough for him to sit and pot in the shade of a boulder, where a breeze off the ocean kept the temperature pleasant. Satisfied. Content. No, *happy*. What more could a guy ask for?

The pot was not the best he'd ever make, he reckoned – it was very much a first effort – but keeping the slip wet was easy with the sea so close, and he managed to give his pot fairly even sides and a flat bottom, working on it until he had something to put out to bake – for which he went up off the beach and onto a ridge where the sun was at its hottest. His legs, his belly, his boxers, his arms and hands were all mud by now, and when the pot had been put on its rock shelf, he ran back to the beach and into the sea with a mighty splash, revelling in its cool cleansing. And now, with his work done, he took his recreation: he swam. Keeping well in touch with the shore he swam north-south, parallel with the land, until the furthest point of land he could see was a high, rocky promontory, where he stopped. But the current was so strong coming back south that swimming his hardest he stayed more or less where he was, in line with a tall hardwood tree he was using as a marker. *Help!* He'd gone further than he should, and that was a vital lesson learned. If he was swept off in the current there'd be no getting back to his island; he'd be taken out into the ocean on a long drift of death;

so he'd be cautious, forever cautious, in the sea. For now, he swam in till his feet touched bottom.

But no experience was wasted; because when he waded waist-deep in the shallows, what were all around him, darting between his legs if he stood still, flicking swiftly away when he made a sudden move? Small fish; silvery grey, about ten centimetres long. So could he catch some and grill them on a hot, noonday rock alongside his pottery? And could a rock get that hot? Whatever, he'd need to catch them first – meanwhile, he was getting hungry again, and the one thing he could count on was coconut. So, coconut it would be, for tea, or supper, or whatever he wanted to call it. *Grub-time!* anyhow.

He went inland and rooted about for another fallen husk; and with more sweat and effort, he attacked this second coconut, smashing down his rock, then eating again; but slower this time, sitting cross-legged, looking out at the ocean as if he were dining, not feeding.

And, differently from the day before, not looking for anything out there on the vast open space that might bring people.

Chapter Five

He didn't get to sleep for ages. He lay awake discovering that, while it was flat enough not to roll him off, this granite ledge was no foam mattress. The bedding he'd brought wasn't nearly thick enough – his body compressed it to a hard pallet within minutes; and something to have on top of him wouldn't be a bad idea. The night wasn't very cold, but a cover gives comfort as well as warmth.

And then there were the noises of the night, although not close or threatening: the clacking of crabs as they mated, shell upon shell, the sudden rainforest squeal of death, and the constant roar of the sea as it came across the reef. While running through his brain were thoughts of the day just gone, and plans for the future. He turned on his side, his arm under his head for a pillow: he stupidly hadn't thought about a pillow; he'd do something about that. And that black rubber dinghy over on the other beach might have its uses: it could be his cover, for a start. If he took it up to the fenced concrete area he could tear it on an upright, and – *great idea!* – he could use some of it to carry water in, couldn't he?

Eventually, in the dark middle of the tropical night he lost consciousness and slept deeply till dawn, unbitten by centipede or mosquito – because a bonus was the place being mozzie-free, even at the fresh water. His beach was on the morning-shadowed west side, and his ledge was overhung by the other giant boulder, so it wasn't the light in the sky that awoke him. It was the urgent need to go to the lavatory; and not just for a pee. Those coconut meals had woken up his digestive workings; and while some calls of nature can be put on hold, others demand immediate action – and this was one of those. In fact, he thought he might be too late already! *Shame, boy, shame!* Jumping from his ledge he had to made a quick decision. Which way to go? Land or sea? Up in the rainforest he'd attract flies – he hadn't found a digging tool yet, plus to clean himself he'd need the right sort of leaves. But the sea was vast, with a good current running along the shoreline, a natural flow to carry stuff away. So the sea was favourite. Quickly, he slipped out of his boxers, left them on a rock and ran into the water, where he let the current drift him down and along from his beach, until, when he reckoned the distance was right, he braced himself against the ocean flow, crouched low in the water, turned himself away from the rest of the world and opened his bowels. *Aaah!* And when he'd finished he cleaned himself thoroughly. Then he took a few strokes back against the current and, well clear of what he'd just done, he washed his head, his face, his hands and torso, before swimming hard for the beach again.

It took him a while, and it exhausted him, enough to have to lean against a rock to dry off before dressing. *Dressing!* Putting on a pair of underpants! But it wasn't his modesty he was protecting; tender parts have to be shielded from thorns and whippy branches! Now, hungry and thirsty, he went to the pot on its baking rock; but it still hadn't dried out. Its colour had changed to something lighter, it had lost its sheen and looked smaller and less finished than yesterday – not at all the pottery object he'd seen in his head. And were those cracks creeping up the inside? Whatever, with or without the pot, a drink meant going up to the spring, because the sky was bright and dry

– there'd be no rainfall on leaves. And as for food first, well, what was that he'd seen when he'd drifted down from the beach with the current? What had he spotted from the sea as he crouched? *Bananas!* Up on a wooded slope he'd seen some small, hanging, green and yellow bunches, which would be a different taste from coconut, and a whole lot easier to get into. The tree had to be in a strip of land somewhere north of here, so to find them he'd head in the same direction as that first day, but strike off at some point to get nearer to the sea. He grabbed his stave and set off in what he reckoned to be the right direction, pushing his way through the same rocky, grassy, spiderwebbed undergrowth that he'd pushed through before, but with everything drier today, the slippery mud already turning to firm footing again. And when he thought he'd walked as far as he'd drifted on the current – which was hard to tell – he turned towards the sea.

It was another climb. The island seemed to have several peaks, and this was the nearest – and the steepest, as he heard the sound of breaking waves below. But he was too high above sea-level for that banana tree he'd seen; that hadn't been far above his eyeline; he'd come either too far or not far enough. About to turn back, he saw two clusters of rocks with the only way forward between them, beneath a lone coconut palm. Well, he'd just go beyond those and see what he could see; but he was sure he was in the wrong place. He pushed between the rocks, eyes-up for fear of a falling coconut, and he prodded forward for the next step – when his stave suddenly hit thin air. *Help!* Whirling his arms backwards he just kept his balance, and stopped – teetering on the edge of a twenty-metre drop onto granite rocks, barely covered by the waves coming in. His stomach leaped, his heart beat fast, he went cold inside – and he backtracked quickly. That was close! If he fell from here, he wouldn't make a splash, he'd make a splat! He *had* come too far. This was the high and rocky jut of land he'd seen in the distance on his first swim. Well, one thing was certain – he wouldn't be worrying about bananas today; bananas could dangle! He'd search out easier trees. Today it would be coconut again.

Or, instead of coconut, how about some of those fruits that the red-flash birds liked? The goat had been eating them, too. But then, goats were notorious for eating anything, weren't they? No, his diet would be coconut, until he found something else he could be dead sure about: with the emphasis on the 'sure' and not the 'dead'! Coconut and fresh water.

Already this morning he'd taken two knock-backs. One, his pot wasn't a clay classic; and, two, he wouldn't be peeling an easy banana. So he ate coconut again, there on the beach as the sun came over the palm trees. And today, as luck would have it, he was left with almost a half-coconut in one piece, which he could use if his pot failed him. So he was making progress! There were always options, alternatives; and with an overriding sense of relief at not lying dead on the rocks right now, he stretched back in the warm shade, contented.

It was another beautiful day, one of several in a row. The sky was an unbroken blue; birds up in the rainforest flashed through the leaves, chirruping and twittering; the sea lapped and sparkled; and the early morning air held a fresh promise. He'd go to the spring and drink, he'd find that rubber dinghy and see what could be done with it, and he'd track down the female goats he truly believed had to be on the island. Yes! Now he had a plan, a *purpose* – and what more could anyone want?

He went eastwards towards the sun, which was still rising through the treetops where fruit bats hung like rags, through rocks and fern and bracken and purple-headed plants, to the spring – where he drank his fill, splashing fresh water down his salty chest and running it into his boxers.

He pulled them open and looked down at himself; and the male sight of himself suddenly made him think, *girl*. What would it be like with a girl on the island? But he straight-off dowsed the prospect with another handful of cold water. There wasn't – so that was an end to it. He stood—

—To be suddenly hit by the sound. And before he saw it, he knew what it carried – heavy with danger, growing rapidly from a slow *clack* close by to a vibrating and relentless whirlwind of mad foliage as the monster shot up from the rainforest and clung there thundering low over his head: a helicopter gunship painted in khaki swirls, its clawing undercarriage almost touching the tops of the trees. Death! Destruction had come in the night! The end of things! He screamed and shouted and dived into the undergrowth, trying to burrow into granite as the terror machine hovered above him like some creature come to wipe out his world. His head spun, he fought for breath and lay shaking violently in the thicket, his skin ice-cold, his chest thumping heartbeats into the ground. And he could smell the monster, he could almost taste its fuel. He had to get away! He had to get away from this deadly *thing*! Still dizzy, his eyes blurred, he pulled himself up, leaped the pool and ran, he didn't know where, falling over himself as he chased downhill through new terrain, jumping, tripping, stubbing – until, gasping for air, he reached the sea and the beach where the black dinghy still lay – punctured flat but with a gap wide enough to crawl himself into. Which was the last he knew as a menacing black shroud fell over the island, wrapping him in darkness.

Mike Symonds OBE, Company Director and Chief Executive, was at his large island of a desk, in the middle of his large marble office. A wall clock without numerals told him that it was half-past eight here in London; and below it a line of smaller clocks gave the time in New York, Hong Kong, Sydney, Beijing, the name of each location inlaid in contrasting pink marble.

His assistant came into the office without knocking, through a door that a visitor wouldn't know was there. She was tall, black, and beautiful, in her early forties. 'Will you take a call from the MOD?' she asked. There was no hurry in her voice; anyone wishing to speak to her boss awaited his pleasure, from foreign prince to British prime minister, and certainly the Ministry of Defence.

'Who is it?' Mike asked, his eyes still on his sales figures.

'Colonel Travers.'

'Rupert Travers? He was close to Rex...'

'Yes, he's on hold.' She didn't give the slightest expression to indicate that the connection with Mike's dead son-in-law had any significance.

Mike closed his folder: his signal that he could be interrupted to speak to someone. Diana Lucky left the office and a few moments later his telephone rang.

'Symonds.'

'Rupert Travers.'

'Long time, Rupert. What can I do for you?'

'Well, this is going nowhere, I'm sure, but we've just had a weird report from the French...'

'They want to sell the Eiffel Tower for scrap. Not interested!'

'That's a pity, sir, it's going for a knock-down price! But what do you know about the French military in the Indian Ocean?'

Mike barked his office laugh. 'Is this a telephone quiz? Or are you phoning a friend?' But his face was suddenly a lot more serious than his banter sounded.

'I hope that's what I am, sir. You know they've got a military garrison on Réunion...?'

'I do.' They were down to business now.

'...Among other functions it services the meteorology in the area for NATO. There are nine French-owned islands with airstrips and remote weather stations – Europa, Juan de Nova, Tromelin...'

'Yes, I know!' Mike's impatience was gaining on his affability.

'French Met officers visit them on a regular basis; and there's one, Solitaire, that's smaller than the others, granite not coral, no airstrip, has to be serviced by helicopter...' He stopped as if for reaction, getting none. 'Are you there, sir?'

'I'm out there already if you're going to say what I think you're going to say!' Mike was standing, twisting left, twisting right, tangling his telephone. 'Alive or dead? *Alive or dead, Rupert?*'

'Hold on, sir! It's unconfirmed. A possible sighting. They landed in the night, but as their Reynard took off from Solitaire next morning, the Met officer aboard thought he could have seen a figure, fair-haired boy, might have been getting himself under some black object on a beach...'

'What?!'

'...But they couldn't land again, they were running five hours behind schedule. All the same, he got the pilot to do a circuit, right around the island, but the figure didn't show itself again. But with your well-publicized quest, sir, the Deputy Commandant in charge of Réunion has sent our people an e-mail...'

'Quite right! Too right! Rupert, I'm coming over for details...'

'I'd rather I came to you, sir. This isn't exactly official.

If it's anyone's, it's Foreign Office, not Ministry of Defence. Lunch at Vera's?'

'Twelve-thirty. Diana will book. I'll bring her with the files…'

'And I'll bring a chart of the area.'

'Good man.'

'Sir…?'

'Rupert?'

'Don't build yourself up…'

But Mike Symonds had already replaced his receiver, and was running across his office towards the door.

What was this? Where was he? This clinging black sheet was so hot it burned, and it stank of old rubber. He could hear water, waves, it had to be the sea, and if he was under a boat he could drown! Desperately, he fought his way clear, and found himself not in the sea but on a beach, and not wet with water but with sweat. And now, coming to, he knew where he was. He was on his island, and he'd had a bad dream – no, a terrible nightmare! A helicopter gunship had suddenly flown up out of the rainforest like a monster dragonfly out of a pond – so real that he'd had some sort of terror attack, and run away from the danger to hide himself inside this dinghy. He must have stood up too suddenly at the spring, and fainted, and had a daytime nightmare! So, still trembling, he told himself to take deep breaths while his hot sweat dried on him. But, up close and squinting away from the blazing sun, he found himself staring hard at the dinghy – because there was something along its welting that he hadn't noticed before; some stencilled lettering: *MV St. George*. Which could stand for only one thing – the name of the ship this dinghy had come from. So – had he once been on a ship called the *St. George*? And did he really care? Well, no, he didn't – and, anyway, that scary nightmare had brought on a headache, so he walked up the beach to the shade of the rainforest. And he stopped. He could hear bleating! His goats were somewhere near – and he wanted to find the goats; so he followed the sounds, carefully trod on inland, until, at last, pushing through a dense undergrowth of fresh, springing ferns, he suddenly saw them. Ten or twelve goats, grazing on a hillock of couch grass; black-coated, long-haired goats, some with white flashes, some with browny-red; a small flock of full-teated females and skittish kids, all the same large breed as the buck. He stopped, balanced himself with one foot in the air before carefully lowering it, as one of the mother goats looked up from grazing, sniffed the air, chucked her head…and went back to her grazing.

Well, he thought, he was going to be all right for milk, then…

Chapter Six

Vera's had an old-fashioned school-dinner menu – meals to make the ex-public schoolboys of Westminster feel young again: pies and puddings, mashed potatoes; and lashings of custard. It was up a narrow staircase in a backstreet near the Thames, one small room – and only someone of Mike Symonds's profile would get a table at such short notice.

When he walked in with Diana Lucky, Colonel Rupert Travers was already there, at a good table by the window: no one kept Mike Symonds waiting. Rupert was in an expensive silk jacket with jeans, a white shirt and a bright, Windsor-knotted tie; mid-forties, shining bald, and on the right side of his face a puffy bloom of grafted skin – the visible sign of a tank fire. *Wounded in action.*

'Mike…' Rupert stood.

Mike introduced Diana Lucky, who sat quickly, putting a briefcase down beside her.

'Describe the boy,' Mike demanded as his napkin was placed across his lap.

Rupert shrugged. 'Fair-haired, a boy – that's all they said. Fourteen, fifteen, sixteen. *Garçon blond.* Ran out of the trees and dived under this black thing on the beach.'

'While what was going on?'

'Presumably while the Reynard was taking off. Spent a few hours servicing their remote Met station, which had conked out. Apparently it's the important one for cyclone warnings…'

'And where exactly is Solitaire? It's not on our map in the office.'

Rupert pulled up a rolled chart from beside his seat. He spread it across the table and, taking out a sharpened pencil, he pointed to where Solitaire lay, clearly seen on the naval chart, to the north-west of Madagascar.

Mike stood to look at it. 'So a current – these faint arrows are currents, yes?'

'They are.' His pencil followed them, running west to east across the chart.

'So a current from *here* where the *St. George* went down, could very possibly take a dinghy – I think that black thing has got to be a ship's maintenance dinghy, others were found – on a route like *this*.' He ran his stubby nail on a curve along the chart, in more or less the same direction as Rupert's pencil.

'Yes, very possibly...'

'A distance of, what? Fifty or so nautical miles?'

'About that. Perhaps a touch more.'

Mike sat. 'Possible!' he said. 'With a strong current, a following breeze – man can survive for up to five days without water.'

Rupert re-rolled the chart as the meal was served; but Mike didn't touch his food. 'I know what you're both thinking,' he suddenly said.

Diana looked up sharply. Because his mouth was full, Rupert's expression asked, *what?*

'You're wondering why a boy like Joseph should hide from help. A helicopter arrives, civilization, people to take him off this solitary island and bring him home... Why scuttle under a dinghy?'

The colonel's mouth was cleared; he lay down his cutlery and spoke with candour. 'No, sir – I think it's you who's wondering that. If he's your grandson, an intelligent, resourceful chap, an Air Cadet – why should he act that way?'

Mike turned to his personal assistant. 'So, *whoever's* thinking it – *why?*' he asked her.

'I'll tell you why.' Diana kept her eyes on her plate, as if choosing her next forkful. 'A possible "why".' The Oxford graduate had their attention, speaking with a firm, convincing voice. 'He's had a traumatic experience, a terrible thing. The ship he's on is sunk by a gunship attack. There's terror, noise, an explosion, deaths. The next time something looking like a gunship swoops above him, what's he going to do? What's his last experience of a gunship? I know what I'd do!'

'Shell shock!' Rupert put in. 'Post-traumatic stress syndrome following some awful experience. I've seen soldiers dive into ditches when a car backfires…' His voice fell quiet. 'We treat them for it. Extreme cases suffer total amnesia – loss of memory…'

There was a long silence at their table; murmured conversation and the polite chink of cutlery on plates coming from those around.

'Thanks, Rupert,' Mike said eventually. 'Gonna let me have this chart?'

'I brought it for you.'

'And your contact in Réunion is...?'

'I brought the top man's details, too.'

Which was the end of the meal. Mike got up, Diana Lucky paid the bill, and Rupert Travers walked them to the door before returning to the table for pudding – after Mike had given him a hug. 'Thanks, Rupert,' he said. 'You're a good friend.'

'I hope this leads somewhere for you,' Rupert replied.

He was among a flock of goats. Having crept up on them quietly and lain himself down a way off, he turned on an elbow and watched them, leaving them to their grazing. Before too long he would get them used to him until he could crouch by one and put a teat near his mouth, squirting in the warm milk. But that wasn't why he was here. He had followed their friendly sound to a place where he could feel safe – goats ran faster than people from danger. And he could think. He could go over what he'd seen and what he'd heard; some horrible dream – the scary sight of a gunship coming up through the trees, the frightening sound of its engines as it hovered above him, the smell of its fuel; which seemed a million miles away from the sounds of these peaceful goats as they ripped at the grass, the musk of their tangled coats, and the lazy sight of a lizard basking on a rock. And as he lay there and the frond-shaded sun seeped into him, the nightmare faded as nightmares do. This was his real world. He was lying in a harmless calm, and he was safe on his island. Yes, he'd stood up too quickly, gone faint in the head, and had a scare; but the scare was over now, and he was all right. There were no sights or sounds in the sky, the big buck was nowhere near, and everything was peaceful. Whatever had happened was in his head, it was past and gone. And as his poor night on the ledge caught up with him, he tucked up his knees, made a pillow of his arm again, and with the goats around him in a protective graze, he closed his eyes and drifted off – into a dreamless, recovering sleep.

Diana Lucky checked that Commandant Daniel Jacomain spoke English and put him through to Mike. They were at home now after the lunch with Rupert, at Sharpe End, Mike's large country house outside Offley, Hertfordshire; and while Magda, the young Polish housekeeper, was preparing dinner, and Diana's daughter Mary was practising violin with the mute on, Mike took the call in his conservatory.

'Commandant, good of you to call back.'

'No problem.'

'Our Ministry of Defence tells me that one of your chaps thought he saw a fair-haired boy on Solitaire, a Met-base island north of...' Mike was kneeling to the map, unrolled on the conservatory tiles.

'Yes, I know Solitaire,' the Commandant replied. 'This is true, the *météorologiste* made this report. But it's very easy to be mistaken in these things. Perhaps some small creature seen from the air – you know, a big disturbance of foliage from the rotor blades – such sightings can be unreliable.'

'But he was convinced enough to do a circuit of the island...'

'Yes. Unfortunately, he could not land again to look. So we cannot be sure...'

'I understand that.' Mike stood up from kneeling, stared into the distance through his conservatory windows, out over his small farm with its goats and pigs, the pink of a glorious English sunset reflected on his face. 'Commandant, how much would it cost to send your chopper back with a couple of chaps – to put a grieving grandfather's mind at rest...?'

The Commandant didn't hesitate. 'I have seen your situation, and my *sous-commandant* also; this is why he made messages to your people.' Now he paused; for a moment or two the line seemed to have gone dead. 'It is true this Reynard does not have so many duties for a while. Our other meteorological islands are serviced by

CASA fixed-wing – we have airstrips every other place, but for this small island we fly the Reynard from here, it refuels in Madagascar.' There was another pause. 'It could be spared for a few days, I think... We could call it an exercise.'

'I can come out and be with them—'

'Not for such an exercise, not possible—'

'But I would pay all fuel costs, and for the men's time – with a *contribution supplémentaire* for your garrison's goodwill. Maybe some new equipment or furniture for your mess...'

Commandant Daniel Jacomain laughed. 'We have what you call a very *homely* mess, this is true. Monsieur Symonds, I will put matters into hand, and I will keep you informed.'

'*Mike*, please. Daniel, thank you very much.'

'It's okay, it's okay.'

Both men said goodnight, and then each went to their supper: the Commandant to his homely mess, and Mike to his dining room which was hung with oil paintings of his grandchildren: one now dead, and the other – well, hopes never had to be raised too high. Except that Mike did suddenly get up from the table to hurry through to Diana's small wing of the house to tell her to find the latest photographs of Joseph to e-mail to Réunion asap.

*

Once more the Reynard went in by night. Mike's fears of the boy being terrified by the arrival of a helicopter had been passed on to the lieutenant who was organizing the search mission. And as usual at night, instead of swooping low above the treetops, the Reynard was instructed to go in high, 'feathering' down as quietly as it could, the landing pad pinpointed using night-vision equipment. If there was a boy on the island there was a good chance he would be asleep at three in the morning. Well, who knew? It was the best they could do.

There was a two-man flying crew – a pilot and a navigator – and a two-man search party. The Reynard men were Air Force and far outranked the army *soldats de deuxième classe*, who were a pair of recent recruits from Marseilles – one Algerian and one from Ivory Coast – taking their instructions from the navigator – an officer from Grenoble. But judging by the banter in the air, all four on board the Reynard were united in thinking this was a far-fetched mission; in fact a bit of *une excursion*.

Skilfully, the pilot put the Reynard down on its pad, a good night-time landing at the end of a well-navigated flight. There was hardly any moon, and after a breath of fresh air, a cigarette, and a pee in the undergrowth, the four French servicemen unrolled their sleeping bags and settled to sleep in the helicopter. Strong coffee and *petit déjeuner* would set them up nicely in a few hours when morning came to the island.

He made a great discovery. Every day there was something new – a skill, a comfort – and today he found a good place for swimming; a calm inlet at the south of the island. Okay, it was a clamber down to the water, but the reward was a pool of cool peace. Here, in the rocky depth he found himself swimming with large, colourful fish, and when he took a deeper breath and surface-dived he was among purple plants, weird suckers and deep, clinging molluscs. The fish were so vivid in the clear water that he straight-off called the place 'Rainbow Cove'; and he knew that he would always take the trouble to trek here for a pleasure swim. After a careful check that the cove was deep enough, he climbed from the water and stood on a rock above it, and suddenly exhilarated his heart with a dive into the deep blue, coming up with a loud shout of 'Fantastic!'

He spent an hour like that; then a weird, guilty feeling that he wasn't 'getting on' with something sent him on a mission. First, he climbed to his freshwater spring, and when, in the damp heat, he'd drunk till the water ran down his chest, he went on beyond it to the 'seal' beach, to the dead rubber dinghy. He was going to utilize a piece of it for carrying water: he'd drag it to the concrete area where he could use his strength to tear it on a metal post. But as soon as he felt the rubber of the dinghy, he realized what tough stuff it was. He needed a knife; but he hadn't got one – so what could he use, some sharp-edged shells? He'd keep his eyes open, he told himself, as he left the dinghy and went off to find the goats…until with the faint sound of bleating to encourage him, and the earthy smell of animal to excite him, he crept up on a couple of skittering kids and five or six females, much the same small flock as yesterday – one mother in particular whose full udder and two engorged teats looked tempting.

Like the day before he lay there, but nearer. He let leaves tickle and ants run as he allowed his own smell to mingle with theirs – that warm goat smell that somehow twinged his stomach. Heads went up, skin shivered and long hair shook, but none of them ran away; and gradually, patiently, centimetre by centimetre, he moved towards the nearest of them – guerrilla fashion on elbows and knees, with an occasional slow, unthreatening roll over; and when the sun had moved further across the leafy sky, he was in among them. A kid sniffed at him. Another trod across him to get to its mother – small hoofs on his belly – and finally, when the kid had sucked, he rolled himself under the mother and lifted his fingers to a teat – just as the kid took a bite at his boxers. His head jerked up and – *Wow!* – she kicked. A hind hoof whacked into the side of his head, the goat ran, the herd scattered – and he lay there with his head ringing and his thirst for milk unquenched.

But he'd been lucky. The kick had glanced off; after a good rubbing better there was no blood on his fingers, so the only injury was to his pride – just when he'd thought he was doing well. It would be even more patience that got him his milk, then. And perhaps he could earn their friendship if he brought them food like coconut that they wouldn't normally get into. Whatever, he'd have to come here day after day to gain their trust. So should he start right away, listen for which way they'd gone, and follow? He cocked an ear. But what he heard was not the bleat of goat. It was the bleat of man.

'*Casse-toi!*' Not far off. And an angry shout. '*Sacrebleu!*' Then the deep laugh of another voice – and goats went out of his head. People! Fierce-sounding men! His skin shock-froze, panic squirted his stomach, and with a life-and-death ducking run, jumping, sliding, branch-whipped, he ran fast from the voices to find some place to hide, some hole to dig in deep sand.

He'd been wrong! All the time he'd been wrong! That gunship hadn't been a dream, not even a nightmare!

It had been real, stark real! Things like that – monster things – could come and go!

This island wasn't his place at all!

Chapter Seven

Wearing army fatigues, one carrying a FAMAS assault rifle in case of snakes or boars, the other a clearing cleaver, the two private soldiers worked together, while the navigator sat under a palm in walkie-talkie contact with them, plotting their progress on the map – as much with coffee stains as yellow marker. As a way of spending a couple of days, this search of Solitaire was next best to a forty-eight hour leave. Marooned kid? *Mon oeil!* The stupid *météo*'s eyes had been blurred by too much staring at instruments – what he'd reported was seaweed blowing about under the helicopter blades. Except, if they did see something that could be wild boar lurking in the undergrowth, they'd shoot first and ask questions afterwards. The highlight of the day would be the building of a fire, and the cooking of something special by Halim the Algerian, who had once worked in a Marseilles kitchen.

They had compasses, and they would search each *vingt-cinq-mètre* square before reporting it as clear. By leaving camp at first light, if the boy were here they'd likely find him as he slept. *If* he were here! What rubbish! By afternoon they'd be swimming, and then making up for lost sleep. *'Nothing to report!'*

But for their prey it was a run for his life – away from danger, from those loud hostile voices. He didn't see the vine looping across his path that sent him crashing headlong into undergrowth. He was lucky, though – his head just missed a rock – and his luck held further as the sound of his fall coincided with a shout of *'Noix de coco!'* and a deep, loud laugh. The men were close – and he knew he had to lie still where he was; he'd be seen for sure if he got up now and ran. When, with no warning, one of his terror dizziness attacks suddenly hit him again; he went hot and cold, gasped for air and shook in a spasm of panic. But somehow he still wriggled and burrowed, and in a desperate bid for survival he pulled himself under a pile of fallen fronds. Trembling in his sweaty panic, he drew his knees up to his chin, and delved into the ground for earth to smear over his face and shoulders. This dirt would make his white skin hard to see. But there's a human instinct to need to know when attack is coming. Lying there with his eyes shut tight would be scarier than seeing who was coming; so he twisted himself to see these men coming on at him through the rainforest.

His breathing was shallow, his body had slowed; but suddenly that breathing stopped altogether – because now he saw them: black soldiers in fighting fatigues, swathing through the trees, grim faces intent on killing with a gun and an axe – the gun gripped ready to shoot, the axe to chop and slice. He was curled rigid like a fossil in a glacier. The soldiers had gone silent now – in their speech; but their boots crashed noisily through the undergrowth as the darker of the two looked straight at him, his head shining in the heat. Yet the soldier must have seen nothing, because he didn't stop but went crunching on through the foliage.

And with them moving away there was only one thing to do: take deep breaths, be sure he could stand and keep his balance – and get to his beach before they or any others did. Get to the bed on its ledge and throw the grasses into the trees, scoop up the cracked pot and the bits of split coconut and toss them into the sea. And then hide again: brush over his footprints with fronds and get himself into the densest part of the rainforest, where he would endure the rats and the giant centipedes and the fierce land crabs, would take all their stinging and biting and gnawing – just to stay alive. Somehow.

The navigator was bored. His pilot was asleep in the Reynard with an air cooler wafting across his face. Military air crew have the knack of sleeping in short shifts; war isn't waged nine-to-five, so sleep hours are built up like calorie intake. Outside the helicopter it was steamy at the height of the day, and in the distance he could hear the tempting sound of the sea. He swatted a pestering fly, and stretched himself upright, his head ringing with caffeine. He radioed the soldiers to take a break where they were, and looking at his chart of Solitaire, put a finger on the beach to the east. He left a note for his pilot and placed it under a stone where it couldn't be missed – reporting that he was going to the beach where the boy was supposed to have been sighted to photograph 'signs'. Any excuse… He was twenty-eight but he looked nearer forty, with the unhealthy skin of someone who lived a lot of his life breathing recycled air. His dark hair was lank, and greying already; navigating for attack or evasion was a stressful job.

Using his chart and compass he made good progress through the rainforest. As he headed east-south-east from the compound, he passed through terrain that his men had already surveyed, so there was no surprise in seeing pink rubs on the mossy rocks, and broken spiders' webs. But he did note them, and when he came upon the searching soldiers sitting smoking and spitting in a small clearing, he refreshed his orders: that they weren't to look just for a boy but also for *signs* of a boy. Although when he'd said that, they looked into each other's faces, nodding seriously, and then they all had a good laugh. *'Ha!'*

The beach was more or less as described in the *météorologiste*'s report: a pattern of granite jigging through the sand, and a flat, black dinghy up above the waterline among old husks and dried seaweed – storm debris. Small piles of excavated sand showed where ghost crabs were hiding, shot away from their task of digging mating holes. But the sea beckoned. He took a quick look around, gave the dinghy the quickest of glances – an old dinghy was an old dinghy – and got his task out of the way by photographing it with wide shots to show its position on the beach, highlighting how close it was to the weed and debris blowing about that could have *looked* like a boy; and, stripping himself naked, he ran into the sea. Not a shiver, not a catch of breath – the warm noon sea welcomed him to a half-hour of heaven. This was a *pique-nique* of a mission!

Hell was a hole in the rainforest floor. His bedding had been thrown back where it had come from, the pot – not a clay pot but a mud crumble – had gone into the sea, and all coconut remains had gone into the undergrowth. He'd kicked across his footprints on the sand and run along the beach in the water to where he could climb onto rocks without leaving marks, then up into the foliage to the depths of the interior.

These soldiers had not been here yesterday or the day before; he'd been all round the island twice. There were no boats in either bay, so they must have come by helicopter, the same sort of gunship that had suddenly shot up from the trees. They had to be hunting him out. The way they'd come through the rainforest with their gun and their axe, they must be guerrilla fighters on the kill – and he was the only person on the island. He had to escape them to live. He couldn't burrow into sand or earth the way the crabs could, but he could burrow under foliage, and this was where he'd go, into the undergrowth at its thickest. But in his rush he'd be careful. He wouldn't break any spiders' webs; he wouldn't put a hand or a foot on a mossy rock to scar it; he wouldn't snap a branch or a twig. What he *would* do was go where the branches bent low, duck himself under the sorts of places where searching soldiers might look but couldn't walk.

There never is the perfect hiding place; but after getting himself into a couple of spots – in one of which he looked up to see too much sky – he settled for a gully under an overhanging lichen-covered tree, whose lowest branches were less than a metre above the ground. Anyone coming under here would have to crouch and burrow, too; there was no natural way through.

Or they could just fire off a belt of bullets into the rainforest floor. Like spraying a hose – that'd get him… Whatever, he wouldn't leave this hole. He wouldn't come out properly until he heard the sound of that gunship taking off. He hadn't heard it come – a mistake he would never make again – but he needed to hear it go.

But it never takes long for the ants to arrive. First the reconnaissance ant, then the backup. The big question is, what sort of ant are they? Black ants would go for the eyes, the nostrils or the mouth, and he could keep those shut tight if they came. But fire ants could kill him if they stung him enough – making it a toss-up between dying here or running out to be shot. The first ant, though, was like the kid with the mother goat; big as he might be, it crossed his chest on the way to somewhere else: so lie still and hope that no battalions come. There were rustles nearby, but he hadn't seen a snake on the island – although that didn't mean there wasn't a viper in the dead leaves, slithering towards him. Cockroaches, millipedes, spiders, scorpions – they wouldn't all be lurking somewhere else just because he was *here*. He was in their territory. As for rats—

He stopped thinking about all that; he'd wait for what attacked him. But he listened hard. His great hope was to hear the sound of the soldiers retreating. His worst was nothing – just the noises of the rainforest for the rest of the day and the night. When suddenly the hiss of a walkie-talkie froze him again – a voice crackling through the trees with the fast, sinister language of soldiers on a hunt. And the live reply, spoken about fifteen metres away. So close!

'*Oui, monsieur? A vous.*'

The static crackle came again. He imagined the two black soldiers he'd seen, stopping to listen.

'*Bien sûr. A vous,*' the close voice said. There was another crackled instruction, ended by, '*D'Accord. Terminé.*' Now the nearby voices spoke to one another, but moving away. *Moving away!*

'*Pas la peine de chercher! Il n'y a personne ici!*'

'*Tu parles! On y est pour rien – autant chercher une aiguille dans une botte de foin!*'

He might not be able to understand the words, but as their voices got fainter, the message seemed pretty clear. They were off! Yes! But he wouldn't break cover until he heard the sound of rotors.

He eased himself a bit, he had to; his arm had gone to sleep beneath him, so he turned himself slowly. The ants were getting busier now, up his legs, into his boxers, and the greatest relief at that moment would have been to jump up and dance them out. But he daren't, so he rubbed and probed and squeezed, more or less kept his position... until – *Pits!* – he saw the beetle: a large, black creature with a sharp horn protruding from the top of its head. It was nearly six centimetres long, coming towards him across the foliage with a relentless march. He had to move! The aggressive way it was heading for him just said, *It's you! It's you!* But no way was this buddy going to get a bite at him!

To be bitten, then – or shot, by a sniping soldier? Their going off could have been a trick: one of the guerrillas might still be slinking close by. Second thoughts. Now he did the bravest thing he could imagine. He lay still. Rigid. He was sweating ice in the heat. He looked down his body as the beetle came to his thigh. He clenched his legs tight together, and pulled his boxers taut with a grip at the back. His neck ached, looking down – as the beetle stopped, couldn't get a grip on the sweat of his flanks, flailed its legs, tossed its horn, stopped; and he tensed himself for the pain of its bite. But it only drank at his moisture – before turning away to go off in another direction.

And now he knew, lying scared rigid on the rainforest floor, that he would stay where he was until the sun had moved a lot further to the west. He'd give plenty of time for the coast to be clear…

For hours he somehow held on where he was, but the night would fall quickly when it came. A terror of invading soldiers with guns gave him the courage to stick it out. But the creatures of the night would bring a different sort of danger – if only because he wouldn't see them creeping up on him. So as soon as it was dark enough – but before it was too dark for him to see his way – he would get back to his ledge. The granite would be hard with no bedding at all, and he wouldn't sleep; he'd be hungry and thirsty, but it was tucked well away, and he could spend the night there and come to hide here again tomorrow – until he'd heard that gunship go. And it *would* go: there was no camp at the fenced area, nor any signs that there'd ever been one. It was his best chance, he reckoned; although a best chance can be a long way off a cert.

He came out cautiously, thinking through every step before he trod it, testing each handhold on a tree – a light skill he had – and at every metre he took a three-sixty stare through the vegetation. But he saw no one, heard nothing apart from the sounds of birds nesting and land crabs clacking out, so progress was good, and knowing that he was moving in a different direction from where the gunship would be, he started to move faster. But he was hungry, and so dried out with thirst that his tongue was swelling again in his mouth. There was no wet leaf to lick, though, and the spring might be where the soldiers drank so he couldn't go there. All the same, what he did could have been fatal. As he passed warily beneath the tree with the purple, heart-shaped fruits that both the birds and the goats had eaten, he took a stupid chance. He picked a ripened fruit from a largish bunch, and with a wipe of its bloom on his boxers, he bit into it for its juice.

Would he die? Would he pass out – and fall into the hands of the gunship guerrillas?

The fruit wasn't sweet, but the suck of its moisture just hit the spot. It quenched his thirst – and it eased his hunger, so he ate another and waited to die, drop dead there and then. But he didn't. He ate two more but he wouldn't gorge – instead he went on his light-treading, sharp-eyed way to his ledge between the boulders, seeing nothing, hearing no one – when suddenly he smelled it. Smoke. And looking into the sky he could see a spine of pale grey rising above the trees into the last of the light: from a cooking fire. The soldiers were eating, a thought that somehow griped the risky fruit in his belly, and made sleep on his hard ledge take a very long time to come. If he went under, would he ever wake up again?

First light – and he woke to a sound that pleased and terrified at the same time: the whining of rotors and the vibration of a gunship going up. He gripped desperately at the rock as that panic terror suddenly hit him again and threatened to slide him off; the hot and cold skin, the breath that didn't want to keep him alive. But he didn't pass out, he didn't forget where he was, and he had the sense to let himself down off the ledge gently and keep himself hidden until the receding sound told him it was safe to look up at the sky, where the gunship was flying off towards the south-east. He leaned against the rocks as the dizziness passed and his breathing eased, and at last he slid his shadow out of cover, and he went into the sea to rid himself of what mercifully hadn't killed him overnight.

If those soldiers had all gone – and he would stealthily check – then all he could ever want would be his again: coconuts, bananas, fruits; his friends-to-be, the goats, and milk to come. So, had that been a bad dream? No way! The scratches and pesky bites on his body told him it had all been too true; and the turmoil of a real shock had left his insides upside down, his brain battered by the fright, almost like being punched. And, okay, the soldiers had gone – but as he stood there in the warmth of the water he shivered with a weird aloneness as a sudden melancholy came over him.

What was he all about?

Chapter Eight

For someone carrying the sadness of his loss, Mike Symonds was oddly able to laugh: a great sense of humour can never be buried too deep. But the sudden shout of his laugh had not been heard at Sharpe End for a long time. This Saturday morning he managed a chuckle – when he went to the smallholding that he grandly called 'The Farm' and saw Diana's nine-year-old daughter Mary running from a head-down billy goat. The girl, slight, black and pretty, ran into Mike's arms; while the goat stopped, tossing its head.

'His own worst enemy!' Mike said. 'That brings de-horning and castrating a few days nearer!'

'Poor William!'

'If we don't keep him as a harmless pet, he'll have to be destroyed,' Mike told her. 'What would *you* rather be: dead, or looked after?'

'Depends on the pocket money!' Which made Mike really laugh. And while Mary, weekend free, fed the chickens, he did what he'd come to do: throw kitchen waste to the pigs.

Sharpe End was a large red-brick house built on farmland by a Georgian earl; and as well as laying out a tennis court and adding a small gym, Mike had converted it to allow accommodation for his key member of staff. As a top businessman owning twenty-four-hour factories in England, Wales, Europe and Asia, he needed a twenty-four-hour personal assistant. High-flying Trinidadian Diana Lucky – with a First in Philosophy, and left alone with a child by a feckless con man of a husband she'd met at Oxford – had been interviewed, and re-interviewed, and had finally accepted the executive job offered to her.

Now she met her boss as he came back to the house. 'The French. Réunion,' she said. 'There's an e-mail report…'

'Yes?' Mike's face lit up.

She shook her head. 'No, I'm sorry...'

He hurried on past her into his large conservatory office. The computer had gone into screensaver mode with a slide show of family pictures: torture – but he could never take them off. He nudged the mouse and brought up the report, in French; but he didn't need a dictionary to get the gist of it. Solitaire had been thoroughly searched and there was no sign of any humans on it. Yes, there was a punctured dinghy on one of the beaches, but that could have been there for years. Pictures of the island in the attachments would show how uninhabited it was.

Mike showed no emotion. He snapped out of his posture, and opened the JPEG picture attachments. They were what he would expect to see: rainforest, blue sky, coral reef, granite outcrops, but all flora and fauna, no *Homo sapiens*. There was a Reynard in a clearing, and several wide-angled pictures of the black dinghy on the beach, showing its position – because this was where the meteorologist claimed to have seen a fair-haired boy taking cover. He clicked in to a closer view of the sad, dead, rubber. And closer. And closer. The sun and strong shadow on the black rubber made seeing detail difficult; but by playing with the image, lightening the contrast... what was that? 'Hold your horses...' He cropped and enlarged the picture, centring on what he might have just seen. *Wording. Small stencilled wording, unlikely to be seen by a too-casual eye.* He reached for his glasses, peered intently at the monitor.

'*St. George!*' Diana exclaimed from behind him. 'MV *St. George!*'

'Yessir!' Mike leaped up. 'Print it! See – that dinghy made it there from the sinking! It's possible!' He went back to the previous pictures of the rainforested island. He swung round to Diana Lucky. 'Couldn't you hide in this lot?' he asked her. 'Couldn't a boy with guts and cadet know-how play cat and mouse with a couple of French squaddies? Someone with the Symonds blood in his veins?'

'Very possibly,' Diana said softly. She put a hand on his shoulder. And she squeezed it, her voice deep and guttural. 'Get out there yourself! Get out there, Mike!'

He stood from the computer, and turned and faced her; and didn't for a second hide from her the fact that he was crying. No slight sob – really crying.

'You know what,' he said, 'I just might!'

The boy crouched by the campfire up near the helicopter pad, his eyes filled with tears. *The filth! The dirty killers!* The spent wood was grey and crumbled, the ashes flaking, the fire stones cold. And, most dead of all, skewered across the embers on a metal spit hung the forlorn, skinned head and hind of a goat, its legs chopped off, the bones lying below in the cinders. He stared at it – the *remains*, what's left after someone has killed and moved on.

Which goat was this? Not the goat in milk that he wanted to tame? Not the big solitary buck? No – it was one of the kids, perhaps the skittish kid that had used his body as a bridge, now a victim left here to feed the rats. *Never!* Not while he lived on the island! These remains were going to be given some respect. He carried them beneath a laurel tree, and with his bare hands he dug ferociously to scoop out a shallow grave, with some dignity laying the flopping carcass into the ground. Soon he would mark this victim's grave; but first, there was something crucial he had to do. He would stop a gunship landing here ever again! No guerrilla hit-squad would come from the sky and do this to one of his creatures. With angry energy he dragged fallen trunks and loose rocks onto the concrete square, vowing as he worked that he would heap more and more obstacles here whenever he could. It would be his mission, his task, his *purpose*. And he would cover the small hut with leaves and branches, and train vines into the fencing, making this place impossible to be recognized from the air as somewhere to land. For now, though, he went back to the fire to scatter the ashes in the undergrowth to stop their smoky smell from ever reminding him of what these brutal attackers had done.

But hello! What was this lying in the ashes? A knife! An all-purpose open-bladed knife with a rubber handle and a point, about twenty centimetres long. *A tool – the vital tool he wanted!* He stepped back to look at the fire again; what else might he find? And now he saw what he'd been staring at since he'd first found this atrocity: the long steel spit on which the goat had been skewered. Surely that could be used as a spear, for fishing; another tool! He stood and stared at it. But – *where would that put him?* If it was a spear and *he* killed to eat – used it as a *weapon* – why shouldn't those soldiers kill to eat? What was the difference between killing goat and killing fish: didn't both creatures have the right to live?

He stared at the dead fire and decided – he would try to live on his island without any killing, ever. And as he made that pledge, it could have been a rustling of the bamboo leaves, or it could have been a voice, a soft and gentle voice, but something came quietly into his head, and another faint dizziness swayed him, but it passed as he heard what the sound was saying, leaving him with a word. *Pax*. And although, up till then, he hadn't thought about calling himself anything, at that decisive moment he named himself. 'Pax'. *Hi Stave, hi Knife, hi Goat, hi Fish. I'm Pax...* And chanting his name aloud, sweaty and ash-grey, he hurried to the sea, to wash away any traces of the killing that had been done on his island.

Mike flew himself to Réunion in his private Learjet 60. The two Pratt & Whitney engines could take him around two and a half thousand miles before refuelling, and Réunion was more like six thousand from London, so he needed stops along the way. He needed sleep, too – so as co-pilot he took with him a young and sharp man-of-few-words from his Merthyr Tydfil operation, Ray Powell. The Learjet finally landed at Saint-Denis de la Réunion early one afternoon – but from the air Mike had already phoned to confirm his appointment with the commanding officer of the French military at the garrison; although Daniel Jacomain didn't much care to see him. As far as the Solitaire search was concerned, the French had done more than could be expected.

The Commandant must have modelled himself on General de Gaulle, the famous French leader from World War II – very tall and aristocratic, outwardly polite, but stubborn. He had known for days that Mike Symonds was coming to the Réunion military offices, and he had tried to put him off; why the need for more than a phone call or e-mail, when all he was politely going to say was '*Non*'? Solitaire had been searched, and there was no point in searching it again. The meteorological satellite station there was functioning well after minor repairs and there was no need for the island to be visited again for another three, maybe six months. And most certainly out of the question was the British industrialist paying to be flown there by an *Armée de L'air* Reynard. Its other flight duties could not be put on hold for the length of time it would take a grandfather to make his own exhaustive search of the island. *Non, certainement!* But politeness and Sir Michael's business influence with the French government meant that Daniel Jacomain would have to turn down his request in person, over a glass of Pernod.

Later that day, in a garrison office, Mike produced the lightened blown-up photograph of the dinghy, which on close inspection could be seen to have come from the stricken *St. George*. In response to which, with a wave of his arms, Jacomain put the point that debris – and, sadly, bodies, some torn apart by sharks – had been found floating on many currents of the western Indian Ocean. '*Desolée!*' Finally came the warning – 'And of course you will please not attempt to fly privately to Solitaire. That would violate our air space…'

'Do you have a grandson, a granddaughter?' Mike asked him, putting a hand into his pocket for a photograph.

Again the wave of the arms. He did not.

Mike finished his Pernod and went from the office with dignity. Outside in the hire car he turned to Ray Powell. 'You were spot on, they're not budging an inch. So it's Plan B, boyo!' They drove back to their hotel, where the Welshman ate in a lively bistro restaurant, and Mike had room service bring him an omelette. But by midnight the determined grandfather was out again, in a harbour bar, where he was doing what he was very good at: a bit of business.

Pax went to the goats to apologize on behalf of the human race. After his wash in the sea, he ate bananas and purple fruits, drank at the spring, then searched out the flock. He'd use the knife to cut up the dinghy later, but for now he carried extra fruits in his hands – to offer to the goats, especially the doe in milk. Does are best milked when they're busy eating; although today wasn't for that, it was too sad. Today was for friendship.

The animals had moved on from where they'd been before, so Pax listened, heard nothing at first, and then thought he caught the slightest bleat on a ruffling breeze coming from the west. Was a wind starting to blow up; were the top branches of the canopy trembling their leaves? Whatever, he followed the sound of the bleating and eventually found the small flock, still not far from the coast, grazing on a granite outcrop where small plants grew between the rocks. Here the goats looked the mountain sort, more vigorous, forelegs higher than hind, better balanced than man could ever achieve; but he still did what he was determined to do – he lay down and scattered his fruits around him, trying to think himself into being a part of the natural scene. Eventually a kid came near, and with a loud bleat went for one of the fruits; but the moment Pax moved his arm to make some gentle contact it skittered away. That didn't deter him, though; he stayed where he was and again willed his human smell to become familiar, one living creature with others. He wanted to share this island.

He was nearer to the east beach than to his bay on the west, so, having given the goats a fair amount of time, he backed off and went east to look at the possibilities with the dinghy rubber. Walking all round it, he could see that it would be quite possible to cut out a circle large enough to fold into the right shape. If he could then pierce the circle's perimeter and lace some supple branches through the holes he'd made, he could bend them into a ring at the top – and great! He'd have a bucket!

'Brilliant!' he said aloud, and headed back across the island to fetch the knife. This route was now becoming a well-marked track because it always passed the spring, and as he went this time – for no reason at all – he gave it a name. *Solar Path* – on the track of the sun. He had a name – Pax – and he was naming important parts of his island, because this place belonged to him. The soldiers had gone, they couldn't land again, and he would have food and drink whenever he wanted. What more could he ask? And, happy in those thoughts, as he walked he started to see other things, pleasing sights: the breeze twisting the fronds green and silver; purple patches of undergrowth where small flowers grew, waving on long stems as if they were being carried by tiny people; unopened ferns looking ready to spring surprises; bluish doves ground-feeding in loyal pairs; and pinky-brown butterflies slowly opening and closing their wings in the sun, waving hello. And he saw a gnarled stump that he passed every day, the remains of a branch broken off in a storm, lying half-propped against a fallen trunk. Which stopped him. Because this time what he saw wasn't a stump, it was a face; if he half-closed his eyes it could be a face, one he'd seen somewhere before; two small hollows giving the look of innocent eyes, and a line of raised bark a mouth; a primal sight that evaporated dinghy rubber from his mind. And in its place came the strong desire to use his knife a different way...

With a lot of rocking and twisting he pulled the stump from where it had settled and found that he could carry it if he grasped it firmly to his belly. Ignoring the scratch of it, he took it to his beach, where, after a dunk in the sea for himself, and a sharpening on granite for his knife, he settled himself in shade on the sand, his feet in sheltered water, and he started to work at the wood. He scraped off the moss and lopped the bark, and with his eyes half closed, already seeing the finished object in his mind, he began to carve. But his carving was a long way from finished when lightning out at sea suddenly took his eye with its flash. He carried his work into the rainforest, laying it beneath the surface roots of a pine that would hold it in place if a storm hit, and he started to think about his own safety. By now, growling clouds and spectacular streaks of lightning were coming his way fast from the west – but where could he shelter that wasn't under a tree? The island was all trees – apart from the beaches.

He blinked as a blinding flash split the sky in fierce veins. Right! If the danger was coming from the west, he'd go east – to the dinghy beach, which would be more sheltered, well away from the trees. Urgently, he took his stave and his knife and climbed back along Solar Path, over the summit, to the beach on the east. But storms travel fast: already the trees along his way were bending, their branches thrashing, every leaf in frenzy. The thunder frightened with its shattering claps, the lightning flashed bright rainforest at him. Trying to be as agile as the goats, he put on speed, jumping rocks, ducking branches, skinning past rattling fronds – as now the rain fell, really *fell*, its force nearly taking the boxers off his body. It hit stingingly hard, lashing down in swathes that made seeing the way almost impossible in the turmoil of the trees. The world had darkened to a false night, and as another huge strike flashed across the sky Pax found himself running through a living nightmare.

And there it was! The beast! The huge buck goat. Standing in Pax's way, looking at him with unblinking eyes, threatening with its two great curled and lethal horns! Pax stopped, skidded and slipped, hurt his back, lay there staring up in horror. It was the Devil, and it spoke – in a loud, throaty bleat: the buck, who must have stood under many nightmare storms such as this.

Pax got to his feet. But what to do? The way around the buck would take him into deep undergrowth and under low trunks and branches; he might never find his Solar Path again before lightning struck a tree and killed him. And the way ahead was barred by this creature that seemed to have grown to twice its size from before. But the goat made the decision for him. With a shake of its head it took off beneath a thick laurel, and Pax could run on his way to the east beach, scared – and angry because he was scared.

It was definitely more sheltered there. Lightning still lit up everything, the water was high and agitated, but the rain wasn't hitting so hard on this side of the island. When – flash and crash! A simultaneous strike cracked the sky open directly over his head. *Help! Any second – fried alive by a million volts!* But what was that – above the waterline? The dinghy – puffing up and blowing about – and Pax couldn't face losing it, he wanted to use it for so many things. He skidded across the beach and dived onto it to hold it down, away from the trees, curling himself into the heaviest shape he could make to keep it on the island, his eyes closed, his fingers in his ears, the sea whipped into greater rage by a shifting of the wind – a cyclonic blast from the north. He forced his eyes open to see the waves growing, the beach vanishing to left and right as the waters crashed and sucked; and in a sudden gust the wind lifted the edges of the dinghy and wrapped it around him. While, with a roar to match the storm, a huge wave surged up the beach and scudded under the dinghy – swirling it into the sea, the cavity in which Pax was curled filling with water as he fought for a way out of the rubber. Like sediment he was sucked down the steep beach into the bottom of the next wave, dragging him out beyond any crest that would wash him back to land. Desperately, he clawed to be free, holding his breath as the next wave thumped him down hard on the ocean floor – in a vicious sea, its bottom strewn with rocks that could smash his head like a gull's egg. In entangling rubber – with his lungs about to burst.

Help! And he found a name that came from some deep place in his head. *Mum!*

Chapter Nine

The Réunion fisherman had a cousin living in Madagascar who was also a man of the sea. Mike's Learjet flew north-west to the main airport there, his journey to Antsiranana harbour completed in a smaller plane and a beat-up Peugeot 'bush taxi'; while Ray Powell parked the jet and waited for further word. When Mike had wiped the blown dust from his eyes he found the yacht moored against the jetty – and with it the man he'd been warned to look out for, an unsmiling, suffer-no-fools-gladly, commander of his craft.

Anyone could see that Mike Symonds was no tourist. Dressed for action, in a jungle shirt and khaki trousers, boonie hat, and with his focused eyes, he looked a military man again.

Dominic Maitrait was a light-skinned Seychellois, currently working out of Antsiranana on the northern tip of Madagascar. Too restless to stay anywhere for long, he took his thirty-two-foot ocean-going yacht all over the western Indian Ocean, wherever someone wanted to charter the *Brume Rouge*. Around thirty-five, black hair cut brutally short, and with a tight mouth, Maitrait spoke as if his words were being counted for engraving, so much per letter.

'Ahoy! I'm Mike Symonds.'

Maitrait grunted.

'Shall I come aboard?'

Maitrait looked pointedly at Mike's holdall. *'Lancez-le!'* he commanded – there would be no carrying of anyone's bags on this trip – and within minutes they were unrolling a frayed chart of the western Indian Ocean across the cabin table. Solitaire was clearly marked, lying west of the Seychelles, about sixty nautical miles from the east coast of Africa. Maitrait put his callipers on the chart, reading off the distance they'd have to sail to get there from Antsiranana. Some yacht captains might have blown out their cheeks or hunched their shoulders at the nautical miles; but he just growled, 'Three hundred.'

'What about sea conditions?'

The man didn't look up. 'South Equatorial Current west, East African Coastal north.'

'That helps?'

'Is what takes dinghy to Solitaire.'

'So, how many days, Captain?' Mike sat, elbows on the table, chin on his knuckles.

'Three day supplies.' Maitrait had already worked it out.

'Times two, for coming back?'

'*Non.* I take you to Solitaire. You stay, I go; one week I go away. Aldabra, Seychelles. I come back—' He tapped his rugged watch to denote punctuality – 'Take you back here.'

'With food and water for three people...'

But Maitrait's face showed no expression, gave no hope. 'We eat now. I know good place. We go first light.'

'So be it!' Mike said.

And that was pretty well all that passed between them for the rest of the evening.

The first thump down onto the seabed knocked the wind out of Pax. He was desperate for air, struggling to get free from the wrap-around rubber, being lifted to the crest again and hugging his head ready for the next crash down. But in a weird slew the wave corkscrewed him within itself and when it thumped him down – miracle! – he was free of the dinghy, fighting for the surface. Could he make it? Could his lungs hold out? He denied them against all the pressures to open his mouth and inhale – until he saw more and more light, held on somehow, and with his heart ready to burst through his ribcage, his brain straining the seams of his skull, he suddenly hit air – and at last took a great mouthful of life. For now! Because he was nowhere near safety: he was out beyond the line of breaking waves in a trough of choppy water, the storm no more than a metre above the sea, the rain pitting the surface like shot, thirty metres from land. He mustn't stop swimming for a second; he knew he mustn't stop. If he was going to save his life he had to go for land right now; being carried further out meant never coming back! Ever! He'd got to use this swell to get within reach of the shore, then get onto a wave that would take him up the beach – ride on top of it, hold himself as flat as a board near its crest – because if he crashed onto the land any other way he'd be smashed against the rocks. He had to bodysurf in, not tumble helpless inside a wave. But first he had to catch the breaker…

Head down, he kicked his legs and threw his arms into a frantic swim against the strong current that was trying to take him further out; aiming himself for the middle of the bay and not the rocks on either side, ready to time the moment to go flying in. Against all the odds. The sea was rough, the current wanted him, he was breathless and exhausted – but a fight for life brings its own desperate strength. He took a huge breath and powered his legs, working his arms with muscle he never knew he had; and metre by metre he slowly gained on the current. Every six strokes he looked up to see the shoreline trees; were they getting closer or was that hopeful thinking? On a seventh stroke he threw a quick look behind him. He was in a short chop between waves, and – yes! – being in a chop at all told him he was nearer the shore. What about surfing the next crest? But the wave coming in was a roller, big but no shape, it'd be a poor choice. The wave behind that was flecking at its top, shaping up better; while all the time he swam with all his strength to hold himself against the powerful ebb. And as the first wave rolled under him, he put down his head and threw himself into a desperate sprint to catch the one following. And *now! Yes!* This wave looked okay; not a great shape but it would do, it would do – if he was skilful. It would *have* to do, because he had nothing left in him, except the will to summon everything and angle himself just below the wave's crest, near the top of the curl. And with one last effort he put down his head and raced the wave towards the beach – in a marvellous and merciful moment feeling the lift of it beneath him, knowing where he was – and as the crest gathered momentum for its crash up the beach he thrust out his arms, tucked his head in line with his body, gave a flailing kick of the legs, and in he went! He raced. He scudded. He flew. In a surging roar at the top of the wave he foamed high onto the beach till the water ran sucking out from under him. His legs shaking, he clambered to his feet and ran up the sand high above the waterline before the next wave could claim him for the sea again, where he lay among weed and wood and coconut debris, and gulped in island air. And in sudden shock, he started to cry, seawater draining from his nose and mouth, his body balled into the tightest ammonite a human could make. And like that he saw out the rest of the storm as it moved across the Indian Ocean to the east.

'We go in at night,' Mike Symonds said. 'If he's there, he's scared of people. When he saw the Reynard he hid himself under a dinghy *here*, so we go in to this beach *here*, on the western side.' Dominic Maitrait had dug out a sheet on Solitaire, on which Mike's stubby nail was pointing to locations. The *Brume Rouge* was making fair speed at twenty-seven knots, riding the coastal current, still a few hours from Solitaire, but nearing the end of a voyage during which Sir Mike and the captain had chopped at each other like colliding currents.

Maitrait was shaking his head. 'You ask, *no noise*. You ask, *secret?*'

'You know damned well I do. We've been over it twenty times.'

'You swim?' Maitrait mimed swimming.

'I swim.'

'So I drop *here*.' He stabbed at an inlet without a beach on the south side of the island. 'No noise. No hull scrape. No trouble I not get off beach, after.' He turned and stared at his passenger with eyes that said his decision wasn't up for discussion.

'You can do it at night? Yes?'

'For sure,' Maitrait growled. 'Stay out of sight till dark, then sail, no motor.' He stared at Mike again, then gripped him on the shoulder with a fierce hand. 'No problem! I do this million times.'

'What if you wreck on a rock?'

'I not wreck on a rock! I wreck on rock, I radio, they send rescue. But –' his seaman's contempt in his voice – 'you not swim? That *problem?*'

Mike knocked the man's hand off his shoulder. 'No problem! I was a senior soldier: I trained for Malaya. If I say I swim, I swim. You can believe the word of an English officer!'

But Dominic Maitrait's expression showed how unimpressed he was by that: so Mike turned away from him to the galley and started slicing a courgette; there were times when it was wise to be busy with the hands...

The girl's head was finished – and he was pleased with it. When the carving was done, Pax went to the beach for sand, and, holding a laurel leaf in his palm, he sanded the features to a fine, smooth finish. It wasn't a gallery work of art, it was still as much 'tree' as 'girl', but there was a beauty, a *spirit* about it that gave him a weird pang – of affection, somehow, and yearning. He found a niche in the beach rocks where she could sit, well away from the high water mark. And as he stared and stared at her, as she came in and out of focus with the intensity of his eyes, her name just came to him. He found himself mouthing it. 'Zuri'. She was called 'Zuri', although he had no reason why that should be; the name simply came into his head.

Beneath the niche was another wider, deeper trough – and for most of the day it was in shadow. Rainwater from the storm had collected there, and, 'Let's get on with something,' he told himself – because the trough would make a good reservoir for a day's supply of water. But, not having the rubber from the lost dinghy, he'd have to carry it in half-coconut shells. So first he'd find some fallen coconuts – there'd be plenty after the storm – and he'd see if he could split them in half, not in pieces. He had both a knife and a spiky rod now; he could pierce the 'eyes' of the nut with the rod and drink the water first – after which he could try to split the shell evenly with the knife. Which meant he could start every day with trips to the pool, and that would be it. There was lots else to do. He had the gunship landing pad to heap more dead branches onto; and he needed to weave something for transporting three or four half-coconuts with water. Plus he had to have regular times to go to the goats with fruits, become one of their habits. He'd do some more carving, too. And having said 'Yup!' to each decision, he laid himself down against a sloping rock in the shade, put a pad of folded fronds behind his head, and rested; and in the calm of the steam slowly rising, listening to the low, slow call of a nearby seabird, he thought how there was nothing more in the world he wanted than to be here on his island, alone.

*

Dominic Maitrait timed the run-in of the *Brume Rouge* perfectly. As the sun went down he took a bearing on the island, but did no more, holding the yacht far enough away to be nothing more than a speck on a distant horizon. It lay low in the water; he wouldn't hoist its sails until after dark when there was no chance of them being seen, then he would tack into the southern inlet of the Isle de Solitaire.

Mike was patient. His years in the army had taught him to leave no room for human emotions like eagerness and impatience. You prepared to the hilt; and if D-Day or H-hour were put back, you prepared all over again. You neither dreaded nor dreamed – you kept yourself busy on the mission, which had started the moment you buckled your webbing belt. So tonight Mike packed and repacked his waterproof survival kit – a torch with spare batteries, jungle survival tins of food, a four-pack of still water, a mosquito-netted sleeping bag, a frame camp bed, and a first aid satchel.

Using its satellite navigation system, Maitrait held the *Brume Rouge* steady until night fell. 'One hour,' he told Mike.

'Affirmative.' Mike looked at the date on his watch. 'I'll see you again on the sixteenth.'

Maitrait grunted.

'And I'll tell you this, Captain...' Mike's soldier face suddenly changed to his softer grandfather look. 'If you take two of us off that island and not just me, I'm going to give you a bonus that'll buy you a fleet of *Brume Rouges*.'

Maitrait's eyes didn't leave the GPS screen. 'Money safe,' he said.

'You've got to have faith!' Mike told him. 'Have you got grandchildren, *petits-enfants*?'

'Too much. I not count.'

'Well, I've got faith in having one precious grandson alive.' Mike looked down and centred the black buckle on his belt. 'It's what keeps me alive.'

'And what keeps me alive, monsieur –' Maitrait turned away from his GPS to stare at Mike – 'is dollars. In dollars I have big faith...'

The *Brume Rouge* sailed silently into Solitaire's southern inlet. Through his night binoculars Mike saw where his easiest scramble from the sea would be, over steep rocks to the right of the cove that looked to offer more footholds than the sheer face dropping to the sea from a great height. The inlet was perhaps twenty metres across, filled with dark water that was probably very deep.

'Take us in as near as you can to those rocks to starboard.'

Maitrait sailed the *Brume Rouge* into the cove, then went-about while there was still room. 'Deepness not on chart,' he said. 'You say you swim...'

'*I swim!*' Mike gritted.

'So you swim now. You tell me, "Come at night-time." We come at night-time, so not see bottom.'

'For a good reason! The boy's jumpy. I want to come up on him gentle, in my own time. After what he's been through, he won't be the Joseph I knew.' The grandfather's voice cracked on a name he hadn't spoken for a long time.

'I come back one week, in day,' Maitrait said. 'Now you go.'

Without any word of farewell, Mike climbed over the stern, used the dinghy ladder to lower himself quietly into the water; and, holding the waterproof pack to his chest, he leg-kicked on his back towards the rocks – to get his first footing on the granite of Solitaire.

By which time the *Brume Rouge* was disappearing into the night.

Chapter Ten

Pax was pleased with his invention. He'd cut young broadleaved fronds from several palm trees and woven them into a carrier divided into six sections. With strong vines lashing it all together and forming the handle, he could transport enough water in half-coconuts to last him a day at a time. He tried it out carrying small rocks first, walked around the beach with the vine over his shoulder, and stood looking at the shadow of himself holding it, well pleased. 'Great!' he said. And as if this success wasn't reward enough, he actually got some milk from one of the goats. Routine and patience had done the trick, never pushing his luck. The doe in milk was his target: he'd lie near her and gently roll the fruits her way, until she was used to being close to him. And on that great day, when he was only half a metre off and she was busy eating his fruits, a kid came to drink. Pax waited until the thirsty, pushing head had finished, then with hardly a pause he reached over and grasped a teat firmly with his thumb and forefinger, squeezing strongly and rhythmically with his other fingers – squirting milk over his face in a short, warm stream, a shot of which went into his mouth. Which was a taste, like the sight of his carving, that suddenly twisted a weird bitter-sweet feeling inside him. The piece of fruit the doe was eating rolled away, she followed it, and so Pax left it at that; tomorrow would come; but that squirt of milk had been a real drink to success.

Now he was suddenly held by what two young goats were doing. They were getting to be billies, not kids any more, their play was suddenly less skittish, more aggressive, and the butting was more than the harmless nudging they'd done before; definitely edgy. And okay, all very natural – except that one was getting the better of the other in a big way. It was a lot stronger, and as well as butting it was pushing and kicking – and as the other fell before it, staying down, submissive, it looked as if it might bite.

Pax shouted, 'Oi! Stop that!' but the dominant kid had already backed off, and the weaker of the two had got to its feet to return to its grazing. So Pax left the goats and crossed the north of the island to the gunship pad, where he spent the rest of the morning pulling a large, rotting trunk from a thicket twenty metres away, laying it on top of his growing obstacle. To make surer than ever that a fighting machine would never land on his island again.

At first light, Mike's immediate move was to make his base camp. His army background served him well for a time like this. An ordinary London boy, he'd done two years' National Service in the Royal Artillery and stayed on, enlisted as a career 'regular', training for jungle warfare in Malaya – later, part of Malaysia – and now, all these years after, here he was in the tropics...

And today nature had also served him well. As the early sun thickened the rainforest with shadows, he crept inland from the cove where Maitrait had dropped him, and fifty metres in he spotted a fallen tamarind tree, split halfway up its trunk. This would make a perfect branch shelter, the trunk not so broken that it would come crashing down, while its dense foliage would make the weaving-in of waterproofing palm leaves fairly easy. While his only other requirement – to get his sleeping bag off ground – was met by his small pack, a frame canvas bed with light interlocking metal struts. His camp was ready within an hour; now he was ready to start looking for the boy. He would search discreetly, no shock or noise, be aware all the time that a frightened youngster could see another person on the island and run scared into the interior – or into the sea. But first he had to locate the beach where the *St. George* dinghy had been photographed, where that fair-haired boy had been sighted. The French military had refused him permission to speak to the Met officer, but the man's description and the later photographs were enough to give a clear picture of what the beach looked like.

Except, when he located the beach using compass and sun – this was it, no question – the black dinghy wasn't there! The place was bare and disappointing, very different from what he'd seen in his head – and he hardly dared think why the dinghy had gone. *Had the boy taken off in it?* 'Oh, please God, no!' He decided to head for the meteorological station and helipad, marked clearly on his map. Because if the boy was still on the island, perhaps he had his camp in the storage shed when no Reynard was there.

He had packed his strong boots – if an ankle went, the game would be up – and now he pressed the release button on his telescopic hiking stick. He pulled the map of Solitaire from his trouser pocket and studied it again, looked up at the sun and consulted his compass. A bearing of three hundred and twelve degrees would get him to the military site. Like a commando, he smeared insect repellent over his face, rolled down his sleeves, retied the black silk scarf around his neck, and stamped his feet on the ground as if coming to attention. His first quick look for the dinghy had been too impetuous, but now his rigorous army training snapped him into service mode. From where he was standing he should get to the *Armée Française* location in forty minutes, travelling at jungle walking pace of three kilometres an hour: perhaps a bit slower, allowing for both the climb and the granite rocks all over the island. This wasn't easy country; and it was little wonder the island was uninhabited. What commercial use would this place be? And what pleasure could anyone get from living here, once swimming and sunbathing had lost their novelty?

Final preparation: seeing the tangly, entrailed way ahead, he took his scarf from his neck and wound it around his left hand. A glove would be better, but a scarf would serve – to push bramble and sharp fronds away, while the other hand held the hiking stick for probe and balance.

We go! By the right...

But it was tough going, and trained though he was, his body demanded more frequent breathers these days. 'Clammy as a wrestler's vest!' he stopped to tell the treetops as he sipped from his water bottle. But finding no dinghy had been a downer and he needed a lift. So on he went, stepping over rocks, skirting boulders, pushing through ferns, and treading where parasitic orchids and tall flower stalks hampered his progress.

And suddenly he stopped. *What was this?* Running at ninety degrees to him was what looked like a track. He inspected it carefully: it was definitely some sort of animal way and not just a gap in the ground cover – its red soil was compacted, and the moss that covered a rock at its side was scarred by something brushing past. It ran down a steep incline – and *what's that?* There on the right-hand side something made his heart flip: a small hole; then a series of small holes at pace-sized intervals, the sort his stick would make if he were descending. *And what animals ever use sticks to help them go downhill?* Could the French soldiers have made these marks as they searched the island? He bent to look at the first hole. The ground was dryish, the humidity on the island allowing nothing on the rainforest floor to go to dust very quickly; but even so, the soldiers had been here over two weeks before: if it had been theirs this hole would have collapsed by now. So it was recent; in fact, its smooth sides told him it had been made in the past few hours...

He puffed out his cheeks, looked around for footprints – sole marks, trainer patterns, boot studs – but he could see none, just this worn track which ran east to west beneath the path of the sun. Should he follow the track, then, or cross it and head for the helipad? He made a note of his compass position and decided to go on to his original target. He could come back here and pick up this fresh trail, if need be. First, he wanted to rule the army shack in or out as someone's camp.

Half an hour later, puffed and doubled, he found the compound. At first sight of it he took off his hat and let out his own small cloud of steam, like a modest signal of success. Here it was – dead reckoning had brought him to the wire-fenced enclosure, with the Stevenson screen, the tall pole with the anemometer cupping on top of it, and the storage shack, all as described. But where was the helipad? There was no sign of a cleared space where a Reynard could land. Instead, rainforest debris was strewn and heaped across the concrete base: branches, rotting trunks, fronds, rocks, vines strung up – and when he looked at it closely, right in the middle, a small space was cleared where the surface was pitted and broken as if someone was trying to dig it up.

He sat on his haunches to think. And before he'd unwound the scarf from his hand to wipe his face, he reckoned he'd got it. There *was* someone here, and whoever that someone was, wanted to stay here alone. Diana had been right! The fair-haired boy who'd taken cover under the dinghy had been scared stiff of the Reynard – and he never wanted it to come back.

Which had to be because he was traumatized: shell-shocked by the attack on the *St. George*, the way Rupert Travers had thought.

Mike smiled, relaxed his muscles. Well, so be it. The cure for that trauma was right here. Him, *Grandpa*, who would track the boy with all his skill so as not to frighten him – because one false move and who knew what a person in that mental state could do to himself? And then he would give him all the comfort and support it was possible for a grandfather to lavish. Mike felt content, happy. Skill and patience could definitely do the trick, and didn't he have plenty of both...?

Pax had never been so hot. The midday sun was scorching down through the canopy, mist rising all around, and that last heavy trunk had taken a great sweaty effort to drag onto the gunship landing pad. Well, the answer was always here. He would relax in Rainbow Cove where he could wallow without having to fight a current. The hot trek there was always worth it for the pleasure to come. According to the sun it took about half an hour to get there from his beach – although, what was time in his world here? 'Great, guys!' he said to a pair of pecking blue-grey doves. He knew very well what time was: *it was his own!*

The thought of that first dive from the rocks made the steamy trek even more enjoyable. And every time he went anywhere on this island he seemed to see something new. Different flowers suddenly appeared overnight, and today he saw a tall, shiny-leafed, unremarkable shrub bursting out in clusters of yellowish green flowers. It was next to the only ugly thing that grew on the island, a thick-trunked tree that seemed to have its roots in the air as if someone had planted it upside-down. But these new flowers took his eyes from that ugliness – and he wondered if later on there might be fruits that he could eat. Who knew? The only problem with living alone was that there was no one to ask about these things...

From above, Rainbow Cove looked as inviting as ever. There wasn't a ripple on the surface, and through his sweat-smarting eyes Pax could see the shapes and the bright colours of the fish he was about to swim among. He shoved his stave into a cleft in the granite and stood with his toes twitching at the edge of his diving rock. With relief from his itchy, smelly state only seconds away, he stopped to relish the moment, looking up at the sky, round at his island, down at the water. And a split second before he dived from the rock he saw it: a sheen, a patch of colour on the surface of the bay. *Hell!* He knew what that was! He'd seen that spectrum of colours glinting on spilled fuel where the gunship had been. Suddenly into his head came the gunship's smell, his stomach rolled with fear as he teetered; but he couldn't pull back, he went into a clumsy dive – to drop with a great splash into silence. Fish scattered and he came up as quickly as he could, trod water, tried to see again what he'd seen from above; but the surface was still rippling from his dive, there was no seeing anything from where he was. And there was no pleasure any more: he was rolling inside with the scare of what this meant. This fuel on the water was recent. It hadn't been dumped by the gunship, and it hadn't come in from the empty ocean: it was still held together, when even the current running past the inlet would have broken it up.

No – it had to have come from a motor vessel that had been right here in this cove. And not long ago, either – a thought that took him clawing out of the water, up the rock clamber, and running doubled-over to his sleeping bay, where once more he was going to have to get rid of all signs of being here. He was going to have to hide himself in the rainforest again – until he knew for sure who or what had come into Rainbow Cove in the night...

Oh, no, no, no, no, no!

Chapter Eleven

Mike headed for the east-west track he'd crossed on his way to the compound; because the sooner he found his boy the better. Let the repair work begin! And he was lifted by the stick holes running beside the track all the way, deeper on the right-hand side – going down; lighter on the left – coming up. Someone definitely came and went along this route! So, was the boy's camp at one end of this route, with some other important spot at the other? And which end would be which? The old soldier went cautiously, didn't tread on twigs or kick loose stones, chose each footstep like a scout in a minefield; he was stalking a nervous prey he wanted to close in on before he was spotted himself; and soon he came back to the scene of his first 'downer' – the beach without its dinghy.

Like forensics he probed around the vegetation above the sand. This could be where the boy had a camp, if he'd been near enough to dive under the dinghy when the Reynard had taken off. Or he could have set himself up nowhere near this beach... Mike shrugged: he mustn't rule anything in or out – he'd never done that at work and it had made him a billionaire, so he wasn't doing it here.

Finding nothing near the beach, he searched along the coast to the south, keeping the sea on his left and heading back towards his own camp, not far from the cove where he'd landed. But he'd covered that ground already today, so he didn't go very far: he'd had his eyes about him from the start and seen nothing that called for a closer look. If there was a bough shelter like his own, or a log or stone shelter, or a sheet shelter or a frond tepee, he'd have seen it. But – *sheet shelter!* He stopped, whistled very low to himself. For a sheet shelter you needed a piece of plastic, or a groundsheet, or anything waterproof to stretch over bivouac poles. So was that where the dinghy was, giving protection somewhere in the interior?

He hurried off in the other direction, keeping the sea to his right this time. His compass told him he was heading north, and his watch said it was early afternoon – which was why he was feeling hungry! But although he knew from his tropical training what plants and fruits he could eat, he wasn't wasting time collecting them right now: he'd got emergency rations in his rucksack that would do him till nightfall. He stopped. He took off his damp hat, hung his shirt on a branch to dry out, and sat on a shaded rock to eat. He checked his military watch and allowed himself precisely fifteen minutes for his break. It was vital to take these rests, keep up his energy – but he felt young and fit enough; he'd never been an *old* grandpa – and right now he was proud to be where he was instead of lying on a settee taking a siesta. He was the Gramps who could outrun his son-in-law; the guy on family holidays who could never be found in hide-and-seek; the adult who was sent out of the swimming pool for 'bombing' his granddaughter. He stared at a piece of cream cracker, closed his eyes – threw it into the air and caught it in his mouth, blind: just one of the party tricks Joseph egged him on to do.

Enough! He stood and dusted the cracker crumbs off his jungle shirt and he put on his camouflage hat again. He stamped his feet for comfort in his combat boots and he slung his rucksack square onto his back. He could still have been the pride of the Royal Artillery. *By the right, quick march!* And almost on the quartz tick to go, he restarted his tracking – to be halted within fifty metres by the sudden sound of animals. Bleating. Sheep or goats – several of them, by the sound of it. Probably goats, he thought, the bleating of sheep was a feeble baaing, while the goats on Home Farm made this same softer cry. Well, he'd take a look. An enterprising cadet like Joseph could well have made his camp near to goats and their milk.

He followed the sounds and found them, not far away: a dozen or so, grazing on a sward of lush grasses on terrain overlooking the sea. But – disappointment – there was nowhere here for a person to camp, it was much too exposed. So he'd go on for now; but he didn't head to the north. A look at the map told him that he'd pretty well covered the eastern sector of the island. That trail with the stick holes had been heading west as well as east, and it was still the most positive clue so far. So he'd backtrack and follow it along the path of the sun. And the more he thought about it, a camp to the west made the fullest use of the daylight: which a bright boy like Joe would know all about. *Carry on!* But the east-west trail was still an uphill slog, the sun was hot, the air clammy, even the birds and the insects seemed to be taking a break, and it was a tiring Mike

Symonds who suddenly stopped and stared at a vital find in a place that shouted *boy!* at him, as loud as you like.

It was a pool of fresh water; spring fed from a granite outcrop, covered in weed except in the most accessible place for drinking. And there they were in the muddy water margin – footprints! A boy's or a small person's, left and right, one set on top of a previous set, around UK size eight or nine, he guessed – which fitted the bill perfectly! And not French military boot, not bush-dweller flip-flop, not tourist trainer, but barefoot and *boy*. 'Oh, praise ye the Lord…!' he sang to himself; and wished for a radio or a phone to tell the Reverend Fliss Bennett what he'd found. But all he could do for now was hunker down at the pool and take a drink himself.

And now Mike knew for sure what he was going to do. The answer was here at his feet, the pool. Where do photographers wait to get film of wildlife? Where do zoologists hide up, certain that at nightfall their prey will come to drink? By a watering hole. And while the boy might not come at nightfall, come here he certainly did – and would again! So this old soldier would hide nearby, and lie in wait.

He scouted around. There were a couple of good places for building a hide – which he'd do before he explored the island any more – then he could come back later, and wait for the first glorious sight of his grandson since the Lewis family had left England to go on that tragic cruise…

Above Rainbow Cove, Pax's head was invaded by the sight of soldiers with weapons crashing through the rainforest as those terrors hit him again, filling his ears with the frightening clack of a gunship. He threw himself to the ground, curled himself small, sweating yet shivering, gulping in great mouthfuls of air, yet panting breathless like a dog, cowering in the spin of his panic attack. All he could do was lay still and hope he didn't die. But after three or four minutes the attack passed – as a red bird burst through the foliage and sang at the top of a nearby palm. The sound of peace – and all at once everything around him seemed normal and calm; fresh, like a new day; and to his own surprise he sat up re-energized, ready to do what had to be done.

He had to know who had come to the island. Someone was here who'd crept in secretly by night; once more, he was not alone – unless the boat had landed no one, which was a very thin hope. He got up cautiously and began searching among the deeper undergrowth that led from the cove, looking for signs, his eyes sharpened by fear. And suddenly there it was in front of him, the chilling evidence – a tall purple flower among a cluster of purple flowers that were held up on long stalks; except this purple flower was bent to the ground, its stalk crushed but the bloom not yet dead. Someone had trodden through here – today! An enemy *had* landed.

His stomach stung again with dread – as he loped back to his bay keeping his head down. Invaded again! Would he never be free to live the way he wanted? Why was this enemy out to get him? He was a person of peace – and they were bringers of war! But was he just going to let them terrorize him until they finally captured and killed him – which was what these hunting guerrillas did? No way!

Shaking, muttering his anger, he destroyed his bedding again, scattering it thin in the undergrowth, wiping out any other signs of him being here – throwing coconut shell far out into the sea. He lifted his 'Zuri' sculpture from her niche and carried her deep into the rainforest, and laid her facing up beneath the same surface roots of the tree that had protected her before: while again that weird yearning stirred inside him, that pain that hurt and pleased him together.

He found his knife, which he had sheathed in thick leaves and attached to a vine belt. This went round his waist, above the boxers. He picked up his stave and his water carrier, because he'd sneak to the pool and fill up with enough fresh water to last tomorrow and beyond – and then he'd decide what to do. When he was stocked with enough to drink he would make up his mind whether to hide again, or go on the attack.

Go on the attack? The sight of the metal rod lying at his feet suddenly opened up that option. Sure! Hadn't he had enough of running from this enemy? There had been no gunship here today, so this was probably a lone soldier sent to do reconnaissance or to make a commando hit – which meant that right now it could be down to one against one. Okay, it could be a scientist, or an explorer, a mapper – although what were the chances of that, after the gunships and those other guerrillas? Anyway, he'd know from his clothes – why dress like a soldier if you weren't a soldier? He would find him, and creep up on him – the toughest troops have to sleep some time – and if he was kitted up in camouflage he'd be treated like the enemy. And suddenly Pax's outrage grabbed him by the throat. He turned three-sixty degrees in swearing disbelief that this peaceful life was being ruined. *So he would find this invader – and if he was a soldier, Pax would get in first!* He didn't know what he'd do, he couldn't tell till he got there – but he had a knife and he had a spear, and if he had to – *if he had to* – he would use them. His love of peace would go on hold if it all came down to either the soldier surviving, or him! When it was Pax or the enemy, it was going to be Pax!

Decision made – so now he thought through a plan: which he muttered to himself to make it real. 'Crack coconuts for carrier, go to the pool, get water, hide up, sleep. Get up, take weapon, track soldier – see where *he* sleeps, what he is; and if he's the enemy – go in at night and attack!' The most peaceful of people sometimes had to fight – and this soldier was never going to get him, nor report to anyone that he was on this island. He would force himself to fight for what he wanted to keep – and if he died trying, then that's the way it had to be!

What Mike made was not so much a 'hide' as a 'blind'. Ten metres from the pool were two large boulders, one half-leaning on the other, both moss-covered across their tops. He measured the gap between them and cut a green palm frond that would stretch between the two like a roof, leaving a small triangular hole to look through; and now he needed to cover his back, although it was unlikely from the state of the undergrowth that anyone came at the spring from the north. All the same, on his side of the boulders he bent the lower branches of a young iroko tree to the ground and tied them with vines to the trunk of a nearby lychee: and, taking several steps back, he satisfied himself that he wouldn't be seen in there.

So what was his plan? He looked up at the sky through the canopy. It would be dark in about three hours at around six o'clock. And, getting into the head of a boy like his grandson, when would Joe come for water? His footprints at the spring had looked fresh, today's not yesterday's – which said a morning visit. That fitted – a sensible cadet trekking uphill from his camp before the heat of the day. On the back of which, then, this old soldier would return to his own camp in a bit, eat and sleep, and come back to the spring at first light. And he knew what he'd say when he saw the boy. When Joe came to the pool he'd call his name softly at first – not showing out, not letting his military look be seen before the kid realized who he was; the last thing he wanted was Joe running off. Then, when he'd got his attention, he'd shout out his own name – *Gramps* – and sing the old song he'd sung at family parties since he first became a millionaire: Abba's 'Money, Money, Money'. Joe would be convinced by that, because no stranger would know about the Symonds's Christmas traditions. And *then* he would come out and show himself, and go to the boy slowly with his hands outstretched; family, blood-tied, someone always to be trusted.

Mike's heart did a little jig. He'd come a long way for this, and now the climax was ten hours away at the most. And so excited was he that he decided not to let anything spoil it – he'd stay up here, wait till night, show the patience that had made him rich, then use his luminous compass to find his camp, say his prayers, and prepare to meet his grandson next morning. And with that decision made, he settled behind the boulders to take a siesta after all. Or, he told himself, a power nap, more like…

Pax smeared his face and his body with mud – for moving unseen between the trees. He gripped his stave and his weapon shaft and hoisted his water carrier over his shoulder – because if he had a clear run to the pool he would collect water for the night. But if he saw someone or spotted any tracks, he would stalk this invader, and then hide nearby and wait for night. The thought of it churned his stomach and sweated his grip, but he was dead sure of what he was going to do. This had to be sorted or he could never live here in peace. Okay, if this person looked like a scientist or an explorer or a photographer – well, that would be different. But if he looked like a soldier there'd be no stopping and asking questions. If it was a soldier or Pax it was going to be Pax: yes, even if it came to using his weapons. His head felt light at the thought, and the tension made his heart beat faster; but it had to be done, it had to be done – so now he would go!

He headed east from Talcum Bay up the Solar Path towards the spring, the sun behind him making visibility difficult in the shadows of the rainforest: nervous, on his toes, at every step on the alert – and suddenly he found that he couldn't trust what he heard any more. What if the singing of the birds wasn't birds at all but soldiers giving coded whistles; was that his own breathing inside his head, or someone else's, close by? And why couldn't the ocean stop its roar for a while, drowning the enemy's whispers in the rainforest? Because he needed to know. He'd run and hide from two, but for one he'd go on the attack.

Bumped-up like that, he trekked the Solar Path until he came to the pool. Here, in the bluff of the huge outcrop, the island was darker, more shadowy still as the sun fell in its dip to the west. And...*what was it?* Was it his nerves, his imagination, or was there a weirdly different feel up here today? He didn't have the scenting sense of a dog, but was there something about this place right now...? Was there something not the same about it – or was that just in his head? Places change with the time of day, and he rarely came here in the late afternoon. Even so...

He stood still at the water-margin and like a nervous bird he looked all around him before risking a bend – looked around again, gently putting his water carrier to the ground. And froze. *There! Certain!* It was nothing he could see – it was something he could hear! He pricked his ears and angled his head, this way, that way. Had the goats wandered up here? Had the great buck come to the pool to drink? *Or else, what was that sound?* He held his breath, straining for what it could be – a buzz of some sort… Bees? Hornets? Not goats – it sounded like nothing mammal at all, more a low humming as if insects were gathering for some attack. A fatal swarm? Killer termites? Or was it a snake? He hadn't seen snakes, but then he'd never stayed too long up here by the fresh water. He came over cold as, ears like antennae, he faced the direction the sound seemed to be coming from. Two fallen boulders lay only metres away with a palm frond arching across the top – was the sound coming from behind there?

He drew his knife, threw down his stave, clutched his steel weapon in the attack position; all at once it was action – every muscle keyed up to attack if this was human, or to run if it was boa or boar. And as his stave rolled and clattered into the half-coconuts the droning suddenly stopped with a snort – the silence more sinister than the sound. Slowly, bravely, he took one step towards the twin boulders, then another: and jumped shrieking as a human voice suddenly called out to him like the word of death.

'Joe! Joe! It's me!'

Enemy! He was right! This soldier was calling to his partner!

And in his soldier's uniform and jungle hat, out from the shadows he came. Shortish. Rucksack on his back – and smiling, teeth shining beneath the hat's shadow like the gleam of some fierce, killing, guerrilla fighter.

Knife! Knife! Throw his knife into this enemy! But he couldn't do it! Fear had gripped Pax and paralysed him there: and something hit him, but not a bullet, not a bayonet – it was that hot and cold terror panic, the trees spinning as he fought for breath. *No – he was not going to sink down!* He was going to control it, strive with the last beat of his heart against sinking down, not get killed in a cowardly curl on the ground. But all fight had drained from him – so he threw down his weapon, and he turned and ran, mercifully keeping his feet as he dizzied away, some crucial thrust of energy spurring him as he jumped rocks, crashed through bushes and chased back the way he'd come, pursued by the soldier ordering him to stop. His legs were weak – with every jump, every run, every step and dodge he thought they'd give out – but when he took a quick look round there was the enemy charging after him with a weapon in his hand. 'Stop! Stop!' Was that the last voice he'd ever hear before he got a bullet in the back? He stumbled and fell, picked himself up, came off the Solar Path into terrain where he'd be harder to follow, pushed through the steep valley that led to the coastal highland, determined to stay on his feet and get away from the enemy somehow. He ran blindly on – his eyes blurred with sweat as he jumped the dry gulch at the bottom of the valley and he toiled up and up, slowing, slowing, but getting higher all the time, until – 'No!' – he suddenly skidded to a stop. He'd come too far! He was teetering at the precipice, centimetres from that deadly drop to the rocks. He turned; listened as best he could above the wheeze of his own breathing. He hadn't heard the enemy crashing after him – had he somehow lost him?

And then came that great bleat, a ferociously angry bleat that drained his blood. Charging from behind the granite ran the buck goat, pawing at the ground, its head down for the attacking butt with those killing horns, staring through slit eyes – and blocking Pax's way back from the edge. Pax looked to the left and to the right. The granite went up sheer on either side, there was no climbing out of here, and there was no branch or trunk to jump at: with this monster still coming on at him, huge in its own aggression. Pax stared in horror. It was as if the creature knew he was standing right on the edge, that he was moving backwards to the last thing he ever did in this world. Pax shot a look down behind him. There was no sea to aim for, a jump would kill him as certain as a fall. He was desperate – what could he do? The buck came on, its anger rising in a bleat at the limit of its range, horns levelled at him, the eyes more fiendish than ever as Pax backed off. To be gored, or to fall to his death, what choices were those? Or to stand his ground and fight the beast? Or – what had one of the fighting goats done in play? Submit! *Yes! Submit!* That's what animals did to end a fight. It was his only chance now. He must lie as flat and low as he could across the ledge, give every look of defeat and submission – and wait for what the buck would do. Either a victorious, piercing butt; or a backing off from a beaten rival...

'Huh! Hoozah! Come off there, boy!' It was the soldier shouting from behind the buck – but not at Pax, he was shouting at the beast. The buck turned its head, and Pax saw the soldier leap to its side. 'Hoozah!' He grabbed its horns, wrestled it like a wrangler – and the buck turned on him, shaking him off with an angry toss of its head. 'Hoozah! Hoozah!' – as the soldier suddenly bent and grabbed the ram's scrotum – and with a great bellow the goat kicked against the rocks, and ran past the soldier to head off down the scree.

Pax was on the edge. The enemy wanted him for himself. So did he let himself get captured, and die another way – or did he roll off the devil's drop and end this nightmare now? He looked up at the soldier, who was crouching – but not to aim his weapon, which wasn't a weapon now but a metal walking stick. He was taking something from his belt. 'Here, Joe—' He offered a flask to Pax; who saw, beneath the camouflage hat, that this soldier had an older face, and was puffed out, sweating; didn't look like a killer any more.

Cautiously, Pax took the outstretched flask, and drank from it. It was different water, not from the pool. 'Thanks,' he said, still on edge for any move the man would make.

'Now let's get that muck off your face, old lad.' The man in khaki drenched a handkerchief from the flask, crawled forward and wiped the mud from Pax's cheeks, forehead, chin and nose – and stopped, rocked back on his heels.

'Oh, my sainted aunt!' the man said. 'You're not Joseph! You're not Joseph at all!' And fell back himself, as if Pax had just dealt him a fatal blow.

Chapter Twelve

They were crouching around a small fire the man had made in a clearing near his own camp. He'd promised 'gutsy grub' and Pax had gone with him – the least he could do after he'd had his life saved. Their way to the camp went past Talcum Bay, but Pax didn't let on about his own place – he wasn't going to show too much of himself until he was dead certain of this sad man from England. And *sad* was so right. On the edge of the drop, while Pax had been picking himself up and rubbing his sore knees, he'd gone behind a boulder, shouting 'Shoo! Huzzah!' at the goat: but that had been cover; his voice had gone high, and when he came back his eyes were red.

'*Who* did you think I was?' Pax had asked, on the way to the camp. Okay, not nice, but it had to be got out of the way.

'Had it in my head you were Joe. Joseph Lewis. Grandson. Missing since the attack on the *St. George*. The French said they'd seen a fair-haired boy on Solitaire...'

'Where's that?'

'Solitaire? Here. It's the name of this island...'

'Oh!' Pax didn't feel good about that. The island had a name that he hadn't given it. But, 'I've seen *St. George*,' he said.

'That was the ship that sank. The name was stencilled on a dinghy, on the beach...' The man pointed to the east.

Pax nodded. 'That's where I saw it.' It fitted – the man's story held up, except why come secretly in the night? 'Got lost in a storm. I was going to make things out of it.'

'Bully for you! Sort of thing...a good cadet...would do.' The man gave himself a few seconds. 'You came here in it, did you? Hit the current?'

Pax shrugged. 'Don't know. I'm just...here. Always been here, don't know anything about before...'

'In Marks and Spencer boxers! You don't remember *anything*? It's all a...blank?' Pax said nothing. The man eyed him with a little nod. 'Shell shock! Know your name, do you?'

'Pax. I'm Pax.'

'"Pax"?' The old man's look said he couldn't get his head round that. 'Like the stuffing?'

'Like...Pax.'

'Ah-hah.'

'What's *your* name?'

'Mike. Mike Symonds.'

'And you're this Joseph's grandfather?'

Mike nodded, holding his mouth tight shut for a couple of seconds. '"Gramps", he called me.' From his webbing wallet he fished a photograph of a fair-haired boy about the same age as Pax; and turned away, his eyes welling up again. 'But...' He took the photograph back and looked into the rainforest, then out towards the ocean – he didn't need to finish the sentence.

'He's not here. I know he's not here...'

Mike stood to attention and nodded, a long, slow nod of acceptance, the end of this hope. The two of them had trekked on in silence, descended to the foot of the valley and on around to Mike's camp – where he got down to realities quickly. From a cord hanging free of the ground

he showed Pax a cardboard box of emergency rations –
nothing in it looking remotely like food.

'Now, sir, I can serve French onion soup for the first
course, followed by chicken paté, and for dessert—'

'I don't eat chicken – or any meat...'

'Ah. A veggie...'

'An against-the-killing-of-creatures.'

Mike nodded. 'Well, *Pax*,' he said, holding up a white
sachet about the size of an A4 envelope, 'then your main
course will be fruit dumplings in custard, with chewing
gum for dessert! What've you been eating so far?'

Pax waved an arm around; it seemed obvious.
'Coconuts, bananas, some purple fruits...'

'Good for you! Fish? Gone fishing yet?'

'Not fish.' Ever since finding the remains of that dead
goat Pax hadn't for a moment thought of killing a fish to
eat. And saving his life or not, he was blowed if this man
was going to change the way he lived. He stood and watched
him as he started hacking away the undergrowth.

'Call me "Mike",' the man said, 'I'm Mike. You've
got to call me something, and I don't want it to end up
being "the old fart"...' And the welling-up in his eyes told
Pax what the man would like a boy on this island to be
using right now. *Gramps.*

'Okay...Mike.'

With a square metre of the ground cleared, Mike used the wrapping from the chosen food as kindling, and with dead twigs and smallish logs, the fire soon took hold. 'Now, water...' he said. He shook his flask, which was empty.

'I'll go up to the pool,' Pax offered. 'I want to, anyway – my stave and pole and knife are up there, and my water carrier...'

'Tomorrow morning,' Mike told him. 'They won't walk off.' He'd been looking around. He pointed to one of those ugly trees that seemed to be planted upside down. 'Baobab – you can eat the leaves and the seeds when I'm having my fish. But tonight we can tap its trunk for water...'

They went to the tree, and, driving in a long, sharp knife which he wiggled about, Mike soon had a brownish water running from it, which he collected in a billycan. 'Now we turn off the tap—' and he plugged the hole with mud; within minutes he was back at the fire simmering the soup. 'Pax – you know what?' he said. 'We'll call this place *The Ritz*.'

And in all his sadness, by bothering with their own name for the camp, he somehow reached out to Pax; which was the moment Pax knew he was going to like this man.

*

Mike insisted that Pax should sleep on the camp bed. What comfort – a bed with a bit of give! Pax wanted to say no – he'd already been told by Mike when he should fetch his knife and stave, and like the man or not, he wasn't always going to have his mind made up for him. But by the time they'd had their meal it was dark, and Pax wouldn't be able to see to collect fresh bedding for his sleeping shelf. *And* Mike was being kind – so he accepted. But once he was lying down there was so much to think about that he slept worse than on his granite and grass. Comfort's not in the mattress, it's in the mind. Tomorrow he would ask Mike why he'd come here so secretly in the night; and he'd find out what war the island was involved in – why that scary gunship had come. But he still couldn't get his head round the place having a name – 'Solitaire'. *No way!* This island was just…where he lived.

Away from Talcum Bay, where the lap of the waves covered most rainforest sounds, tonight Pax's sharp ears picked up the flapping of bats and the snuffle of small hunting creatures – whistles, clackings, croakings – and what could be the scratching of rats and the slither of snakes, things he'd only imagined – and he longed for his shelf on the beach. But Mike's softer bed at last gave more comfort than snuggling into his grasses, and eventually he slept.

To be woken by the sounds of swearing. *Which was who, which was what?* He opened his eyes to see this Mike trying to bandage his right hand with his left, and getting in a state about it.

'Stupid bandage! Blasted thing!' Mike's face was red, he was kicking at a log, swearing deep in his growly throat.

Pax came out to him. 'What's up?'

'Cut myself on a sharp leaf. Stupid daft thing to do…' Mike was holding a small rolled bandage, trying to wind it around the third finger of his right hand, and since he was no good at using his teeth as a clamp he kept dropping the other end.

'Let's have a look.' Pax saw a deep cut bleeding through a browny-yellow stain.

'Iodine antiseptic,' Mike said.

'I'll sort that.' Pax sat Mike down, and, crouching in front of him, started again with the bandage. 'Cut looks clean,' he said. As he skilfully dressed it, Pax's mind wasn't so much on the wound as on the whole man – who'd woken this morning to that big disappointment: because the boy doing this first aid wasn't the boy he'd like to be doing it. Pax fixed the end of the bandage with a neat piece of sticking plaster. 'There you go!'

'That's an A-one job you've made of that! Like having

my own bush medic. Got the pro finish of Accident and Emergency.'

'Keep your hand up as much as you can for a couple of hours.'

'Yes, doctor.'

Pax shook his head, felt ashamed. 'Should've washed my own hands first.' Which prompted the thought of cleanliness, which in turn rumbled his bowels, signalling his morning routine. 'And I've got to go and clean up…'

'Where'd you go for that?'

'In the sea.' But Pax still wasn't up to giving away too much – partly conscious decision, partly a weird feeling that had just come out of nowhere, dressing Mike's wound – the same twist he had in his stomach when he looked at the sculpture of Zuri. 'I'll see you later. I'll come back here and find you…'

'Dried egg and smoked bacon for brekkers?' Mike was trying to be cheerful, but Pax could see how sad the man was; his shoulders were slumped, his eyes small and rimmed red, his head low, as if he'd moved from being a *young* old man to a *real* old man. Pax smiled, but shook his head. 'Not bac on, thanks.'

'Right. Yes. Got you. The old fart's sieve of a brain. I'll rustle up something else…'

Pax gave the canvas bed a brush-off, and went for his

morning ablutions; but he headed for his usual place by a roundabout route, and then only after he'd made sure that Mike wasn't following him.

So, now what? Pax asked the small fish that swam around his ankles. *When is Mike going? And who'll come next – another gunship, and real soldiers on the search?* He loved his life here when it was calm and normal; although it seemed there was never too much calm before one of the rotten terror things happened. Whatever, he'd keep his word for now – he'd go back to Mike's camp to eat – but only when he'd done his own thing, the way he always had.

He came out of the sea and put new grasses on his ledge before leaving the bay and climbing up Solar Path to the pool, where he retrieved his knife, his stave, his steel rod – and his carrier, which he filled with fresh spring water. It tasted miles better than the water out of the ugly tree. And only when he'd done all that did he go back to Mike's camp, to find the man was sitting on a log by the morning fire eating an egg and bacon mix from his billycan.

'Thought I'd lost you,' Mike said. 'Where've you been?'

Pax was about to show the water in his coconut halves when Mike quickly held up both hands in front of him, and stood – an apology. 'No! I'm sorry, old lad. You don't have to tell me where you've been. It's your business. I'm not your father, or your...' And he was trying hard, he rode it. '...I'm your friend, an equal friend. You go where you want, when you want. You don't have to take any notice of me.' Pax found a small smile. 'Get some breakfast down you. You haven't just eaten a dozen coconuts?'

Pax shook his head. 'I brought water –' and he showed Mike the slopping coconuts, setting them down in the shade – 'from the spring. Fresh.'

Mike looked at the woven carrier. 'That's a clever piece of work. Inventive.'

Pax didn't know what to say to praise. So he asked, 'What's my breakfast going to be?'

Mike spooned up the last mouthful of his own, and, using a fleshy leaf, he took from the base of the fire a small foil parcel, looking like a baked potato. 'Fried dried egg with roasted sweet potato.' From behind him he picked up a spindly tuber, held it up, and pointed into the rainforest at a vine-like plant. 'One of these...'

Pax opened the parcel in a series of hot grabs. The heat steamed out, revealing a yellowy mash.

'Taste it.'

Using the blade of his knife Pax put the mash to his mouth. It was okay. He could taste egg, although the sweet potato didn't have much taste. 'It's great. Thanks.'

'I wasn't trained for jungle survival for nothing. Comes in handy...' Pax was silent: the food was very hot. '...Like here and now.' Mike started boiling water for coffee. 'This place, Solitaire, it's not been lived on for a hundred years – gone back to rainforest. French rainforest. Not used as a military base as such, but one of a series of islands they use for weather stations. Europa, Juan de Nova, Tromelin, all coral, all got airstrips – they fly in and out on fixed-wings; but Solitaire, being granite and mountainous, they access by helicopter.'

Pax said nothing; he was urgently fighting to keep the image of 'helicopter' from getting too sharp in his head. Helicopter was just another word for gunship.

'The guy who spotted you is a meteorologist. The others who came were soldiers – looking for...my grandson.'

'They looked like killers...'

Mike filled two of Pax's half-coconuts with black coffee, gave him one, and sat on the log next to him, put an arm around his shoulder. 'You've had a bad time,' he said. 'A Gambellian attack Puma went for the *St. George*. And you must have been on her – there's no other rhyme or reason for you and the dinghy being here – and it's my opinion the experience has shell-shocked you.'

Pax burned his throat on a hot mouthful.

'Which is no disgrace. No, sir! Heroic, more like. But that's why the sound of a Reynard had you diving under that dinghy. That's why the sound of one takes you back to that terrible night...'

Pax's eyes hadn't left the man's face. 'Does that mean I'm mad?' His words seemed to rise into the air above them.

'Certainly not! You've lost your memory, sort of...'

'And will I find it?'

'*Yes!*' Mike gave him a huge hug, shook some reassurance into him. 'Oh, yes. I should say so. No doubt at all about that...'

But Pax wasn't so sure how he felt about that himself. If he had some terrible memories and he'd lost them – why should he want them back? Wasn't he all right as he was, where he was? *Wasn't he happy here, on good days?*

'In England – your people and me – we'll get you to see the top man...'

Pax screwed his eyes at Mike. 'Is my...er, shell shock... the reason you came at night, then? In secret?'

'You've got it, old lad; but read *secret* as more *quiet* than *furtive*. Honourable intentions – for my grandson.'

Pax got up, walked away, thinking, kicking at the undergrowth; at least, he *wanted* to think but Mike interrupted it. 'Your feet... Now, my grandson's—'

'*"Joe's."* You've got to say his name, Mike...' Somehow, Pax knew that to be so.

'You're right. You're a bright kid.' Mike blew his nose thoroughly into a khaki handkerchief. 'But Joe never went barefoot; on holiday he hopped about on shingle like an Irish dancer on a stove. How come you don't need anything on your feet? You're running about like a native...'

'Don't know. I just do.'

'Stupid question! Sorry! If you knew the answer to that sort of thing you wouldn't need Queen Square, would you?'

'Queen Square?'

'Where they hang out – the top medics for your sort of thing.'

'But what if this place is my top medic?' Pax suddenly found himself saying. 'Okay, so maybe they can tell me who I am – but will that make me happy?'

Mike had started raking over the fire, now he stopped and stared at Pax. 'You're telling me you're happy here...?'

Pax thought about it. 'Yup, I s'pose I am.'

'...Except when the French helicopter comes...?'

Pax nodded.

'Well, I've got bad news for you, old son, because it'll come and it'll come and it'll come. But a real doctor would cure you of aversions like that.'

Pax hated the sound of that helicopter; even talking about it now made him go hot and cold. 'But if I went to London, and got better…could I come back after, and live here again? On my island?'

Mike wrinkled his face. 'The French could be asked,' he said. 'I can't say more than that…'

'But is there a chance?' This was crucial to Pax.

'Everything's possible,' Mike said. 'Everything's possible, old lad.'

And for the time being, the two of them left it at that.

Chapter Thirteen

It wasn't a bit weird for Pax, not having a past. He had lost his memory, Mike said, but that was all right by him – he was fine, living the way he did. He knew what he wanted to happen, though – he was very clear about that. He would go with Mike from the island, and he would be cured of the terrors in his head – and then he would come back here to live.

Great! He was on his back in Rainbow Bay, the sea holding him up as he pushed back his head, stretched out his arms and legs, and lay floating on the flat surface,

closing his eyes in the sunlight. He was where he loved to
be, doing what he loved to do, relaxed and at peace with
the world. If it wouldn't mean him going under, he would
nod his head at the bliss of it.

'Watch out for that sun on your face!'

Pax let his feet sink, and trod water. Squinting, he saw
Mike at the top of the rocks, his hat pulled over his face
and his sleeves rolled down.

'Fair skin – you were spared it in that dinghy, you
don't want to get sunburned now...'

Sunburned? That hadn't bothered Pax so far; most
things he did were in the shade, it was a lesson he'd
learned from somewhere; besides, the sun was his friend,
it shone comfort on him, it was like having a warm arm
around his shoulders. But he ducked his head under,
and came out of the water – he was going to, anyway.
When he got up to where Mike was standing, the man
suddenly whipped out a pair of black underpants from
behind his back.

'Have these new Calvin Klein's before those others
disintegrate!' But he turned his face away as he handed
them over, and Pax could see why. It was nothing to do
with the underpants – it was because his face was red
and swollen. Mike did that, he'd noticed. He went off on
his own without saying why, and came back broken up.

Every sight of the wrong boy had to be making the man so sad and miserable.

'I'm sorry I'm not Joe,' Pax said. 'I really am. I should've been your grandson.'

'Eh?' Mike took off his hat and wiped his sweating face with it, taking a long time over his eyes.

'I wish in all the world I was Joe. Not for me, don't get me wrong, I'm fine like I am, but if it'd make you smile instead of cry, I'd swap being Pax to be your Joe...' He broke off. 'Sorry – I'm talking rubbish...'

'No you're not.' Mike's eyes glistened like the sea in shade. 'You're talking from your heart. I appreciate it, old lad, I really do.' And he put an arm around Pax's wet shoulders.

When the moment was right, Pax slipped off his tattered grey boxers and put on the black pair. He pulled them up, took his hands away with a flourish, and they shot straight down to his ankles – sizes too large.

'*Todger alert!*' Mike exploded into a single gunshot of a laugh. Pax laughed, too – and while Pax reverted to his old boxers, they stood and nodded at each other, at the vulgar humour of a dropped pair of pants.

'We'll put your picture in the papers,' Mike said, 'we'll find out who you are. You'll have friends, relatives, grandparents who thought you went down with the

St. George. So you'll be their equivalent of Joe...'

But Pax didn't fancy the thought of relatives; the only thing he wanted was to be without those terrors in his head. He didn't want to be handed over to people he didn't know, relations to *belong* to. He was his own man here, and all he wanted in this world was to be alone again. 'When are you going?' he asked.

'A week yesterday. The *Brume Rouge* comes back on –' Mike consulted his watch – 'the sixteenth. But I hope it's "us" going, not just me.' He sat on a rock and looked up at Pax. While Pax looked at the ground. He'd worked out his future, swimming there in the cove, but now that it was put into words, was he so sure? Was the chance of getting better from the terrors worth the chance of never coming back here? Could he live with the attacks in his head if it meant staying free on his island? He couldn't be forced to go, not by Mike – and Mike would know that, too. If he chose to, Pax could dodge, hide, disappear for long enough to upset Mike's timing with the boat and its owner – it wouldn't stay long, especially since it wouldn't have Joe in it. Anyway, Mike hadn't asked him a direct question, so he didn't have to give a straight answer.

'So what's for supper tonight?' Pax asked.

*

Mike took Pax with him to get the ingredients. And the ex-soldier knew what he was about – he collected their supper from trees and plants that Pax had only thought of as parts of the jungle.

'Eh? How about this for a slap-up, sit-down do? Lychee for dessert, tamarind-pod pulp for a sauce, and – ta-ra! – for the *plat du jour*, roots of the goa bean, roasted and served with its own boiled pods and leaves. Tastes like spinach!'

'Great!' Pax had never even thought about eating such things. He said so to Mike as they crouched over the evening fire, cooking.

'Just as well you didn't experiment, old lad! You've got to *know*, or you could wake up dead. But with a bit of know-how, no one should ever starve in the tropics.'

'Tropics?'

'Where we are, Indian Ocean. And before we leave it,' Mike said, stirring in the pulpy sauce, 'there's a job I think we ought to do.'

'What's that?'

'I think we ought to clear the helipad. If we don't let the French helicopter get in to do their weather stuff, they'll only send a ship and a task force to clear their landing space – which won't chuff them up to heaven, and unlikely they'd look too fondly on anyone asking permission to live here…' He shot a quick look from under his hat as if he realized how much that sounded like a threat.

Pax picked up on it quickly. 'I do want to come back, Mike. You think I won't want to when I'm better – but I will. I will, I can tell you that for sure!'

'Hell's bells, why not?' Mike looked around him. 'It is paradise, isn't it?' And Pax nodded to that. 'Now, tell me about your carving…' Mike had seen it when Pax replaced Zuri on her ledge by the sea. 'What's it all about?' He leaned back and put his hands behind his head, one pal being relaxed with another.

Pax shrugged. 'I don't know. I just…saw a sort of face in the tree stump, and wanted to see her better…'

'You've got a real skill with the old whittling knife! Are you sure about your name – can't I call you Micky Angelo? Or "Pax the Knife"?'

'It was just something to do,' he lied: because he knew he'd *had* to do it.

'And what about *her* – have you given her a name?'

But Pax wasn't sure that he wanted to share her name. To tell Mike the girl's name would make her public – and she was private. But Mike was looking amiably at him – and the grieving grandfather *had* saved his life. So Pax said it. 'Zuri,' he told him.

'Odds on, someone special to you, if you only knew it.' Mike grunted, deep in his throat. 'And I tell you what, Pax, old lad, I know what you've just done...' He was looking closely into Pax's eyes. '...You had to think about telling me her name, didn't you? Your Zuri *is* special. You know she is – even if you don't know why. And you just shared her with me.' Mike rubbed his nose, as if he was a bit embarrassed. 'And I think a lot of that. I can't tell you what that means to this sad old man, coming from you...'

The fire crackled and a log popped, which set them to making safe the embers. But later, back on his sleeping ledge, Pax felt strangely uncomfortable about giving out Zuri's name; when he got his memory back he might not want people to share her. And the thought came to him – couldn't he fight his own battle against the terrors? Wasn't there something he could do for himself *here* instead of going to England? Couldn't he try to think of something good when those bad things hit him? Mike had tricks for jungle survival; well, couldn't he have some, too – tricks in his head to help him stay on his special island?

And as the ocean washed in on the beach, lulling, calming, in a sudden lift of his spirits, Pax knew he could succeed. He had beaten thirst and hunger on his own; he had beaten the sea in the storm; he was a survivor –

and he could beat his terrors! And on that surge of hope, a plan started coming into his head; not complicated, but it would just take a bit of skill and patience. And lying there, he went over it and over it, added to it, and ended up well pleased.

Whatever he was doing on the island, with Mike or on his own, he would keep his eyes skinned on the ocean, looking for a boat. Mike had pointed to the south as the boat's likely direction, so that's where he'd look the most. Plus, next time he got the chance, he'd try to get a glimpse of the date on Mike's watch, and he'd count the nights to the sixteenth – and on that night he'd be sure to lie awake, just in case the boat came in the dark. Meanwhile, bit by bit he'd hide water and fruits and coconuts deep in the interior, and then as soon as he got wind of the boat he'd disappear. He'd stay hidden until they'd searched the island for him, and hadn't found him, and until he'd seen them go.

Because, yes! He would stay, and let Pax and the island be the doctor.

He carried out his plan. Whenever Mike had his 'power nap', or Pax was on his own for his swim or his ablutions, he started taking food and water to his hiding place. The place he picked was well off all the tracks, chosen because no one could follow a trail there. It wasn't deep in the interior at all; it was along the rocks, west of Rainbow Cove, where he found a narrow niche three metres down which couldn't be seen from the sea, or from the land, not even from above – a great hiding place, its choice clinched by the rocks leading to it, which were always wet from the sea, leaving no footprints. Here, deep in the cleft, he put his coconuts and purple fruits, and, secretly splitting more shells, he lined up enough drinking water to last him about three days. That should be enough: much longer than that would mean Mike wasn't going to go without finding him, and he'd have to come out, anyway.

So he was ready! Pax had made up his mind. Mike could leave – and he would stay. This island was going to go on being his home: and he would never think of it as Solitaire, he would think of it as *Mine*.

But the boat came a day early! Pax knew it was early because he'd double-checked the day before by using Mike's watch to see if he could find the compass direction of the dinghy beach from Mike's camp, just for the sake of it.

'Horizontal, remember: point the twelve o'clock at the sun – and then the mid-point between twelve and the hour hand gives you your north-south line.'

'Ah.' Pax had done as he was told, but his eyes had been focused on the date in the window. *14*.

'So, what direction does that give us for the beach?'

'East-north-east,' he'd said.

'You're a bright boy. Finish your education, go to college, and then come and tell me when you want a job.'

'What sort of job would that be? I don't know anything about you.' Which he didn't. What Mike did in England hadn't seemed important here on the island.

Mike had taken back his watch. 'Import-export; mainly export – all over the world.' And then he'd gone back on himself. 'Dammit,' he said, 'I'm a blooming billionaire!'

'Are you?' said Pax. 'Does that make you happy?'

And Mike had suddenly twisted his face, and Pax had realized what a crass thing he'd said. As if money could make this grandfather happy…!

Pax thought it was a breaking wave, out beyond the reef, a flash of white on the surface of the ocean; but he looked again from the top of the rocks where he'd just jammed two half-coconuts of fresh water into his secret store. And now he saw it clearly, a blue and white boat heading his way! *A day early! A day early!* He had to hide! He had to get back down there into his deep crack! He was right here. He could get into his hiding place within seconds.

But he mustn't – he wouldn't! He'd been caught out – with something vital he had to do today. *He had to bring Zuri here to the niche.* It had to be a last-minute thing because Mike knew she was on her shelf, but now Pax wanted her safe with him. What might Mike do with Zuri when he couldn't find Pax? He might take her back to England as proof that there was still a boy on Solitaire who had made this carving. Or – more likely – knowing Pax's feeling for Zuri, he might use her as bait to get him back. *'Come out, or I go off with her...'* Okay, there wasn't a great chance of that – but he just might, and Pax wasn't going to run the risk.

Stupid early boat!

He knew where Mike was right now. He was up at the gunship pad sweeping off the last of the twigs, and packing mud down the hole Pax had dug to grow a tree. So, without wasting a second, Pax had to fast-trek from the rocks to his bay. He kept well back from the sea. The trail went inland, anyway, but he didn't want the boat's captain to get a glimpse of him. If the man had never seen him, he might doubt Mike about a boy being on the island at all... Stealthily, knife at belt and stave in hand, he slipped back to his bay; and there, up on her own little shelf she sat –

Zuri, beautiful with her half smile and her sleeping eyes. She didn't change, she never moved; her expression was always the same, coming out of the wood from which she'd been carved as if she were peaceful in some private way. Now, just looking at her, the spirit of the girl within the piece touched him, and his heart began to beat a little faster – and as he took a step towards her, reached up, and lifted her off her shelf, that weird feeling came into his stomach again. It didn't hurt at all, it wasn't a pain, it was a yearning, good, yet sad in some way, and it spread and reached into him. And in that moment he knew without any doubt that Zuri was real, somewhere in the world – he was absolutely certain of that.

He stood there and stroked her head, cradled her in one arm, smoothed a hand down her cheek, and he lifted her to where he could look into her closed eyes.

And in that moment he changed his mind completely. He threw out his plans and resolved on something else he was going to do.

He would go with Mike to England, and he would get help. Yes, for himself and the terrors, but more to get a clue on his life from before he came here; enough to help him go in search of the real Zuri – because she was very real somewhere – and he would bring her back with him one day to share his special island.

Part Two

Chapter Fourteen

Where am I? Pax hadn't woken to the familiar roar of the waves – so where was he? Seconds later he knew, of course. He was in Mike's house and feeling okay about it – although living in a house in England was very different from being on his island. He'd come here for a purpose, though, and now here he was, kitted out with new clothes and trainers, and a comfortable guest bedroom to sleep in.

But the same as before, the first sight he saw on waking was Zuri, now sitting across the room on a marble-topped dressing table – looking more primitive against the straight-edged world of a house, with its square-cornered doors instead of openings between rocks, and where light shone through windows instead of filtering through foliage. But whenever he looked at her that same old yearning came into his stomach; and always with it his promise to find the real girl who had made him want to carve her. He could never forget; especially since there was a girl here at Mike's who had a slight look of Zuri about her. She was just a little kid, though, called Mary, the daughter of Mike's assistant, Diana. And although Mary's eyes opened wide when he came into a room and although she was always kind to him, there could only ever be one Zuri.

They were all being kind to him, letting him get used to his new life. Mike left early for work in a limo, but every day there was a note outside the bedroom door, always saying the same thing, in different ways. *Have a good day. Relax, recharge your batteries.* And, *We're soon going to find your people.*

Mary went off to school in a Land Rover driven by Pedro, the odd-job man, long after Mary's mother had gone to London with Mike. So Pax hung around, got to know the goats and the pigs at Mike's farm, read Mary's books, and watched the television. But whatever he was doing, his mind was on his island, daydreaming of drinking from the does or sitting on the beach, carving – and he always came back to Zuri, wondering who the real girl was, and where she might be right now. Well, he had his plan, his determination to find out those things: it was his deal for finding out more about himself. Meanwhile, Mike was being really good to him. He was great about food. He never once made a fuss of Pax not wanting to eat a killed creature. When they all sat down together, Pax's food was a tasty vegetarian alternative to their meat or fish; and when it was just Pax and Mary eating early evening, Mary would have the same as he did. In fact, everyone had been kind to him since leaving his island. The British Consulate man in Madagascar had listened to Mike's story – of finding a shell-shocked boy instead of his own grandson – and after hearing Pax's good English and the stuff about the *St. George* dinghy, had issued an Emergency Travel Document for a 'distressed British citizen'; which allowed Pax to travel to England in the Lear with a nurse as medical escort. And at Cranfield Airport, where Mike kept his jet, the immigration officer had notified Social Services and the police, and let Mike take him home.

On the second day, Mike had photographs taken of him: not digital snapshots but special pictures set up in the drawing room, with a tripod and lights and a woman called Tam. It took ages, the posing and all the focus, everyone standing behind the camera and saying this and saying that – until Tam caught Mike pulling faces and sent everyone out of the room. She turned off the photography lights and came to sit opposite Pax with a camera in her lap, talking quietly, asking him questions about his life on Solitaire; and when he was relaxed and telling her about Rainbow Cove and the freshwater spring and his sleeping shelf, when he began enjoying going over his times with the goats, she started to click quietly away.

The next Saturday, the pictures came by post. Mike spread them on the dining table, and everyone was at them. Mary liked this smiling one, Mike thought he looked scared in that one, Diana preferred a sober, formal shot. But there was one that Pax liked best. He could remember the feel of his face muscles when Tam had taken it, when he was telling her about his carving – just about the knife and the wood, no naming of Zuri – but this picture, Pax thought, this was *him*.

'Fair dos, old lad. It's your mug, so it's your call. I'll get this to the news agencies first thing on Monday.' Mike scooped up the rest and bundled them into their envelope; and then, instead of having breakfast with them, he disappeared in his sports car somewhere, and came back three hours later with his eyes red and his face swollen. Pax guessed where he'd been; not to a business meeting, more to some private family place.

All the same, 'You work mega hard, don't you, Mike?' he said – for something to say. But it was true. Saturday was the only day when Mike wasn't doing business – in London, at one of his factories, or in the car or the train or the plane. He even spent Sundays in his office, shouting at his laptop and doing what stuff he could without Diana.

'You've noticed, old lad? Well, you know what they say – money doesn't grow on trees.' Mike pulled out a handkerchief and blew his nose, hard. 'If you want it, you graft for it, and if you want more – you graft more! Hah!' But it was a laugh about nothing funny.

'Doing what, then?' Pax wanted to know. Which, to be honest, was a bit more than taking Mike away from his sadness – he was quite keen to know where Mike got his money from.

'Running "Symonds's Systems", old lad. Retired from the army and set myself up in business. I'm a hands-on man, me! And not just counting the takings…'

Pax grinned. Of course Mike *ran* something: he couldn't picture the man sitting in the back seat of anything. 'No – I mean, *making* what, *selling* what?'

Mike had wandered into the kitchen; now he started

filling the coffee machine with water. 'Well, take this. Example. All the options for a cup of coffee – espresso, cappuccino, milano, turino, roma, napolino, mafioso – whatever crazy coffee you want, what do you do? You push a button...'

'Yeah...'

'And in lots of these machines – definitely this one, brand-spanking latest model – it's one of my sensors that makes the machine obey your finger. Switches, timers, pressure pads, modems – that's what we make...'

Pax nodded wisely. 'So everyone needs you...'

'Or people like me. Companies, governments... But there's more than one of us about – and contracts don't hang around on street corners – they've got to be winkled out, struck, good deals done...' Now Mike was Mike again – the manufacturer rather than the grieving grandfather.

And Pax felt happy at having helped. He found mugs for the two of them.

'But I tell you what. I won't give my office the time of day tomorrow. Let Lithuania wait!' He sipped and turned to Pax as if he'd just made the finest mug of coffee in the world. 'You and me – we'll jaunt off somewhere, how about that?'

'Great! Sounds all right.'

'You won't mind missing church?'

'I won't mind missing church.'

'Right then.'

And the next day, when Diana and Mary went off for a drive on their own, Mike took him to Surrey Adventure Park. But they drove out of the electric gates of Sharpe End with Mike staring at the way ahead without a sideways look at Pax. 'One of Joe's hot spots, the Adventure Park!'

So he was doing today what he'd done with his grandson. Making something less special? Getting stuff out of his system? Correct. He was at the wheel of his red two-seater, soon telling Pax how Joe used to drive an old car off-road at Sharpe End, how they watched the rugby together, and Joe played for the Marlow Thirds. What was in Pax's head, though, were his treks up Solar Path, his swims in Rainbow Cove, and his bed between the boulders. But once they were on the motorway Mike stayed in the outside lane tight up the back of anything in front of him – and life was suddenly too precious for memories. No ride at the theme park could possibly water the guts like Mike's driving. And, true enough, the Adventure Park's head-in-your-feet rides seemed tame in comparison with the motorway. On the Sky Diver, Pax shouted as his body hit a G-force; he screamed as he was doused with water upside down on The Devil's Sluice;

and his legs didn't belong to him on the Tarantula –
but none of the fearsome rides had the real-life chill of
overtaking a Merc already doing ninety. And as he'd
expect from such a driver, Mike was strapped in next to
Pax on all of them, shouting and swearing, and laughing
his head off like a big, childish brother. Or an ace
grandfather... 'Did you see my backside go? It just took
off over yonder hill!'

Still in the park, Mike took them to a fast-food place
for veggie burgers and fizzy water. After which, 'as an aid
to digestion', they went on the quiet Bush Railway – an
aerial train that took them around and over the Adventure
Park Zoo. And it was this last, gentlest ride of all that
churned Pax's stomach the most. Lions, tigers, seals,
gorillas, penned into enclosures that gave them no room
to roam; creatures of the wild slumped bored and
meaningless for the pleasure of people who'd travel home
over smaller distances than these animals would cover
searching for food in the wild. He saw a small herd of
goats with no greenery to eat, just buckets of 'meal', and
he thought of the freedom the goats had on his island –
yes, even the diabolical buck. He went quiet as Mike
pointed out the different species: the sights upset him –
but he wasn't going to spoil things. By the canny way
Mike had geared-up the rides, he knew he'd shared this

day with Joe a few times before; but the man said nothing of that, and if his face ever looked swollen and his eyes red, it could have been a ride that caused it. But Pax *knew* – and there was no need for disagreement. They'd come on this juvenile adventure to get something out of Mike's system; and they would never come here again, he was sure of that. And when they got back to Sharpe End, Mike went up to his room and stayed there till dinner. Like the rides, every experience has a cost to it.

Pax's photograph was in the Tuesday papers. True to his word, Mike had e-mailed his picture to the news agencies, and there it was, larger or smaller according to the editors' layout.

DO YOU KNOW CRUSOE BOY?
THE WRONG KID – BUT WHO IS HE?
TOP BOSS RESCUES GRANDSON WHO ISN'T!

But it was much the same story written beneath all the headlines – because Michael Symonds had given them as much as he was going to: his brief version of the background to the appeal was his final word, and he refused to give any interviews. His Hertfordshire home might be photographed from the air, reporters might be at its gate, but no one was going to profit from his grief. And he protected Pax from it all like a responsible guardian. Their story was definitely not up for sale.

The only paper Pax saw was the *Daily Telegraph*, where he was on page one.

IDENTITY APPEAL

The tragic loss of industrialist Michael Symonds's family in the *St. George* sinking earlier this year – his daughter, son-in-law, and grandchildren – has taken a dramatic twist, *AP reports*. Seeking his teenage grandson Joseph, whose body has never been found, Symonds followed a chance sighting of a fair-haired boy to the French-owned Isle de Solitaire in the western Indian Ocean. The *St. George* survivor found there, however, was not his grandson but the boy pictured, who appears to be suffering from amnesia.

The boy, officially in Social Services' care, but currently living with Symonds at his Hertfordshire home, can remember nothing of his life before his resourceful existence on the uninhabited island, which is used for meteorological research.

Anyone recognizing the unidentified boy is asked to contact Michael Symonds at Symonds's Systems.

Our science correspondent writes: *Amnesia is unusual forgetfulness that can be caused by brain damage due to disease or injury, or it can be caused by severe emotional trauma. Sometimes memory returns of its own accord, triggered by familiar objects, or music, or photographs. Otherwise, skilled neurological or psychiatric treatment is employed.*

'You're famous, Pax – can I have your autograph?' Mary passed him the newspaper as they ate breakfast, him in his tracksuit and her in her school uniform. He'd hardly finished reading it, though, when the telephone rang and Mike came on to speak to him.

'Pax, you're in all the papers today, old lad; and later on your mugshot will be on the TV news...'

'I'm reading it right now.'

'Damned good show overall – but don't get brought to the blower again. Let Pedro field all calls – he knows what to say – those press blighters can be as devious as a Sunday train. And don't go to the main gate – the long-lens boys are camped all along the King's Walden Road.'

'Okay.'

'We had the blighters before, over Joe not being found.' There was a painful silence on the line. Mike was getting better, but he still got caught by sadness attacks, as sudden as a hiccup. 'But who knows, old lad, I might come home tonight with your name in my pocket...'

'Thanks, Mike.' *But no thanks!* That was the deal, though – he had to know who he was if he was ever going to track down Zuri and go back with her to his island one day; what he didn't want was the family that went with his name.

The call was interrupted by Pedro coming into the

breakfast room. A small, bent Spaniard, with skin like old bark. 'Big cameras, front end,' he told Mary, miming a camera the size of an accordion. 'Quick, eh, we go the long way round, back gate.' Half a kilometre away, the farm entrance to Sharpe End was hard to find and would be a lot more private.

Mary got up from the table. 'If I'm late for school I'll blame you for it! Being in the paper.' She stared at Pax. Pax frowned. Was this some sort of dig? Was she jealous of his times with Mike? 'Then you'll have to pay a forfeit,' she went on – and she put a finger on his nose, pressing it like one of the buttons on the coffee machine. And her face opened up in a smile. 'A game of swing ball.'

'Okay by me!'

But when Mike came in that evening, it wasn't with the *who he was, who he'd been* that Pax was dreading – it was with an appointment to see the doctor who was going to get him better. Against which Pax was already prepared with a plan. It had been forming over the past few days. He was going to be selective! When he saw the doctor, he'd work hard to get better from the gunship horrors – enough to get his own private clues about his past – but he'd pretend *not* to get better enough to have to go off with a family. The newspapers and the hospital might tell him his name – but he was still going to stay

'Pax'. His family couldn't claim him till he was better. Like the purple fruits and coconuts, he was going to pick what he wanted to survive. It was his life, *he* would decide just how much better he was going to get.

After supper Mike drove himself to the church of John the Baptist at Little Fletching. He knocked at the vicarage door and interrupted the Reverend Fliss Bennett watching a DVD with her family.

'I'm sorry, Fliss, I should have phoned,' he told her in her study.

'You've done me a good turn.' She smiled, and touched his arm. 'There's only so much I can take of funny American kids.' Quickly, she came to his obvious reason for coming. 'I saw the *Guardian* today. I was going to telephone you – but I said a little prayer over in the church. It must have been a terrible disappointment for you...'

Mike's handkerchief was out and he was blowing his nose heartily, ending with a brave done-and-done-with flourish. 'This lad's a nice boy; calls himself Pax...'

'The Roman goddess of peace – he's probably heard it somewhere. And it's got to be said – a better name than Mars!'

'And he's got problems you'll have read about...'

'Yup. And what about your problems, Mike? You're

my concern.' She was facing him, out of her dog collar and clerical grey shirt looking no different from any young mother.

'You talked about closure...'

'I did. I think it would be good for you.'

He sniffed. 'I'm starting to think myself there's little chance another boy's going to be found like Pax somewhere...'

Fliss was shaking her head, but in agreement with what he was saying. 'No, I don't think there is, Mike.'

'So I'm thinking – just thinking – of putting Joe's name on the headstone. It'd give me somewhere to come and... talk...to him. With the others.'

Fliss put a hand on Mike's arm. 'Yes,' she managed. 'That's always a very real help.' She could hold herself together in funeral services, but in her own home she was as emotional as anyone.

Mike took a big, broken breath, and together they stood there hugging: until he led the way slowly to the hallway and opened the front door. He stepped into the porch. 'Just to let you know, Fliss, early alert,' he said, 'I'm thinking about closure...'

'Good.' And as Mike drove away from the vicarage, Fliss came out of the house and shut the front gate, with a positive push.

Chapter Fifteen

AMNESIAC BOY REMEMBERED

The boy found by industrialist Michael Symonds when searching for his grandson is named as Peter Foster, the son of British expats living in Port Elizabeth, South Africa. Peter's father, Leonard, was a pharmacist and his mother, Cathryn, a doctor – both working with *Médicins Sans Frontières* in Gambellia and reported missing after the *St. George* sinking.

It had been feared that Peter, in Africa with his parents while on summer holiday from Cottingham Manor School, Grundisburgh, Suffolk, was missing with them. Now he has been found alive.

It is possible that the East African Coastal Current carried him more than sixty nautical miles to the French owned Isle de Solitaire, where he survived alone for almost a month before the ex-soldier sought his grandson there.

Hertfordshire Social Services said that members of Peter's extended family would be contacted as soon as they could be traced.

Peter Foster? *Peter Foster? Who was he?* Pax was Pax, *him*, *himself*! So this Peter Foster's parents had been killed the same as Mike's grandson Joe and his family – but somehow Pax felt less sad for two dead people he didn't know than he'd felt for the butchered goat on his island.

'It'll be all right,' Mary's mother told him – sort of *buck-up-young-man!* 'You'll soon have family come to claim you. Mary's without a father, and we cope. We cope very well, don't we, Mary?'

Mary nodded across the dinner table. 'Specially with Pax here.'

The three of them were eating without Mike that evening – he'd driven to Peterborough that day to visit one of his factories; but when he came in later, 'We've put out feelers, old lad,' he told Pax. 'And on Friday you and I are off to Cottingham Manor, to your old school…' His eyes sparkled for the pair of them. 'See how that stirs up your noodle pot!'

'You're meeting "the Persian" on Friday,' Diana told him. 'The robotics contract.'

'With this terrible sciatica?' Mike did an old man's shuffle – before jumping over an armrest onto a settee. 'And hush your mouth – that's supposed to be secret. I'll see "the Persian" next Monday. I'm in the driving seat.' And that was settled. Diana opened her eyes wide with a *what's-happening-to-the-world?* look; and Mike changed the subject – told them how he'd overtaken a Porsche GT2 on the M1. In all ways, it seemed, Mike was racing to sort out Pax's needs.

Was Pax pretending? Pax thought he could sometimes see the doubt in Mike's eyes – and definitely in Diana's. But no way was that the case. Right from the first turn-off into the driveway of Cottingham Manor, Pax felt confusion and frustration at being somewhere he was supposed to know – and didn't. The sights, sounds, and smells of the place were supposed to bring back his past: but, negative, dead negative! This front entrance could be any front entrance – definitely nothing special – and the school secretary was a total stranger. The way she looked at him said, *you know me!* But he didn't, and his stomach churned with embarrassment. What was he supposed to say? How was he supposed to look – smile, and pretend?

It must have seemed so rude to her, but he couldn't do that: he truly didn't know her from anywhere before. Nor did he know any of the boys in the school photograph she showed him – and he felt lucky it was the half-term holiday or there'd have been kids around who'd have got mad at being blanked. It all fuzzed his brain and twisted his insides. What with him not answering to Peter at home, and now failing this memory test, how could he blame Mike for having doubts?

'Nothing, old lad?' Mike asked. 'You don't remember the charming Mrs. Cassidy here?'

'Sorry, Mike – no. I don't.'

The looks between the two adults were sympathetic, but Pax could see that raising of eyebrows an infant gets when he says he hasn't trampled the flowers in the border. But he knew nothing of this place – and as well as feeling a fraud, Pax was brought down by the thought that his brain was in a worse state than even Mike believed. *Had he got some serious disease?* Whatever – all ways up it was a horrible visit.

Mike said hardly anything all the way home, just concentrated on winning every race along the A14. Except, as they turned into the back entrance of Sharpe End, 'Funny old thing, the brainbox,' he said. 'But we'll get you sorted, Pax old son – not a doubt about that. Clever chaps, these brain merchants – and next week we'll make a start!'

But bright and certain though his words were, there was no denying the Hertfordshire house seemed a doubting place that night.

And Pax was doing some frowning of his own. To get the school visit out of his system he made himself think of something else – and a niggle came back into his head from when Diana had talked of some secret meeting with a man called 'the Persian'. Why should it be secret, he'd asked himself, to the people at home at Sharpe End? Or was it just from him? But the doors in the house were always open, including Mike's office door – so why would he keep something secret from him? Which again made Pax ask himself who 'the Persian' was. Well, he could do a bit of digging in his bedroom. Mike had given him a new laptop with a wireless internet router. He could easily get online and look up *Persian*. That would be a start.

Which puzzled him when he did – because a Persian would be someone who came from Persia, yes – which was Iran before it was Iran. Was 'the Persian' Mike's nickname for an Iranian? *Or was it a code name?* Whatever, according to the internet, Iran was regarded by the west as a dangerous state, developing its nuclear industry. So why would Mike Symonds of 'Symonds's

Systems' have a secret meeting with a businessman from a country like that? And what were the 'robotics' Mike would be selling him? Well, Pax didn't know – it was probably just to sell him a few thousand remote-control sensors for HD television sets – but he went to sleep that night with a thing or two on his mind.

Mike took him to Queen Square to meet Dr. Mughal, a two o'clock appointment with a 'treat' lined up for later – meeting up with Mary and her mother after school and doing something 'a bit special'. 'Dolly mixture after the medicine,' Mike said. 'Make a pain a pleasure – it always worked with Penny.' And as he said it he kept his voice as steady as anyone can who has stood by their daughter's grave.

They didn't wait long to see Dr. Mughal; private patients don't. She came out to them herself and showed them into her small office: youngish, dark eyed, pale skinned, with abrupt black hair. Pax had expected a long white coat and a stethoscope, but Dr. Mughal wore a fussy cardigan and a long floral skirt that didn't seem to match.

'Hello, Peter,' she said. 'I'm Aysun Mughal. Please sit down.'

Pax sat, Mike stayed standing. 'Peter likes to be called Pax,' Mike told the neurologist. 'We all call him Pax.'

'That's an interesting name.' Her mouth smiled at Pax, but he wasn't sure about the eyes. 'I'm fine with that.' Which marked the start of her course of treatment to help him become Peter Foster again. It could be a slow process, she told them, but today would just be getting to know him, to explore his neurological state. She talked of a brain scan another day, but now, with alert eyes and encouraging nods of the head, she took Pax through what she called her standard tests. Mike was allowed to stay in the room – although she'd see Pax on his own the next time – but they went on for so long that at one point Mike had to take a break, 'Before I fail the waterworks test!' They seemed endless to Pax as well, all the while trying to keep on top of what he should and shouldn't know if he was going to carry out his private plan.

She asked him where he was, what date it was, and what time. He had to repeat strings of numbers to her, which got as long as telephone numbers – quite easy – except when he had to do them backwards as well. He had to answer questions like, 'What do you call the large African animal with a trunk?' He was shown pictures of everyday things like a tap and a pillar box for no apparent reason; till later on he was asked if he could remember them – which he could. He had to read aloud, and spell some words – 'manoeuvre' defeated him – and he had to add up and take away numbers, like forty-one minus thirteen. All okay. But he felt stupid when he had to stand up and do actions for her – mime using a saw, and saluting, and typing. She got him picking out patterns within shapes, and she tested his sense of smell from a cluster of little bottles. And she ended up sticking a pin in him. 'Ouch!' – and she laughed. But he hadn't tripped himself up on those tests – given nothing away – and 'No little surprises there!' she pronounced.

He told her about his life on Solitaire – from first finding himself on its beach to the final push-off in the boat, all the while Dr. Mughal's questions coming in a soft voice with silences, letting him run on when he got to talking about his gunship terrors – the dizziness, the hot-and-cold skin, the not being able to breathe, the terrible feeling of horror-to-come rolling in his stomach. But when she asked him about things before that – did he remember going onto the *St. George*, or anything of the Gambellian war, or helping his parents with the wounded? – all that was closed off to him; genuinely, no danger of tripping himself up. It was like trying to see into someone else's head. Mike had told him what the *St. George* had been doing that night in Moebane; he had explained how Peter Foster's parents, and Peter, had been on the sun deck when the ship was attacked. But Pax remembered nothing of that – and that was the truth. The only lie he told was through what he didn't say. He didn't tell Dr. Mughal about Zuri. He deliberately kept Zuri from her, and he was always going to do so. The special way he felt when he looked at Zuri was for him only: it was private, deep. He wasn't sharing Zuri with anyone who couldn't understand what she meant to him – especially when he wouldn't understand himself until he found her one day.

'Did you have a knock on the head, or anything like that?'

'I don't know. I don't think so. I had a headache first off, but that went away.'

Dr. Mughal stood and felt his skull, looked into his hair. 'No sign of a healed wound. It wouldn't fit, anyway…'

'How not fit?' This was Mike, back from the gents' and sitting behind the door as upright as a juror.

'If this were a typical post-traumatic amnesia – the sort sometimes caused by injury – it wouldn't produce loss of personal identity. And he's got his motor skills.'

'You're not driving my car, matey!' Mike laughed. 'So you're talking *psychological* condition?' he asked her.

Dr. Mughal sat again, firmly. 'I'm talking nothing yet. But you'll be following up on the personal details, won't you? Any information you get on those – the home, the parents' work, Pax's role in the African medical aid – that will all be very useful.'

'Goes without saying.'

Dr. Mughal stood finally – so did Mike, and so did Pax. The session was over. She organized some routine blood tests and a brain scan for another day; but this woman had searching eyes – she wouldn't be easy to fool, Pax knew, when he had stuff he didn't want to let on about...

Now, after the medicine – the dolly mixture! They met up with Mary and Diana and walked across to the South Bank, where Pax could see the huge wheel of the London Eye going round so slowly that he had to stare at a cloud to see its movement.

'We're booked on that!' Mike told them, and Mary did an excited jig. 'But, first, a down-to-earth surprise...'

Parked by the roadside just in from the river stood a covered yellow vehicle with rows of seats in it. While others queued, Mike flashed his pre-booked ticket at a young attendant, and the four of them were shown up the steps into the back, where Mary ran straight to the front.

'What's this lorry?' she wanted to know, wrinkling up her nose at the smell of diesel. 'Not very comfortable.' She wriggled into her seat as if that might make a difference.

'Wait and see!' Mike told her. 'We're off on a tour of

London Town...' He held his face very still, his eyes staring ahead; which could have been him keeping the surprise to come, or it could have been his memories of some other ride on this vehicle – it was the look he'd had driving off to the adventure park. After a few minutes the driver came through the seats to sit at the front. Next to him, a snappy young man with spiky hair picked up the microphone. 'Welcome to the London Duck,' he said, 'which gives you more than any old sightseeing tour! It gives you me for a start!' And the tour guide started his spiel about the landmarks they passed: Westminster Bridge, the Houses of Parliament, then lumbering on down Whitehall. The guide was keener on his string of jokes than any history, but Mike made sure they saw the window through which Charles the First had been brought for his execution. 'The bloody end of a civil war – like Pax's war in Gambellia.'

'It wasn't my war,' Pax corrected – 'and I don't remember anything about it.' It wasn't comfortable, people knowing stuff about him that he didn't know himself. He'd never felt like that on his island. And he hated war – conventional, or the nuclear conflict the TV was always saying the Pakistanis or the Iranians were involved in.

And thinking Iranians, that Persian came into his mind

again. What *did* Mike's company have secret meetings with him about? What could be secret about coffee machines and TV sets?

'Anyway, war happens – and war means killing. It's a straight fact of life...' Mike pointed at other landmarks. 'That's the War Office – all those statues are of great soldiers – and on our left, Horseguards' Parade: cavalry dressed in ceremonial gear, but underneath, all tooled-up fighting men, fit as fiddles! And up ahead is the great admiral, Horatio Nelson...' Pax squinted at the distant figure on top of its column. 'It's all around us,' Mike went on, 'martial history...'

'Ol' Nelson only gets off at night when he's got to come down for a pizza!' the guide chirped into his microphone. Mary laughed, but after that the ride seemed to bore her, until the 'duck' drove across the front of Buckingham Palace – and she stood up to look for the Queen but didn't see her; and ten minutes later they went over Vauxhall Bridge, and Mike was starting to look twinkly in the eyes.

'Wait for it! Wait for it!' he warned: and suddenly the 'duck' ran off the road and took a surprise dive into the river – down a muddy beach and, splash! – into the Thames. The lorry had turned into a boat.

'See – the duck's another war relic,' Mike told them.

'We built over twenty thousand of these for the D-Day landings. Stuffed with soldiers. Out of the sea and up the Normandy beaches…'

'Clever invention!' Diana Lucky said.

'In its day,' echoed Mike.

Pax enjoyed the river more than he'd enjoyed the streets of London. Being at water level reminded him of Rainbow Cove, when he'd floated on his back looking up at those granite rocks. They cruised down to Westminster Bridge and back upriver, to drip out of the Thames and chug up the foreshore to the street – and, with the surprise of the splash behind them, to head without delay back to the London Eye.

'Did you like that?' Mary asked Pax.

'Terrific!' Pax said. 'For us. But how about those soldiers who once sat in here, going to fight and kill?'

'It's what men and women do – to preserve their way of life,' Mike said. 'If we like our way of doing things over some foreign way – if we hate dictators like Hitler and Stalin – then we've got to stand up to them. We'll kneel to no foreign power, however mighty and dangerous they are!'

'Like the Iranians?' Pax suddenly heard himself asking. And he could have kicked himself for letting his mouth run away from his brain.

Immediately, Diana swung round on Mike – and Mike gave Pax the sort of look he'd never given him before; like, *where do you think you're coming from?* But he switched it straight off for a friendly, grinning, shake of the head. 'If you ever want to be rich,' he told both Pax and Mary, 'you don't pick and choose. I'll take Iranian money, much as some dodgy regime isn't mine: if it's legal to trade with them, why shouldn't we have some of it?' And he clapped his arms around the pair, and suddenly swung them in to face him. 'And now for the big one!' He waved up at the impressive London Eye as if he'd constructed it with his own two hands.

Diana produced an internet printout and showed it to an official. The queue for the London Eye was marshalled fifty metres along the river walk, but the four of them were taken right to the front and shown onto the next arriving capsule. Which was all theirs: while all the other capsules were full, theirs was just for them. Mike had to be someone with lots of pull.

Mary squealed as the capsule swayed while they got into it, but the wheel's smooth movement took them up slowly and gently: up to roof level and then beyond, with Mike the most excited. 'Look at that river,' he said. 'London's river.' And he started singing,

'"*All hail to our school on the bank of the Thames,*

And those far-sighted men at its source,
O Riverside School, O Riverside –
Where the tides of our learning course..."
The old school song...'

'This is such a special experience!' Diana said. 'How few people in history would ever have seen their city from above like this?' She lifted her face to the sky. 'People were grounded – but we can fly and see everything like the birds...'

'Beg to differ!' Mike disagreed. 'Remember the Montgolfiers and their balloons – seventeen hundred and how's-your-father? And German airmen dropping bombs from balloons in the First World War? Man's commandeered the air ever since the Wright brothers grew our feathers.' He suddenly pointed. 'Aye-aye! Look! There's Alexandra Palace – shown our wares at a few fairs there!' The capsule had reached a great height, but Pax could still see three capsules in an arc above them – there was further to go yet.

'I don't like it!'

Pax, Mike and Diana were looking out in different directions – but Mary was sitting on the oval seat in the centre, away from the windows and staring at her feet.

'What's not to like?' Mike asked. 'It's marvellous up here! Pretend you're a little bird...' He flapped his arms, one then the other. 'See – I'm a swallow!' He made a loud gulping sound in his throat.

'I don't want to be a bird! I'm too squishy inside...' Mary was on the verge of tears.

'Now, who's being a very silly girl?' Diana sat next to her. 'You're perfectly safe—'

'Perfectly safe!' Mike reinforced. 'We're in the safest of hands.' He smacked the side of the capsule. 'Engineered to perfection...'

'And you've been in Mike's aeroplane; we're nowhere near as high as you went in that...'

Mary was crying now. 'That was different!'

Mike patted her hand. 'Okay, I'll tell them to take us down. It won't take long. I'll tell them...'

'That's right, Mike, tell them to take us down,' said Diana.

But Pax knew Mary wasn't buying that. Mike was pretending to send a text from his mobile phone, but they all knew they wouldn't get down till the capsule had gone round at the usual pace. Pax looked at the young girl, crying down into her T-shirt, trying to be brave but failing, her chest heaving with great gulps of air, and a look of real terror in her eyes. Now their capsule was at the top of the arc, as if they were balanced alone in the sky. He sat by her, and put his arm around her.

Diana gave her a sip of bottled water. 'That's right, Pax'll give you a cuddle while Mike makes them take us down...'

Mary's small face looked briefly up at Pax, intelligent disbelief in her eyes – and he knew how she felt; at any second she would go hot and cold, and she wouldn't be able to breathe. He knew those panicky feelings.

'Listen – there was once this kid,' he started telling her, quietly. 'She lived in a big house with a big bedroom – and you know what was special about this bedroom?' Mary didn't look up. 'It was high up in some rocks, sort of carved out of a mountainside. And she didn't have stairs, she climbed this rope ladder to go to bed, and the bed itself was on a special ledge, with a deep mattress of the softest grasses; and to go to her bathroom she slid down a smooth slide to where there was a door with bushes and leaves growing all around it...'

'It had *Privet* written on it,' Mike said.

'And guess what she had instead of a garden? A beach, a sandy beach as soft as talcum powder. One step, and she was at the seaside, with all the most beautiful fish in the world swimming between her feet when she paddled...'

Mary twisted slightly on the seat, turning herself closer to Pax. She took in a long, deep breath.

'And when she went into the kitchen for breakfast –

where the food was cooked on a sort of campfire – she had sweet potato and fried banana, followed by purple fruits and sneezing nuts: you know, cashew...'

Mary hiccupped into Pax; or it could have been a very small laugh. The capsule was on its descent now, and in the blustery evening it swayed in a gust from the west.

'And instead of going to school she learned all about nature, and how to live with it. So it was all perfect – until these big birds came flying over her house, big, noisy birds with wings that went round and round instead of flap-flap-flap.' Pax felt the gust, heard the capsule creak, and a mild dizziness of his own started to sway him. He looked down at Mary's small, listening face, her eyes closed in trust – as his vision blurred and he lost focus for a second or so – and in that moment she seemed to become someone else: someone also black, and beautiful, whose eyes were closed, whose mouth was slightly open with a smiling look of utter faith in him. And as he went on talking he heard his story coming from somewhere else... 'But there was one special path from her house that she had never been along before. And on this day she went along it – and guess where she was? Not at the seaside, and not where the leaves were green – she was in a very hot country, where the ground was hard and no one had any shoes, but went around with bare feet.' He closed his own eyes to describe the scene he could see. 'There were mud huts in this scorching hot place, and the girl didn't know where her mother or her father were – she was just running with this boy who was sort of looking after her.' Pax opened his eyes and looked around him. But there was no one else in the capsule except him and the girl he was cradling, a long way from London. 'And the girl was frightened. But it wasn't ghosts, or monsters, or wild animals she was frightened of. Nothing like that. It was men, soldiers who suddenly came shouting through the trees with big loudspeaker voices—'

'Thank you, Pax,' Diana interrupted.

'Well, that was a good story,' Mike said. 'Time to get ready to get off!'

But Mary was shaking her head. 'Go on!' she urged Pax. 'Go on!'

'...And worse, over their heads was a gunship, a swirly green and brown helicopter, with men hanging out of its doors pointing their machine guns, shouting down about going to death...'

'Definitely enough!' said Mike. 'Good story, Pax! But a bit old for Mary – and, hey, look! They did what I asked – we're down again!'

'Back on the ground!' said Diana, lifting Mary up and away from Pax. 'End of made-up stories. All safe and sound in the real world...'

Where Pax's feet were the most unsteady, his balance gone; and for a few seconds he truly didn't know where he was.

Chapter Sixteen

The bad news came to Mike at his West End office. With a knock on the door – and she never knocked – Diana came in to where he was reading a specification by the light of the window. 'I'd like you to sit down, Mike,' she said, quietly.

The hand holding the specification dropped to Mike's side, and his face said that he knew what this was about. He didn't sit, though, he turned to face her, his chin up. 'Well?'

'Joseph...' she said.

He nodded, just once.

'Someone in a hospital in Madagascar, a victim, a woman who's been in a coma since the tragedy…'

'Yes…?'

'She's come out of it. After the *St. George* tragedy…she saw a boy in the water…floating…face up…before he went under…'

A big clear of the throat. 'And?'

'The boy had a badge on his shirt, on his chest. It was a swan…'

There was a very long silence; but the implication of a boy with the emblem of Marlow Rugby Club on his top was fully understood. 'Her description tallied in other ways – hair colour, the blue shirt with a white rugby collar. There's no room for doubt, Mike.'

'Swimming? …*Dead?*' It was as if Mike's eyes would never blink again.

Diana's voice came from somewhere deep. 'Dead, Mike – but not drowned; a casualty of the attack. From his injuries he'd have known nothing, no pain…'

Mike turned back to face the window, and the sight of an empty Wembley Stadium. 'Thank you, Diana.'

She went quietly away; and following that message no one at Sharpe End saw Mike for five days.

*

Mike's absence wasn't all a private mourning. Wherever he went immediately – and Pax guessed it was to the house where Joseph had lived – Diana made sure to tell everyone at Sharpe End when Mike was back at his business. 'However much he's been expecting that terrible news to come some day, it's no less awful when it does. But he's keeping his chin up; and today he's at work in Castlemartin, and we must all be very kind to him when he gets back.'

'Castlemartin? Has he gone to a castle?' Mary wanted to know. 'He could have taken us!'

'And you're a self-centred little girl!' Diana frowned at her. 'Right now he'll be thinking of poor Joseph, not of either of you!'

Which set the tone for the next few days at Sharpe End. Guilt all round for being still alive.

They lived in Australia. Pax's nearest relatives. Mike brought the message when he came back later in the week, hurrying into his conservatory office to print up the e-mail from London. Not a word about where he'd been – and Joseph he didn't mention.

'This is from your aunt, Jenny Lancaster,' he told Pax, like a solicitor reading a will, with Mary and Diana standing listening like witnesses, 'younger sister of your mother, Cathryn. Married to Stephen – that's Jenny, not your mother – emigrated from England to Australia ten years ago, lives in Perth, got two sons, Alan and Ryan.' Pax watched Mike's eyes scanning forward and back on the e-mail as if he was on the alert to censor something. 'Your mother was a doctor, and your father was a pharmacist. Leonard. You all lived in South Africa – Port Elizabeth – but you spent school terms back in England... all of which we know, don't we, old lad?' He squinted at the tight print. 'Now – the nitty gritty: what are their plans? What do they want to do about things...?'

Pax knew what he wanted to do – right now. He wanted to grab the e-mail from Mike's hands and read it for himself. If this was bad news, he should be the first to see it. It affected him most, didn't it? What this Aunt Jenny wanted to do was all about *him*!

'She's coming over to the UK pronto.' And Pax suddenly felt the way he had on first seeing that oil slick in Rainbow Cove; stomach sinking at the first sign of the end of something. 'She says, "If you can get what reports and grades you can from Pete's school" – that's me she's talking to – "I'll stop over in South Africa" – that's her – "and dig out his birth certificate and see what happens re death certificates for Cathryn and Leonard. I guess I can do a formal adoption back here in Perth." Et cetera, et cetera, et cetera.' Mike looked over the e-mail at Pax. 'So start standing on your head, Limey, you're going down under to Oz...'

Pax felt sick. *He was Pax.* If he belonged anywhere in the world he belonged on his island in the Indian Ocean. He'd been brought here to England by Mike, which had been great – but now he felt like a fifty pence piece being passed from person to person to person: from Mike, to some aunt and uncle and two Aussie cousins he didn't know! What were *they* like – and *did he care?* Did he want to go to live with them? No, he didn't! He wanted to be cured of his terrors just enough to go looking for his Zuri.

'Have you *got* to go there, Pax?' Mary asked.

Pax shrugged.

'It's a long way away, Australia.'

'But the world is a very small place these days...' said Diana. She smiled sweetly at Pax, but ten spoonfuls when one would have done.

'Well, it'll all come out in the wash.' Mike folded the e-mail and put it in his pocket. 'We'll look up this Stephen Lancaster chap. He might own half of Swan Valley – one of the best wine-growing regions in the world...' But his optimism was still more of a try than a success.

'If you're the only son – which I guess you must be,'

Diana told Pax – 'they'll likely sell up the house in South Africa and put the money in trust for you.'

'Less their outlay in bringing him up,' Mike mused. 'If Stephen Lancaster's not a millionaire.'

Which Mike was. Pax was learning fast that it wasn't the words people used that mattered so much, it was what didn't get said that carried the meaning.

Pictures came through next. There was one of Cathryn, Peter Foster's – *his* – mother, a smiling young woman in a graduation gown; and one of Leonard, the father – a snapshot of a frowning young man in a sunny garden; and there was one of the three of them together, a young Pax sitting between the others on a shingle beach. And, printed bigger than any of the others – perhaps to show its importance right now – was a picture of this aunt's home in Perth, Australia. A narrow three-storey building with a red tile roof, a balcony, a glazed front door, and, standing in front of it, two kids – one with long hair, about sixteen; one about twelve in a football kit, sticking his thumb up at the camera. And there was a message underneath it: *Al and Ryan looking out for their cousin, Peter!*

'That's very welcoming,' Diana said; and, 'Nice-looking family, Peter...'

'Pax,' he corrected.

'Pax.' She went from the room with the others, leaving

him alone with the pictures of his family. Which he wanted to rip up. Instead, he dumped them on the sideboard and got out into the open. Air was what he needed. Air, and freedom.

He didn't have jobs or responsibilities at Sharpe End – there was staff for everything – but he helped with the dishes, made his own bed, and he'd sometimes give the farm manager a hand feeding the animals. But tonight they'd been fed – although Tommy Hopper always left a bucket of specked apples near the pigs' pen for Mary to throw in.

The evening was calm. Far across the fields to the west, a line of smoke rose into the sky where a farmer was burning off stubble. In the tops of the beeches to the east a rookery cawed, and somewhere a large dog barked; sounds of being about, and alive. Pax stood by the farm fence and thought of this time of day on his island. The land crabs would be clacking, the scarlet birds would be shooting from branch to branch, and the frogs would be croaking. While instead of the day and night hum of a distant motorway, the ocean would be roaring in endlessly across the reef. He stood in gloom at the prospect of losing all that to go to live in a town house in Australia.

'You won't go, will you?'

Eh?

Mary had followed him out and crept up on him. 'You mustn't! You can hide here in the fields and woods, and I'll sneak out and feed you every night, after the pigs...'

Pax should have laughed that off; but it seemed a great idea right now: to be alone, and be himself again. He picked up an apple from the bucket and threw it towards the goat that had come running.

'I'll say you told me you were going to London – so they won't go looking for you here. Then, when your auntie's gone back to Australia, you can jump out again!' Pax gave her an apple to throw to a pig – which she did, too hard, and hurt its snout. 'Oh, sorry, Tam...' Pax walked away, on around the farm fence and out towards the beech copse, hoping Mary wouldn't follow. 'Oh, fiddle! I hurt Tam – that's bad for doing the accounts...' She trailed behind him.

'*Doing the accounts?*'

'In bed every night I do the accounts with Mum. I say the good things I've done – they're the plus side – and the bad things – they're the minus side – and if I end up "in the red" she ticks me off.'

'Help! That's tough!'

'Her mum did that in Trinidad – and if she ended up too much on the bad side, she had to go outside and cut a switch from the tree for a beating...'

'Mega-tough!'

They had come to the edge of the copse where there was a fringe of longer grasses and nettles, and here, where the nettles were thinnest, Mary sat herself down, cross-legged, and pulled Pax next to her. 'Right!' she said. 'Before he runs away and hides from his auntie, we'll do Pax's accounts!'

'Oh, no we won't! And he's *not* running off!' But why shouldn't he? He didn't *belong* anywhere, did he? He didn't feel either English or Australian, and he wasn't going to be part of Mike's family for much longer, so he had no real bonds at all. He belonged nowhere and he belonged to no one. What he was, was a boy from Solitaire, someone on his own. He looked at Mary's upturned face in the evening sunlight. A shaft of brightness struck through the branches, making her close her eyes in the glare. And there again, seeing her small face angled up, he had a glimpse of that special face – and with it that old, weird feeling swelled inside to tell him that he was wrong. He did belong somewhere, and to someone.

'Get on with it!' Mary opened her eyes to say.

But Pax heard nothing. The distant traffic had stilled, the rooks had roosted, the dog no longer barked, and he wasn't here any more; he was somewhere shaded but hot, and a girl was with him.

'I thought I did a good thing,' he heard himself saying. 'I took her away from the village, I told her to run with me...'

'Who? Who did you tell?'

'I thought the soldiers were coming through the bush, and she had to get away. We all had to get away...'

'What soldiers? Who did you have to get away from?'

Pax could see nothing of Sharpe End, or Home Farm, or Hertfordshire. These trees were other trees, this shade was from a stronger sun. 'I made her run away with me as fast as she could go. I ran her so hard I hurt her, I pulled her off her feet, made her knees bleed...'

'Who? Where was this?'

'...And we were getting away. It wasn't soldiers chasing on the ground, it was from the sky...'

'What was?'

'It came over the trees, and the soldiers hanging out of it saw us running...'

Mary clapped. 'That was your story before. The London Eye story, the helicopter...'

'I ran her on to try to get to the next trees. I let go of her hand so we could run faster. And suddenly there was a great explosion – and we were both blown off our feet...'

'They fired! Pax! Did they hit you?'

But Pax's throat had closed up, he couldn't speak at all, could hardly breathe; the girl's face was swimming before him, and inside his chest his heart was thumping like a frantic drum.

'What happened to her? Is she all right?'

The question hung. But his mind had gone blank. A rook cawed close above and Mary jumped up, scared – and now Pax was back on the edge of a copse in the English countryside, where all he could see were the nettles and grasses in sharp focus. He got up, too. 'So, how's that for my accounts?' he asked her roughly – and with long strides he hurried back to Mike's house, leaving Mary to follow.

Through the windows of Mike's office they'd seen him coming back, the tall, slim boy striding the length of the farm fence, pursued by Mary running to keep up. Diana Lucky had been opening up her computer, ready to click on the next day's diary. After dinner they did an hour in the office before Mary was put to bed. Being PA to this powerful man was the reason she and her daughter lived here, on the company.

'There's something about that boy,' she said.

'Yup – he's a fine lad.'

'He's got Mary in his thrall, but I've got to say, as her mother, I've not been sending up happy balloons...'

'No?'

'He's *weird*!'

'You think so? Well, that kid's been to hell and back!'

'The story he told on the London Eye...' Diana persisted.

'Sure...' Mike put his head on this side and then on that. 'I think things are starting to come out.'

'And could that be because he's deciding that they should...? I've got experience of things coming out when it suits someone. Mike, you mustn't mix up your grieving for Joseph with the rescue of that boy...'

Which were the words that arrested Pax as he went through the house to get to his bedroom. He hadn't meant to listen – he wouldn't spy on Mike to save his life – but passing by he heard that phrase, and he had to stop. He heard the click as Sir Mike closed his hard black briefcase. 'I'm not an old fool,' the man was saying, quietly.

'I know. But already Mary's changed. You've given so much to the boy...she talked about wanting to be taken to Castlemartin – that's not her.'

'She thinks it's only a castle?'

'Well, she wouldn't know why you went there, would she? She's only nine, Mike.'

Pax wanted to get away, but he couldn't move.

'And I wouldn't want her to know why,' Mike said. 'But it was nothing illegal. Symonds's Systems doesn't deal in anything illegal, you know that, of all people...'

'Except perhaps in Nagpur, Mike...'

'And that wouldn't be illegal, either – not there!'

Pax had almost stopped breathing. Listening in to a private business conversation was not what he wanted to be doing, and it was a relief when a filing cabinet was opened and he could get away on the toes of his trainers. And never mind Mike's world tonight, Pax's head was filled with his own weird life right now. That experience with Mary out there by the woods had been very spooky... He went to his room and closed the door quietly behind him.

'Anyway, as the mother of the girl who's just been trotting behind that boy like some devoted fan, and the ex-wife of a liar who could con a guide dog off a blind man,' Diana was going on, 'let me say it straight – I shan't be sorry when Peter Foster goes to his family in Australia.'

Mike looked up at her and slammed his briefcase shut again. His voice, when he spoke, was chilly and thin. 'I think that will be enough for tonight, thank you, Diana.'

She turned in surprise from the filing cabinet.

'Goodnight,' he said. 'Seven a.m. at the door.' And Mike watched without a word while she silently left the room – before he slumped in his chair, and covered his face with his hands.

Chapter Seventeen

How real are dreams? Pax asked himself. Those thoughts he deliberately put into his head for going to sleep on, those stories he wanted to tell himself, they were one thing. And the terrifying scenes he sometimes saw in the dark – they were nightmares as crazy as fantasy stories. But that night he had an experience so real that he knew it was different from anything before.

He was somewhere hot with his mother and father, who he seemed to know better – although the two of them were still more like characters in a story than real people. They were in a baked village, the huts made from mud blocks, with open doorways and dried-grass roofs. A female goat was tied up in the shade of one of these huts, and a girl of about his age was feeding her, with a small boy sitting gripping a teat and squirting milk into his mouth.

'–A kitosha!' An old woman in a tattered dress came chasing out of the hut and waved the boy away, to leave milk for others – which he obeyed straight off. But the weird thing was, he didn't run off, he had to pull himself by his hands and scuttle like a crab: because he had only one leg, and that had no foot to it, just a stump above the ankle.

In the centre of this village a tent was set up, with Pax's father standing at its doorway, dressed in shorts and a white T-shirt. He wore a wide-brimmed floppy hat, and squinted in the brightness the same way he squinted in his photograph, and he was coming along this queue of people asking them questions. They were all shading themselves with broad leaves and squares of old cloth, some standing, some squatting, some sitting. Women and old men held children in their arms, or stood by them, but none of the bony kids showed any spark – none of them were tugging to run off and play. Because what was most prominent in that sad queue were the sticks – the crutches, the staves, the bentwood frames, holding up people in half-empty skirts and flappy trousers. Like the goat boy, most of those people were maimed.

Pax saw all this as his father went along the line making notes of the answers people gave him, and inside the tent Pax could see the woman he knew was his mother leaning over a table, dressing wounds.

And Pax himself? He was part of all this, and he knew what his job was. He was patrolling a rope beyond which no one was allowed to go. It stretched fifty metres between the village and the scrub of the bush, and hanging from it was a big skull-and-crossbones sign, the international symbol of danger. He was the sentry at the boundary of safe ground. This side was okay, but the land on the other side of the rope hadn't yet been made safe by the mine-clearance people.

'The adults know not to go there, but you guard it from the children.'

Now in his own wide hat and cotton clothes, Pax was walking up and down on the safe side of the boundary rope, keeping away the kids who still had two legs – one of whom was the girl feeding the goat. And he knew her well. She belonged to that village where the medics were set up. She lived with an old grandmother and a small brother – the mutilated goat boy – and she and Pax had

become friends. In the evenings he played cards and
fivestones with her, and sang songs, and they told each
other stories.

And tonight, in his head, in his Sharpe End bed, as he
saw her beautiful face looking at him across the village
clearing, he quietly said her name aloud. *Zuri.*

When suddenly from over a low hill came the deadly
clatter of a gunship, loud-hailed voices shouting out in
violent language. His stomach leaped as the first cries
went up in the clearing, people scattering as best they
could – they'd been surprised, the war was flying like fire
through the bush and catching up with them!

And there was Zuri's beautiful face, staring up at him:
pitiful, frightened – and trusting. Straight off, he grabbed
her hand and pulled her towards the scrub on the safe side
of the rope. But he pulled her too fast and she fell, grazing
her knees on the hard ground. He lifted her, half carried
her – as the gunship came roaring in low over the trees,
its terrifying roar drowning out the sound of Zuri
screaming.

Enough! –A kitosha!

The scene in the village vanished as Pax deliberately
pulled himself away from what was in his head. But he
didn't sit up – he rolled out of his bed like someone hunted
dropping into a ditch; and as he hit the floor, crouching on

all fours in his room at Sharpe End, he knew that he hadn't been dreaming at all; he had been lying wide awake, remembering. And the hand he had been holding so tightly wasn't Zuri's, but his own.

Chapter Eighteen

Pax was at Queen Square, alone with Dr. Mughal in her small office. It was his third visit to the institute – on the second he hadn't seen the neurologist at all, but had spent nearly a day on a blood test, a brain scan, and an examination of the electrical activity in his head. He'd been slid into a noisy, claustrophobic tunnel, and later had a net of small electrodes placed on his scalp, looking like something out of a sci-fi movie. At least it ruled out any serious disease; but Mike must have known how tiring it would be, because that day there was no treat to follow:

just a chauffeur-driven ride in his limo, home to Sharpe End.

Today, though, he was seeing Dr. Mughal again – but on his own, with Mike working on his laptop in the corridor outside. The neurologist had a little green book of memory tests which they went through together, and he seemed to pass okay – although she didn't say too much. And she also had a folder marked *PICTURES*, which she brought up from a carrier bag on the floor.

'Tell me if you recognize or remember any of these people,' she told him, showing Pax the top photograph, which was of a woman he'd never seen before.

'No, don't know her.' He shook his head. She put the picture at the bottom of the heap, revealing the next. This was of an unknown man, and, like the first, a snapshot rather than a portrait. Again, Pax shook his head.

'How about her?' The same thing again, to reveal a woman dressed like a performer in a black choir.

'Nope.'

But the next was the man he now knew was his father, in the same photograph that had been attached to the e-mail from Australia. Dr. Mughal's manner was exactly the same as it had been for the first three photographs.

'I know him,' Pax said.

'Who is he?'

Pax went on looking at the picture, at the face squinting in the brightness in a garden somewhere. 'I know he's my father – but I don't, like, *know* him.' He paused. 'I've been told,' he said.

'So you don't remember him in any situation other than this picture? You don't remember seeing him anywhere else?'

Pax stared at the picture till it blurred. 'No,' he lied. He had to be careful. He couldn't say he didn't know stuff that she knew he knew; but he didn't want to go to Australia. At the same time, he did want all this to go on till there was no fear of more terror attacks. Only when he was really better would he be free to go looking for Zuri.

Dr. Mughal moved on through more pictures – of men and women he didn't know. As he expected, his mother's photograph soon came to the top of the pile. 'Yes,' he said. 'I believe that's my mother. I'm told that's her.'

'You're *told*? You have no remembered connection with her?'

'Nope,' Pax lied again, and he wondered how clever Dr. Mughal might be at spotting the signs of lies being told; there had to be giveaways that a brain person like her would pick up. He was glad he wasn't in his sci-fi hairnet.

'Okay.' Dr. Mughal closed the folder of photographs. 'So now go into your mind and tell me about what you saw—'

What? Was she on to him? Was she inside his head?

'I don't know what you mean.'

'You didn't let me finish. Tell me what you saw in here the last time you came. This room.'

'Oh! Sure. There was you, and Mike – he was in here then...' But where was she going with this?

'And, furniture...?'

'Um – this desk, and that cupboard, and these chairs.'

'Is the desk the same one?'

Pax looked at it carefully. 'I think so – but it's in a different place.'

Dr. Mughal smiled. 'Good – I can move it back when you go; I hate it over here.' Pax's bewildered expression must have asked a great *WHY?* 'I've shown you photographs you saw a few days ago, with some distractors – which were those other people – and you named your father and mother. You can describe my room as you saw it over a week ago...'

Yes, and he could have told her that she was wearing the same long skirt, with the same coffee stain in one of the swirls!

'So your ability to form new memories is fine. And you know language, know facts, know how to hold a knife and fork – you just don't know who you are, nor anything connected with who you are. The indications appear to be against a simple amnesia.' She looked towards the door, on the other side of which Mike would be sitting waiting. 'Which means, Pax, that I don't think you need me. Your brain could well be protecting you from a painful memory. But we're all still somewhat ignorant about many aspects of memory function, and the ways emotional states interact with them. I think you need a psychiatrist rather than a neurologist.'

'Oh.' Well, it was all the same to Pax, so long as he got over his terrors enough to do the things he wanted to do.

'You are denying certain things to yourself – or, rather, your subconscious brain is. If you like technical terms, I'm inclined to describe you as being in a "dissociative fugue".'

'Great! Good to know I've got something, and I'm not just scared of helicopters!' But – *hell!* – that had just burst out! He'd got to be more careful than that.

Dr. Mughal looked at her hands, which were holding the folder of photographs upright on the desk, tapping it on the surface in an over-and-done-with sort of way. 'Although a lot of people – people in my profession – aren't altogether convinced that such a state as dissociative fugue even exists.'

'Doesn't exist? How can people say it doesn't exist if I've got it?'

Dr. Mughal was putting the folder of photographs back into her carrier bag. 'Oh, they say some patients might be making it up. Pretending – so as to rid themselves of some guilt-evoking event in their lives…'

'You mean…?'

'Perhaps even lying to themselves. So some practitioners think.'

Pax stood up. He'd had enough of this. Practitioners could think what they wanted. And if she was finished with him, he was finished with her!

She stood, too, as if no one's behaviour ever fazed her. 'Would you kindly ask Mike to come in when you leave? I'll fill him in on some of this.'

Pax grunted, and gripped the door handle hard, twisting it the wrong way first in his hurry to get out of the room. *Lying!* He wasn't lying – not about the terrors. And – no kidding – he didn't really *know* those people as his mother and father, not even from that memory in the night. He didn't remember the school, or anything about a house in South Africa, or what had happened on that ship. But before he could slip out of the door, she continued.

'The good news is, dissociative fugue often gets better on its own. Things will come back – perhaps through the help of a psychiatrist, perhaps by seeing a face, or a certain look; perhaps by a voice, even a feeling.'

Which had happened, hadn't it? Seeing Mary's face with her eyes closed on the London Eye, and near the woods at Sharpe End, had brought those pictures of Zuri into his head. It was with an enormous effort that Pax kept his face straight and his eyes unblinking.

'Piece by piece the past returns, sometimes triggered, sometimes not.'

'Then you *do* believe in it?'

Dr. Mughal smiled. 'I don't like wasting my time,' she said. 'And I don't think I've been wasting it.' She held the door open for him. 'Goodbye, Peter.'

And he went, with the rotten feeling in his stomach that by not telling the truth he'd just made a mess of his treatment to get himself really better from his terrors.

All the same, he had his treat – without Mary or Diana this time, as it was too early on a school afternoon. 'I'm really up for it myself,' Mike told him. So it was a short journey on the Underground, a walk alongside the Thames, and they were there: looking at a long, grey, warship, moored in the river between London and Tower Bridges.

'Look at that piece of history! HMS *Belfast*,' Mike said proudly, as if he'd shot the rivets into the vessel himself. 'Thirty-two knot cruiser with a gun for every knot. Meaty enough to leave the convoy and go cruising around on its own. Moored up here as a permanent memorial to our Jolly Jack Tars.' He waved an arm at it, but his eyes were on Pax: who suddenly thought Mike might be looking for how he'd react to the sight – probably the first big ship he'd have seen since the *St. George*. But he wasn't going to ask if that was why they'd come. He'd just go along with the treat.

The big thing Pax realized as they went round was that the ship was like a small floating town, and the jobs the sailors did were the same as on land. There were bakers, butchers, doctors, a dentist, engineers, wireless operators, carpenters – all with their 'shops' and special spaces. Okay, there'd be the sailors who manned the guns and fired the torpedoes, but they were well outnumbered by the people whose work was to keep the ship at sea. He said so to Mike.

'Aha! Till they went to action stations,' Mike baulked a party of schoolkids to tell him. 'If the ship was under attack, they all became part of a fighting machine, every man jack. And think how a butcher might be a bit of use to the ship's surgeon.' He reached for a handhold and swung himself up the rungs of a companionway ladder, nimble as a sea cadet. 'Coming aloft, matey?'

Pax was impressed. For the first time after the tragic Joseph news, Mike was the old Solitaire Mike today – on his toes, climbing up and sliding down ladders, darting about the decks like a schoolkid himself, poking his head in here, going where he shouldn't in there – this treat just as much his as Pax's. He pushed Pax in the back when he was peering into a punishment cell. 'Fourteen days for you, old lad, bread and water.' It was like any boy and his granddad on an afternoon out.

Until they got down into the Shell Rooms – and here Pax stood back. They were on the lowest deck, way below the waterline, down where the ammunition was stored. Shells as thick as tree trunks were stacked horizontally on top of each other in row after row of wooden units, and in the centre of this arsenal were two lifts for sending the heavy ammunition up to the guns on deck, forty or fifty shells all ready to go. It was a huge cargo of death that opened Pax's eyes wide.

'Awesome!' Mike enthused. 'That six-incher up top could hit a target fourteen miles away – and that was sixty years ago. Think what we can do today.'

Pax looked around the small space. *Hell!* he thought – all this deadly stuff ready to be shot at other people. But

Mike was admiring the lifting gear, so he kept that thought to himself and quietly backed off and led the way to the ladder, relieved when they were up from the depths and in the open, on one of the foredecks. He took deep breaths and stood waiting for his heart to stop beating so fast. The killing side of things, those shells lined up to send death and destruction into the air, had really upset him. Mike didn't seem to notice, though, and from the deck he pointed out the London landmarks ashore: the Gherkin, the Tower, and City Hall; while all Pax wanted was to get off the ship.

'Come on, Mike – I'll choose you an ice cream.'

When – *help!* – out of nowhere a helicopter came flying in at them. Black and heavy, it swept low over the riverside buildings, circling the warship, not twenty metres above the top antennae. Pax's eyes shot up to it. He ducked his head. It sounded like the helicopters on Solitaire, and like the gunship coming at them above the African village, its engines clacking and vibrating, that deadly noise cutting deep inside and rattling his spine.

'Yank tourists!' Mike said – taking Pax's arm to pull him into the compass room. 'Let's get out of this…' His voice was urgent as he pulled, staring into Pax's face as if searching for signs of the terrors hitting him.

But they didn't! Pax's heart thumped hard thinking

that they would, but miraculously he didn't go dizzy, he didn't go cold beneath a sweating skin, he didn't have to fight to breathe: in fact, he had more control over his voice than Mike. 'I'm all right,' he shouted in the din of the rotors and blades, 'I'm fine!' – his surprise doing for both of them. 'It's no bother to me.' And he came out of the compass room to watch as the helicopter made three circuits of the ship, each time as it came over its engines rattling the ship's rails and bouncing off her armour plating; but Pax stood tall on the gun deck, unaffected.

'Crikey!' he said, when the helicopter buzzed away downriver. But it was more to himself than to Mike.

She was coming the next day – his Aunt Jenny from Australia. Back at Sharpe End, Diana informed them that the aunt would fly into Heathrow at six a.m. and be with them by noon. Jenny Lancaster had enquired about taxis and trains and had refused all offers of Mike's car meeting her at the airport.

'What time does she get to the station?'

'I don't know. But she's insistent on getting a cab.'

Mike shrugged his shoulders. He walked from the dining room through to the kitchen where Magda was putting dinner plates in the warmer. 'Maggie – where's Mrs. Lancaster going to sleep?'

The young Polish woman leaned forward. 'What does she like to eat? Vegetarian like Pax? I got so much meat in the freezing I can start a market.'

'Wait-and-see pie,' Mike told her. 'So, bedrooms...'

Magda turned down a gas burner. 'Pax he is in the best guest room. What you think I put Mrs. Lancaster in the sleepover room?' She asked it softly, because this was the room Joseph or Rachel had used when they stayed with Mike; unused since the *St. George* went down.

'Yup. Time we blew those cobwebs out,' Mike said, lifting his chin.

'*No* cobwebs in this house, sir!'

'I mean, good to use it again.'

Magda touched his arm gently, and turned from him, nodding.

'Yeah...' Mike said – and left the kitchen, dodging Mary and Pax to go to his conservatory office.

'Pax – want to know what I did in school today?' the girl was asking.

'Was it something different, then?' Thoughts of school had started to give Pax a twist inside: on her last visit, the woman from Social Services had talked about him needing to restart his education, if he didn't go to his relatives in Australia fairly soon.

'We did history in the morning and IT in the afternoon. And history was castles – we're going to Warwick castle soon.'

'Watch out – they lock cheeky kids in the dungeons!'

'Then in IT we looked up castles on the internet.'

'Very good.' But Pax's head was too full of his Australian aunt coming.

'I looked up Rochester castle – did you know it's got three square turrets and one round one, because after it was sieged and one turret fell down, they built the new turret with a better shape? To make the cannonballs skid off?'

'That was clever.'

'And Corfe castle...'

'Gives you a bad throat, that place...' Pax coughed, but Mary didn't laugh – as if she was too full of something she wanted to tell him.

'And I looked up where Mike went the other day – Martin castle. Except it's Castlemartin... The teacher helped me.'

'Very good. Did you print it all up so you can use it for your coursework?' Pax was ready for a breath of air outside.

'And guess what's there?'

'Where?'

'Castlemartin! Keep up!'

'What's there, then?'

'A castle...'

'Surprise, surprise!'

'And miles and miles and miles where people can't go. Aren't allowed. Where there's army stuff. Tanks and guns and shooting into the sea...'

Pax closed his eyes to the image. He'd seen enough gun and shell business on HMS *Belfast*.

'Well if soldiers actually live there,' he said, finally, 'I suppose they need fridges and tellies and coffee machines the same as everyone else.'

'Yup.' And Mary suddenly changed the subject. 'Play swing ball?' she asked.

But the thought of HMS *Belfast* had sent Pax off somewhere else in his head. He and Mike had driven all the way home from the ship in silence – apart from a swear about some slow driver; nothing had been said about the appointment with Dr. Mughal. But Pax guessed Mike's thoughts had been the same as his own: wondering how that helicopter hadn't brought on a terror attack. Okay, they'd seen and heard helicopters since Pax had come to Britain – but they'd been small, light stuff, and usually flying high. That helicopter today had been heavy and low, noisy and close and threatening – just like the one he'd thought was a gunship on Solitaire. Yet he'd been okay, he hadn't gone into an attack, nor even the start of one. Other kids on that ship had shouted louder and ducked lower than he had. *So what was that all about?* Was he better? Had Dr. Mughal shown him up to himself in some way, and she'd cured him? And did Mike think that, too?

'Pax! I said, do you want to play swing ball?'

Pax came back. 'I'm not very good at it. Probably be better at proper tennis…' But there was definitely time to do something before bed. 'Come on, then!' he said. 'Got the tennis balls?'

'It's on the end of the rope, silly!'

'Stupid!' He laughed at himself, and she went out through the French windows with him, holding his hand – which reminded him of the last hand he'd held, in his head, in the night. It was a fine evening with the sun's redness deepening, and they were soon on the back lawn.

The game was simple. A sliding plastic ring on a steel spiral held a long cord with a tennis ball fixed at the other end of it. They each had a bat, and they had to hit the ball alternately until the ring got to the bottom of the spiral and the ball fell to the ground, a point scored if your opponent was the one to let the ball die. First to twenty-one. And Mary was very good at it. She had a keen eye for the ball, and once they'd warmed up she started hitting hard, sending it careering around and swaying the post with its force. She stepped in and stepped out, her bat held in a champions' grip, squealing with every hit like some of the women at Wimbledon.

Pax started off by going easy. It was her game, and he wanted her to win; but his efforts were so puny that when he was three-nil down Mary wrinkled up her nose and complained. 'You're not trying, Pax! You're *letting* me win!'

'I'm not!'

'You are – it's like playing against Pedro. You want to hit it like Mike does.'

'Oh yeah?'

'He never wants me to win. He never wants anyone to win over him!'

Pax wound the ring back to the top of the spiral and stepped back, holding the ball with the cord taut. 'Okay, watch this!'

'Right! Hit it hard!'

Pax threw the ball into the air and lunged into it, pulling back his bat and bringing it in with a hard, centred hit. The ball swung fast around the top of the post as Mary skipped in and whacked it on its way with a solid hit of her own. 'Yow!' she squealed. 'That's better!'

Pax stepped in again, and hit it with another good strike – and off went the ball around the post, gaining height. 'Take that!' In came Mary for her turn, and 'Yow!' again – as she stood for a split second to see it go hurtling round – and just didn't move fast enough as Pax came in for his strike, hitting her around the back of her head with his bat, full strength.

'Ow!' Mary crumpled to the ground, stunned, then screamed with the pain.

'Mary! Sorry!' He'd really hurt her. Was there blood? Was she conscious? He bent over her as she writhed and cried. 'All right, all right, you're all right – I'll get your mum...'

But Pax didn't need to get her mum. Diana Lucky was already running across the lawn, shouting at Pax. 'I saw that! I saw that! You stupid boy! Why can't you take care with a little girl?' She pushed past Pax and kneeled to the ground, where she put her face to Mary's, and cuddled her, and felt for the lump at the back of her head. 'No blood. No cut, honey – but it's an egg for breakfast...' And she smothered and kissed her daughter.

'I'm sorry, Mary...' Pax began again, wishing like heck she'd hit him instead.

'And so you should be!' Diana Lucky was looking up at him, still cradling Mary on the grass. 'Why don't you use some common sense – a big guy like you, playing with a little girl like this? Why don't you *think*?'

Pax hovered. There was nothing he could do – Mary's mother wouldn't let him help. She led Mary into the house, who walked on weak legs, leaning into her mother, ignoring Pax, giving him no forgiveness.

He picked up his bat, and hers – and then he picked up the ball, which he suddenly hit so hard that the post came out of the lawn, looping in the air – and for a while swing ball was off the options list as an activity at Sharpe End.

Chapter Nineteen

The Sharpe End house might have been traditionally Georgian in style, but its facilities inside were very modern. In the best guest room – Pax's bedroom – Mike had put a false wall along one side, and behind it an en-suite shower and lavatory, which was great for Pax. Once he'd gone to his room he could shut his door and not come out till morning; he could be private. And tonight he desperately needed to cut himself off. He'd written a 'sorry' note to Mary and slid it under her door. He'd apologized to Mike for the accident – who had gripped him around the shoulders. 'Put it behind you, old lad. I broke my brother's nose once, biffing about – and he still can't sniff without someone answering their mobile!' As soon as he could, Pax had got away – and shut himself in his room to try to sort himself out.

And there was a heck of a lot for him to sort – his mind was tumbling with it all. Number one – poor little Mary: he *should* have been more careful with her. Number two – was he really better from his terrors? And if he was, did Mike think he'd been shamming all along? Number three was this aunt, Jenny Lancaster, who was coming here tomorrow to scoop him up and take him back to Australia – *doing her family duty!* – when she might not even want him. And the house in the picture didn't look very big, which could mean having to share a bedroom with a cousin! Urgh! All he wanted in life was to find Zuri and one day go back to his island. Until then he wanted to stay here with Mike, who'd been showing him love, not family duty; and have fun with Mary – who would forgive him tomorrow, he knew she would. And then there was item number four – Mary's mother, Diana Lucky, who was treating him like a centipede who'd crawled under her backside. Hadn't she been lightning-quick to have a go at him after the accident? And tonight there'd been something else about her, too – something weird and close-to-home that made him feel extra uncomfortable, but no way could he get a grip on what that was.

All in all, it was a really rotten state to be in. So thank goodness his bedroom door was shut until the morning. He kicked his trainers across the room, and got out of his tracksuit. Off came his sweatshirt – and he stood staring at himself in the wardrobe mirror. His eyes went down to his smart black boxers – and he remembered that tattered grey pair he'd lived in for so long on Solitaire. Those dear old boxers! He took in a deep, sad breath and turned away to look at his carving of Zuri. Special Zuri. He narrowed his eyes, and tonight he could see – now that he'd seen her in his head a couple of times – how the carving didn't actually *look* like Zuri, yet in a strange way how it was somehow more real. Because that carving was the *spirit* of Zuri, it always had been. And from standing there staring, staring, his mind becoming a confusion of the real and the longed for, he backed away into his bathroom and turned on the shower tap, stepping in under the warm water – but leaving the door open a chink so that he could still look at Zuri and feel her spirit. He let the water run over him, as comforting as the ocean when he'd swum in it, as heavy as the tropical rainfall when he'd stood and let it drench him. He still had his boxers on, but he didn't care – that was how he'd been on his island, and that was how things were going to be again one day.

He lifted his face into the water's fall, closing his eyes. And in its comfort he thought of how little Mary must be aching right now, poor kid – when suddenly into his ears came the cut of her mother's voice. *'Why don't you use some common sense – a big guy like you, playing with a little girl like this? Why don't you think?'* But more than Diana Lucky – as he heard that criticism, somehow, under the run of the water, her voice became someone else's, also striking at him with hard-edged words.

'Peter! Peter! They weren't firing, they were shouting at us to stay! They weren't the rebels, they were government! What made you do that?'

And he knew without any doubt whose voice it was. It was his mother's, going at him – more real than in any photograph, and more lifelike than some memory of a medical tent. She was here with him – and in just the same way as Diana had bent over Mary, she was bending over Zuri. The girl's eyes were closed, her mouth was open, and her cheeks were puffing slightly as she breathed, as if she were lying there in the deepest of sleeps, her head cradled by his mother. As the life ran from her. As Pax watched her dying…

'*Thank heavens you're all right – oh, I thank God for that – but you ran her into the minefield!*'

Pax couldn't bear it. Zuri was dead! Seeing her in his head before – on the London Eye and in the copse with Mary – until this crucial moment he hadn't realized that the girl was dead. He clutched his hands to his face and slid down the shower side, his legs failing beneath him, his brain going round and round in dizzy confusion, his body turning icy cold under the hot water, and his breath so hard to draw that he thought he was going to suffocate, or drown. And there he lay in the shower basin until the panic finally passed – who knew how long? Oxygen came back to him, and with it the ability to think. Slowly he pulled himself up and turned off the shower, ripped off his sodden pants, and found a towel to dry himself. Like a figure in a dream he walked to his bed and lay on it to stare up at the ceiling. And with a shudder that sent his body into a sudden rictus, now he knew. He knew why that helicopter hadn't frightened him today, he knew why no panic attack had happened on the deck of the *Belfast*.

It was because all along it hadn't ever been a helicopter that had caused his terrors. With his first real memories returning, he was starting to clutch at the true cause. It was himself, it was what he had done. He had run Zuri the wrong way beyond the rope, and when they'd dropped hands to make a harder target and to run faster, she had trodden on a mine that had ripped up and into her belly. Until now, until the vivid memory of his mother's snap, he had thought it was all down to a gunship giving him the terrors. But just now in the shower he'd had another terror attack, and that was after something different – after the memory of him running Zuri into the mines. *What gave him the terrors was something that had happened at the same time as the gunship coming over –* and his brain had mixed up the two.

So was that the nasty incident Dr. Mughal had been talking about? Was that the thing his mind wanted him to forget, wiping out everything that had gone before? Was his shame at causing Zuri's death the trigger that made his mind want to destroy the past?

Now, lying there, he knew that it was. And there was a word for it. *Guilt.* It was his guilt. His own guilt brought the terrors on. And no Dr. Mughal, no psychiatrist in the whole world, would ever be able to cure him of that.

She was with them by late afternoon. Pax had spent the day taking his guilt for a walk around the country lanes, finding excuses for himself – like having done his best at the time. But he knew he should have realized his father wasn't running, his mother wasn't chasing out of the treatment tent, none of the other white T-shirts were diving for cover. All he'd seen was Zuri, and she was all he'd thought about. So was that weird – or what? Whichever way he tried to see it he could never forgive himself. And at the end of a long trek skirting fields, he told himself he had two choices – to go back to Sharpe End, or just walk on, north, south, east, or west, and do what Dr. Mughal said some other people did – *pretend* he didn't know who he was.

But he found himself back at the house before Jenny Lancaster arrived, getting a small smile from Mary, just in from school, whose headache was, 'A bit better, thank you very much.'

Aunt Jenny was short, plumpish, sun-lined, nothing remarkable about her; brownish hair, and a mouth that pursed and unpursed as she walked from the taxi carrying a large rucksack. So far as he knew he'd never seen her before – but then she'd gone to Australia when he was very young. He didn't know whether to go into the hallway and meet her, or shoot up to his room. But Mike and Diana weren't home from London yet, so he hovered behind Magda as she opened the door and greeted.

'Come in, you're welcome. Mr. Symonds is not home yet. I will show you your room, then have some tea…?'

Pax stepped forward. 'Hi.'

'You're Peter!' Jenny Lancaster slipped her rucksack to the floor and gripped Pax around the waist, suddenly crying into his chest – all the more embarrassing because Pax didn't feel any emotion at all.

'I'm okay,' he said, to a question she hadn't asked.

'Well…' Jenny stepped back. 'I bet you don't remember me.' Her accent was definitely Australian, but it was English, too.

'No.'

'I'm your Aunt Jen.'

Magda was still very welcoming. 'Would you like a cup of tea?'

'A cup of tea would truly hit the spot. I haven't had a real cup of English tea with English water since I don't know when!'

'I have one for you when you come down.' Magda clapped her hands and Pedro appeared, all arms. He picked up Aunt Jen's rucksack as if it were an Armani item and led the way up the curved staircase.

'Don't you go away!' Aunt Jen told Pax. 'I'll be right down in a jiffy for a proper catch-up.'

Pax stared after her. So where did she think he'd go? Any one of a million other places would do right now, thank you very much! Okay, she was pleasant, putting herself out to be nice – but she was like Mary when he'd first arrived here, sort of, *at him* before he was ready for it. He mooched off into the large sitting room and lounged by the side of an armchair, already waiting obediently for his Aunt Jen to come downstairs again.

When she did, she'd changed, with her hair left wet from the shower and combed off her face. She was in a loose T-shirt and jeans with sensible sandals – very much at home. She was carrying two large photograph albums – which must have weighed her rucksack down – and she didn't waste a second in getting Pax to sit next to her on the sofa. Magda brought in her tea, but never mind the 'don't know when' since she'd drunk one, she let her English cup of tea with English water go stone cold while she went through the first album of Pax's family.

He sat there and ached. He half closed his eyes when she wasn't looking and he thought of his island. She showed him baby Pax, school uniform Pax, Pax and cousins, Pax and parents – but in his mind he was on Solitaire with the goats, the fish in Rainbow Cove, and a crumbled clay pot that was only dried mud.

'How about that?' Aunt Jen was throwing herself back and laughing, clapping her hands at the merriment of the picture on her lap.

'Yeah.'

'Uncle Stephen and I never thought they had it in them.'

Pax had to focus on the photo. It was of his parents in grass skirts with strings of flowers round their necks, sticking out their bottoms in some sort of dance. He smiled, too – and suddenly realized how people can *think* they've got a memory. He'd have known who these people were just from what he was told about them. This was his mum and this was his dad. Fact.

The session ended with the second album unopened – as Pax heard the Symonds's Systems's Jaguar draw up outside. He was on his feet in a shot. 'There's Mike,' he said. 'It's Mike.'

Aunt Jen was standing, and pursing and unpursing her lips.

Diana Lucky had peeled off as usual with the briefcases, and Mike came into the sitting room alone, smart in a city suit.

'Mike Symonds?'

'Jenny Lancaster?'

'Jen, please.'

'I bid you welcome to Sharpe End. And England.' Mike sounded a bit precise – and false. His normal manner was casual, but tonight he stood almost to attention, and when he nodded his head it was like a formal bow.

And Jenny Lancaster spoke slowly, as if she was filleting her Australian. The atmosphere had all the heaviness of a storm across the ocean. While the nonsense talk went on – how was the flight, had she managed to sleep, what was the weather like in dear old England? – Pax stood behind a sofa and yearned to be whisked out of the place, to hot sand, squishy mud, the clack of land crabs, and the sudden dart of a fiery bird.

'Now, let me get out of this suit...' Mike was saying, and Pax swiftly said he would change, too – although he didn't need to; but anything rather than more of this, or sitting down on that sofa with Album Two.

'How'm I? Do I need to...?' Aunt Jen looked down at herself.

'Not for me you don't. There's no top table stuff here.'

'I feel so much at home already.' Aunt Jen turned to Pax. 'Like you will, Peter, within minutes of me getting you home to Perth.'

And Pax smiled. But he didn't know how he did it, or why.

She told them a load of stuff that Pax would need to know about his life. Over dinner, no one tasted what they were eating: food turned out to be an encumbrance to everything coming out.

'You lived in Suffolk when your mum and dad worked at Ipswich General – then they wanted to do more for humanity and moved to South Africa.'

'Why move to South Africa for that?' Mike asked.

'To be nearer wherever they were sent. They joined up with the *Médecins Sans Frontières* outfit – sadly, there's always a need in Africa.'

'Which is how they came to be in Moebane, taken on to the *St. George*?' Diana Lucky asked.

Mike gave a loud clearing of his throat.

'Yes. Cathryn and Leonard went wherever they were sent, doing their medical thing – and sometimes taking Peter with them during the long school holidays.' Jenny Lancaster drew up her shoulders in a slight gesture of criticism, but dropped them. 'To be fair, at the time they went into Gambellia everyone thought the conflict was over. Well over. Till someone provided the rebels with fresh weapons in exchange for diamond-mining rights. We were collecting back home for the Gambellian Peace Fund; our choir gave a "War Requiem" recital in Perth Concert Hall...'

Pax's mind had to be the furthest away from the table – because things were coming back to him at weird moments like this. Somehow the fresh photographs he'd seen of him with his parents, together with his dreams and his memory fragments, his visions in the shower, they were all suddenly fastening him on that time spent in Gambellia. Sitting here, he saw through a sort of mist some of the things he'd done out there: how he'd helped his mother to dress wounds – no wonder he'd been good with Mike's thumb – and drunk milk from goats and worn strong boots alongside the minefields, but run barefoot with the kids so as not to be different, and played football in the open spaces, and lain in a mud hut and heard the roar of lions in the night. And while Aunt Jen talked on in a voice that sounded a bit like his memory of his mother's, now he was seeing Zuri's village again, and that medical tent, and that goat with the footless boy drinking from her, and Zuri herself...

And Zuri!

And all at once he was gripping the sides of his dining chair. *Help!* Don't let him go into a panic attack here at the table. *Please, no!*

'...Yes, I think Peter was very much heading for a medical career...'

'Pax!' Mary came up out of her custard. Which was as well, because otherwise Pax might have lost it. 'His name's Pax, not Peter.'

'*Mary!*' Diana reprimanded. 'You know his real name's Peter, and so do I, and even so does he – now.' She looked across the table at Pax – who managed to sit himself up with a very straight back.

'All I've got to say,' Pax fixed Diana Lucky with a stare, 'is that I've read in one of Mike's books that it doesn't matter what name's on your birth certificate, day-to-day you're actually allowed to call yourself whatever you want.' He looked defiantly around the table because he somehow knew that he had a special reason for calling himself what he did. 'And I am always going to be Pax.'

Diana looked sideways and down with a twist on her mouth. Jenny Lancaster opened hers to say something – but the next voice was Mike's. 'Dead right, old lad. You're Pax. You want to be Pax, you're Pax by me.' And he stared hard at him as he added: 'Good on yer!'

'Speaking of which –' Pax's aunt diplomatically changed tack – 'birth certificate. I've been to the house in Port Elizabeth – which is all shut up and secure, for whatever we're going to do about the place – and I've found your birth certificate. You just get me an ID picture and I'll pay to fast-track you a British passport for coming back home.'

By now the cheese and biscuits were sitting untouched on the table, and Mary was hanging off her chair ready for something more exciting to happen. But for Pax one fact had been confirmed – which was going to keep his brain whirling all night. *He was his parents' son! He had worked with them in the thick of things in Gambellia.* They spent their lives picking up the pieces left by warfare and killing – while those six-inch shells on HMS *Belfast* had turned his stomach over, that slaughtered goat on Solitaire had made him feel ill, those limbless Gambellians had made him ashamed to be human. *Yes, he was one of them!*

And the knowledge that he was so like his parents suddenly gave him new courage, as if they were both standing in that room, one on each side of him. 'Come on, Mary,' he heard himself saying, 'want a game of tennis or something?' And he made sure that he again stared Diana Lucky in the eye as he said it.

He was Pax! And Pax was the son of Cathryn and Leonard Foster – determined to be his own man!

Chapter Twenty

After a game of catch with Mary out on the lawn, Pax was with Jenny Lancaster and Mike when she told them that the next day she'd see Social Services in Stevenage, and go to the school in Suffolk to collect Pax's things – formally sign him off the roll. And she had brought a couple of gifts for Mike that she knew were small, but how could she ever thank him enough for what he had done for her family? They were tokens – but clearly meant to mark the end of Mike's care of Pax. She produced a small gift bag, which she handed over.

'Hello! What have I got here?' From a skein of tissue

paper, Mike unwrapped a luxury leather wallet, marked with the Perth City insignia. 'Thank you, Jen.' He sniffed it. 'I love the smell of real leather...'

'And this is for fun, but it's part of our history out there...' From behind her back she brought a painted Aborigine boomerang. 'That's for your wall, somewhere.'

'Wow – I'll have to think hard where to put this for maximum effect.' While Pax knew just where *he'd* put it, for sure.

'Tell you what, while your Aunt Jen's doing her business tomorrow,' Mike said, 'you and me – we'll shoot off somewhere special. I'll tell Diana I'm going to one of the factories – but it's an outing, old lad, a first-class outing...' although his face suddenly looked as sad as any man's would, coming up with a last-ever treat.

But Pax didn't spend the night spinning 'treat' possibilities in his head – things were coming back to him from out of nowhere, just the way Dr. Mughal said they would; things he desperately needed to know if he was ever going to understand himself. Going to bed every night, he wondered where his mind was going to take him before morning. And that night he was back in Gambellia, in a village whose name he didn't know, where he was helping to bury Zuri. But this was no nightmare – again, it was memory returning, and he was in it as clearly as the day it happened. Every jar of the shovel was felt as he dug into the hard ground, and he saw every throw of the spoil onto its small heap; he felt the jut of his jaw as he insisted on them going deeper than they did for the dogs, wiping at his tears as they rolled down his face and onto his arms. And into his heart came that ache again as he lifted Zuri's light, sheet-wrapped body into the grave. Her grieving grandmother's wailing drowned the short prayers read over her, and Zuri's mutilated little brother insisted on Pax and a village boy holding him up between them for the final covering with earth. Tonight, lying there in his bed, Pax relived it all, bright and vivid under the African sun. And while the tribal war for the diamond mountains was not Pax's fault, none of the cold facts of the killing could ever take away his own terrible guilt.

Jenny Lancaster's bedroom was next to his, and he was very grateful for the bathroom between them, because she was less likely to hear his groaning as he remembered the terrible thing he'd done. Whether he slept or not he didn't know; time had no meaning any more – until Mike's rap on his door suddenly brought him back to Sharpe End. A different person. Every morning now a different person came out of his room.

*

Before they shot off, Mike told Diana he was putting his diary on hold that day and going to the factory at Milton Keynes to look at a problematic production line – and he was taking Pax with him: two pieces of news that had her frowning. But there was an obstinate look in the boss's eye, and she got alone into the limousine to go to the London office wearing a very straight face.

'Let's chase some clouds!' Mike said as her car pulled away.

Without saying much more at all, Mike had the red Chrysler Crossfire brought round and drove them fast up the M1 for about twenty-five miles to a place Pax suddenly realized he knew. As they got nearer, and he saw a couple of private jets coming in, he remembered it was where he'd landed in England those weeks before – Cranfield Airport, the Learjet's home. So this was going to be a jaunt in a jet! And the question that then hit Pax was quite mad. Was Ray Powell waiting for them? Was Mike working a great bluff – and taking him back to Solitaire? Did he think Pax was better from his terrors – and letting him off Aunt Jen's Australian hook?

Which *was* crazy thinking – and pushed right out of Pax's mind when he saw the plane they were going up in that day. It wasn't the Learjet, but a single-engined 'prop' Cirrus SR22, which Mike 'kept for fun'. And the flight plan, when he filed it, wasn't four or five days' international, but an hour over the Midlands.

'We might give the Milton Keynes factory a buzz at five thousand feet,' Mike told Pax, 'just to keep on the angels' side of the truth!'

And in case Diana Lucky or Mary might start quizzing him when they got back, 'So what do you make there? Anything special?' Pax asked.

'Oh, variations on the usual stuff. What we make all over – England, Wales, Scotland, Europe.' But, Pax noticed, he didn't say that place with the Indian name which was supposed to be secret. 'Switches. Timers. Sensors. Micro-silicone circuit boards. Things that nothing works without, these days.' Mike pointed at the Cirrus that had been taxied outside the building. 'Aircraft fuel tank sensors. You name it, anything digital needs what Symonds's Systems make.' He was being handed a meteorological report by one of the airport staff. 'All the gadgets the world uses – we and others make the vital parts.' He waved a hand at Cranfield Airport, with its line of executive jets. 'See why I'm a billionaire?'

'Beg pardon, sir?'

'Sorry, talking to my grandson...' Mike smiled at the man as he studied the Met sheet, leading the way out onto the tarmac.

With Pax walking like a robot beside him. *Oh, help! Who had the wonky mind, him or Mike? 'Talking to my grandson...'*? Pax said nothing for a long time. For one thing, he couldn't find the small talk to fill the huge hole opened up by Mike's slip. And, for another, Mike was doing his pre-start checks. However often anyone flew, these were vital to ensure that everything was working properly; and, jet or prop, no one talked through the checks. Satisfied, Mike kicked the Cirrus into life and, with the engine running up, Pax looked at the displays – one screen with the flight instruments on it, the other with the navigation information. Until Mike suddenly gestured for Pax to plug in his headset.

'Golf-five-seven-eight-five ready to taxi,' he said, stowing his checklist. They were off on their final treat together.

'Clear to taxi, Golf-five,' Pax heard the tower tell Mike, and with careful hands Mike pushed the throttle forward, released the brakes and took the Cirrus along the white line to the far end of the jet-length runway.

'Used to fly bombers out of here in the war,' Mike said. 'Blenheims, that sort of thing. Made a concrete runway out of the grass flight path, which got shot up by Jerry a couple of times, but a damned fine outfit according to my old man – RAF Cranfield.' There was all this pride Mike had about the army, and the navy, and the air force – which had to be his generation, Pax thought, because all he ever saw himself was the ugly, death side of war.

They waited at the runway's end while a business-class Astra landed and taxied off – and with the Cirrus revs pushing at the brakes, Mike got clearance for take-off. Which was always exciting – and always predictable. Pax had done it three times in the Learjet, and it thrilled rather than frightened him – not once had it threatened a panic attack. Well, the science was simple; he'd looked it all up at Sharpe End; he understood it. With the aerodynamic design of an aircraft giving lift under the wings, at the point they hit the right ground speed they'd get airborne – as simple as that.

Now Mike's hand was on the throttle and his concentration on the runway ahead, with glances here at this display, and there at that. Pax saw the engine revs creep higher to three hundred brake horsepower, and suddenly the plane spurted forward, a push in his back as it gained speed fast – until, when the dial showed sixty knots, lift-off speed – back came the control column, up went the nose, and they were airborne.

Mike climbed rapidly. It was a beautiful day, just a few puffs of light cloud cover, low enough to have some white-outs to climb through – until, when the displays in front of them showed eight thousand feet, there they were in a clear sky with only the sun above them.

'Just think – it's always like this up here! Weather? That's for the groundlings!' And Mike set the direction at forty-eight degrees east-north-east, heading for the North Sea, just south of Norwich.

It was a good flight. Once they were up and cruising, Mike paid less attention to his ear-cans and more to Pax. 'Got a unique safety feature on this little beauty,' he told him. 'If all else fails we've got a parachute.' Pax's eyes widened. 'Not for you, not for me, but for the plane itself. The whole thing comes down like a field-gun dropped for troops!' It was a bang up-to-date, really comfortable light aircraft, two more passenger seats behind them, a luxury job. She flew straight and level; but as they headed away from the sun, Pax noticed how the smart display of screens and dials could actually be narrowed down to a crucial three: height, airspeed and direction.

'Keep your peepers skinned!' Mike said. 'Radar's good, but you never know what Hooray Henry might come up in a hot-air balloon. Eye's best on a clear day.'

And it was – England looked beautiful below them, green and open, with a small cluster that was a town, and roads and railways like toys. Pax felt the exhilaration of being in a small plane, that sense of owning the sky.

There was nothing else in sight up there: the world was theirs.

'Put your hands on the stick,' Mike said quietly.

'Eh?' In front of Pax were the dual controls, the control column moving when Mike's did. He reached forward and took it.

'Get the feel.'

'Okay.' It was neither stiff nor loose – it just seemed right.

'Relax on it, don't clamp it. Now, hold it straight and level, just the way it is.'

'Right.' This called for deep breaths, all the same. Pax held the stick lightly but firmly, kept it exactly where it was.

'You're now in control, old lad!'

What? Pax glanced to his left. Mike was holding his hands off his stick like someone surrendering – and then he made a show of folding his arms.

'Just keep the nose of the aircraft on the horizon. Do nothing and it'll fly along straight and level.'

Pax kept things as they were. Doing nothing gave a powerful feeling of control.

'Now move the stick to your left, steady as you go, and…see? The nose comes round forty-five degrees…'

Which it was doing in splendid obedience. 'Wow!'

'Now straighten the stick, resume our course... there...'

Pax followed the instruction, glancing at the navigation display to take the preset mark as his guide.

'Now push the stick forward – not too far...' And the plane's nose began to dip. 'Now we're going downhill.'

'Brilliant!'

'And pull back gently...'

Pax levelled off the Cirrus. He even had the confidence to look out and to the side as he held the plane steady. They were over flat, open countryside, and in the distance was the sea.

'I've got to say, you're better than Joe was. He learned to fly – but you're a natural!' Which was matter-of-fact. There was no choke in Mike's voice up here. 'I think you stay,' he said.

'Help, no! I couldn't land this thing!' He might be a natural at wiggling a stick up here in the sky, but no way could Pax be a first-time natural at putting this thing down onto the ground.

Mike snorted a laugh. 'No! You're not that good yet. I mean...I don't think you go to Oz.'

'*What?*' The Cirrus wobbled.

'I've got her now.' Mike took over the controls. Pax folded his own arms, just for something to do in the tension. 'Till you're better. I don't think you go back with Auntie Jen till you're properly better. You're making damned fine progress with me, and going off with Mrs. Lancaster's only going to get in the way of curing your dissociative fugue...'

So Mike *had* been fully debriefed by Dr. Mughal. *But what had the man just said?* Not go to Australia with Aunt Jen? Stay at Sharpe End? Live with Mike till he was 'better'? *Yikes!* What a turn-up was this?

'There's a long way to go on the brainbox front – you know it, and I know it. And to shoot off Down Under as soon as a passport comes through – that's going to stand everything on its bally head. Literally. You included!' And with a pull back on the stick, a rev on the engines, Mike took the Cirrus up into the clear sky, up and up – and suddenly into a dive like a ride at the adventure park – the G-force hitting Pax at the bottom as Mike pulled out of it.

'Fantastic!'

'We're birds of a feather, you and me.'

Mike put the Cirrus into a wide turn over the North Sea and headed her back the way they'd come, into the sun, leaving the talk at that. And Pax left it, too. He didn't want to be brought down to earth by any second thoughts from Mike. Except, before the runway came into sight –

when he knew Mike would have to give all his attention to the Cranfield tower – he turned to him and said, 'Solitaire.' His voice was quiet in his throat; in the hum of the engine sounding to himself no louder than thinking. 'I love Solitaire.'

Mike was nodding as he checked his displays. 'I know you do, old lad. I know you did. And I know you nearly didn't come off it with me.'

'What?' Pax frowned. 'How come?'

'I was keeping an eye. You were worried about your carving...'

'Zuri,' Pax said in a whisper. 'Mike, I dug her grave and buried her – the real one...' And now he was crying, up there in the glare of the sun, his chest heaving.

'And...I'm...' Mike was filled-up, too – and he spared a hand to clap Pax on the shoulder. '...I'm going to put you back on Solitaire one day, old lad, or damn-well buy you an island of your own. And you can take your Zuri there...'

Pax closed his eyes.

'They come on the market. Islands. There's one up for sale in the Seychelles... After university. Pax, old lad, you stick with me, get yourself better qualified than this old soldier, and I promise you – *I promise you* – you'll have your Solitaire, one way or another. And in the meantime, in the long holidays – you can visit. I can see to that with the French...'

Pax choked back his tears, as miraculously Mike kept the Cirrus firm and steady on its south-west course. 'But what about Aunt Jen?' he had to ask.

'Nice lady.' Then Mike gave a laugh, one of his small explosions. 'But I've made a few enquiries out there – and she's biddable, biddable,' he said, adjusting his ear-cans, ready to talk to the tower. And with a loud 'Tally-ho!' he waggled the Cirrus's wings in a left and right victory flap. With Pax knowing very well that 'victory' was exactly what it was.

Chapter Twenty-One

He took her out to dinner at the top of one of London's tallest buildings – Freddie d'Orsay's at The Heights. In this exclusive setting, up among the stars – with the capital city spread out three-sixty degrees below them – Mike cast his wealth like bait on a line. The tables in the smart venue were set well apart for privacy, and the cuisine was masterminded by the international TV chef, Freddie d'Orsay. So who wouldn't be impressed? But Mike acted as if this was something run-of-the-mill for him, and he talked of Pax, not of power.

'He's doing great, all things considered. Dr. Mughal's been pursuing a very stringent course.'

'So what is it, exactly,' Jenny Lancaster asked, 'what he's suffering from? You said diss-something. The papers say amnesia, but we all know there are lots of different amnesias...'

'Traumatic, dissociative fugue,' Mike said tapping his forehead. 'Also known as psychogenic fugue. That's our boy.'

'Caused by – what?'

'Ah!' With a gesture, Mike ordered the ice bucket with the white wine to be brought to the table. 'That's the point. When the psychiatrist Dr. Mughal's recommended uncovers that, that's when the cure kicks in. Our lad begins remembering, and Pax starts becoming Peter again.'

'But they're on the right track, she reckons...?' Jenny Lancaster looked at her watch, a time query, but of weeks and months, not hours and minutes. 'Only I've got...'

'It won't be quick. Dr. Mughal warned that it won't be quick.' Mike poured the wine himself, wrapping the chilled bottle in a napkin. 'And, of course, it isn't cheap...'

Jenny Lancaster pursed and unpursed her lips.

'You don't get it on the NHS, not at the speed we're getting it, and health insurance leaves a pretty hefty hole in the kitty… But if a job's worth doing…that's what I say. Yes, very good,' he added, to the wine glass. 'I guess you have top people like Aysun Mughal in Perth…?'

'Bound to have.' Jenny Lancaster took a sip of her wine. 'The Aussies are as nutty as anyone.'

Mike exploded a laugh. 'So long as the same approach is taken, that's the key that fits the door. Trouble is, the people here at Queen Square – neurologists, psychologists – have got their own specific lines on things…' Mike said it like a skilled peddler selling a Bible to a clergyman. 'They're pioneers in the world of mental stress…'

'Sure…'

'You've only got to read your *Lancet*. And Dr. Mughal is very confident that a psychiatric approach will bring a breakthrough – though it might be later rather than sooner… However, she sees that as a strength, not a weakness,' he added. 'Deeper, and more secure, you see, with less chance of a relapse…'

The hors d'oeuvres arrived – Yarmouth Island lobster – brought by a young man with flame-red hair gelled up in spikes, but wearing a discreet dark grey suit. As Jenny Lancaster contemplated the stainless steel shellfish crackers that he'd brought with the dish, the man walked round to greet Mike.

'Mike!'

'Freddie!'

And Jenny Lancaster's eyes opened wide.

'I'd like you to meet Jenny Lancaster...Jenny – Freddie d'Orsay.'

'It's...*you*!' she said. '*Yourself!* We get you all the time on ABC! I was watching you only the other week...'

Freddie d'Orsay bowed, and smiled. 'So what was I cooking? Were you paying attention?' He waggled a forefinger. His name was left-bank Paris, his voice a smartened-up south London.

'I was. It was a new way with a shank of lamb. And you've brought us our starters yourself...'

'Because the hors d'oeuvres is the red carpet to the eating event,' Freddie d'Orsay said. 'So we'll have our photo taken!' And a waiter snapped him leaning over Jenny Lancaster. 'I'm shooting off to Downing Street, so I had to catch Mike early... Let him know if I've got the edge on your barbie boys down under!' And he laughed his famous laugh and went away.

'Wow!' Jenny Lancaster looked impressed; while Mike put on the blandest *this-is-simply-my-world* face. 'Nice kid,' he said. 'Unspoiled.'

'I can't believe that just happened.' She went with her cracker at the seafood.

'Now,' the billionaire said, getting in forcefully at a

lobster claw himself, 'how can we ensure our boy gets well again – in a smooth, uninterrupted sort of way?'

Jenny Lancaster was nodding her head. 'That's what we want, isn't it? That's what we want.' Her eyes were all around her, looking out at London, and the privilege of the world in which Mike lived.

'Park Lane! I've got Park Lane!' Mary was out of her seat at the joy of landing on a second prime property. She already owned Mayfair – now she was set to be a Monopoly millionaire.

Diana waited for the pretend money to be counted into her hand before she released the deeds. 'That puts your Bond Street portfolio in the shade,' she told Pax. 'And the best card I hold is Get Out of Jail Free!'

Pax rolled the dice and played on, moving his silver car along a trio of properties he already owned. But this game wasn't going so well. Not the Monopoly itself, but the fact of who was playing. When Mary had wanted to play a game after dinner, he'd jumped at it. She'd been a bit strange with him since the swing-ball accident, even though they'd played catch the following night, and tennis on the court later. She'd been different, and Pax was as sure as he could be that it wasn't the hit with the bat. She was being got at by her mother, who didn't like him;

at least, she definitely didn't like him being *here* – as if he was putting Mary in the shade at Sharpe End, as well as taking Mike's attention away from his business affairs.

'Six!' Mary wrinkled her nose at landing on Euston Road. 'Don't want it.'

If he'd been alone with her tonight they'd have played a real-life game like hide-and-seek out in the fields and the wood – and he'd have made it *fun*, like playing a game on Solitaire. But Diana had insisted on staying with them and on playing, too: not allowing Pax to get close. And Pax knew that if Mike won Jenny Lancaster over, if he didn't have to go to Australia, he was going to have this woman to win round – a hard old job. But, then, his getting here in the first place hadn't been a piece of cake, had it?

'You've certainly got a lot going for you,' Jenny Lancaster said, as the coffee and *digestifs* came – a Cointreau for her and a Cognac for him. 'I don't know – he's going to find a big difference, coming to our old town house in Perth…'

'It looks spanking smart to me,' Mike smoothed. 'And it's what's inside here that counts.' He laid his hand on his heart, like a general stopping his medals from jangling.

'You don't know quite all of it.' Jenny Lancaster shut her mouth in a flat line.

'No?'

'There's Stephen's father…'

'Your husband's…?'

'His dad, Alan. He's been with us since his wife died, came over from King's Lynn, but he's not an old man. I mean, not *bodily* old…'

'How old?' Mike prompted.

'Late sixties. But—' She paused; a touch of drama – 'Alzheimer's! Poor old Alan sometimes doesn't know whether it's eight o'clock, nine o'clock, or Anzac Day.'

'Which has got to be very hard on you.'

Jenny Lancaster went silent, looked into her hands. 'But I truly want to do what's best for my dear Cath's family…'

'Of course you do. Which is why I think I might be able to help.'

'I don't want charity.' She looked up sharply.

'Hold those horses – I'm not talking charity! I'm talking hard sense.' Mike signalled for more drinks to be brought. 'Although I'm in a superb position to be very, very helpful over Peter and the future…' Which was obvious. He was giving her dinner at a top restaurant, served personally at their table by a world-famous chef; he had a handle on the best psychological treatment and could pay for it, no waiting; and he lived in style in one of

England's most beautiful counties. This man with whom Jenny Lancaster was dining was superbly placed to give a kid a huge leg-up in the world. 'I've got a little proposition to put to you,' he was saying. 'Now, see how this idea goes down with your Cointreau…'

'Houses and hotels aren't everything,' Diana Lucky said. 'You spent all your money building up two properties, and neither of us landed on either of them. So now you've got to start selling! And I can tell you, my girl – I don't know about him, but I'm going to drive a hard, hard bargain.'

And what a hard, hard woman she was, Pax thought – who still couldn't bring herself to say his name! If Diana hadn't been here, he'd have made sure that Mary came out on top – he'd tried to help her by miscounting the taps of his car around the board so as to land on her Mayfair, but her mother had been watching with her bank-statement eyes. 'Count that again! If a game's worth playing, it's worth playing fairly.'

All the same, Pax thought, Diana would be a marvellous problem to have, if having it meant he was staying at Sharpe End with Mike – till one day he got back to Solitaire. He'd take problems like her with open arms if it meant he wasn't going off to Australia with Aunt Jen.

'You're *so* like your father,' Mary's mother went on. 'Feckless. Think, girl, think!'

Mary looked bewildered, stared at Pax, then at her mother.

At which Pax had a sudden warning surge inside him to keep quiet; but he didn't – somehow he couldn't. 'I'd have done the same as you,' he told Mary. 'You just had bad luck.'

'She gambled – and she lost,' Diana said. 'This is the real world.'

At which Pax got up, leaned over the table, and kissed Mary on the forehead. 'Anyhow, it's only a money-grubber's game,' he said – and walked out of the room.

He went to bed. Mike and Aunt Jen would be back late from London; and although he knew what was in the balance, he couldn't wait up especially for them; it would only tell her he was in on Mike's plan. But, like most nights now, sleep wouldn't give his brain any rest; he was as alert as he'd been on Solitaire, listening for the crush of soldiers' boots. He tried to read for a bit. Mike had found him a copy of *Treasure Island,* but after a while he realized that what he'd read that night had made no sense at all; he wasn't reading, his eyes were running over print while he thought of other things. He put out his light, put it on again for a stare at Zuri, switched it off – and shot up in bed at a sudden rapping on his door. *Knock-knockety-knock-knock*. And before he could get up, Jenny Lancaster came in.

'Are you asleep?'

'Not quite.' What was this? He didn't wear anything in bed – now he couldn't get up. He switched on his bedside light. 'Is everything okay?' *Had something happened to Mike?*

'All's fine!' she said. 'Lovely evening!' She came over and sat on his bed, pinning him beneath the duvet. 'I hoped you wouldn't be asleep.'

'Couldn't get off.'

She leaned towards him, her voice slightly thick in her throat. 'I guess you realize Mike and I have been having a good old think,' she went on, 'about what's best for you...'

'Yeah?' *And what's that?* he wanted to yell. *What's been decided?* This was mega-crucial to him.

'Well, it's going to be a bit of a surprise – and I've darned well got to get it off my chest before I go to my bed...'

He wanted to sit up, but he was in a straitjacket.

'Being your own flesh and blood, you can guess how badly I feel about this – and I hope to goodness you won't take it the wrong way...'

'Take what?' He rubbed his eyes to pretend he wasn't

too alert – but his mind was as focused as ever it had been.

'We think…I think, and Mike thinks, too…'

He lifted his chin in an encouragement to her to spit this out. 'Uh?'

'That your best interests would best be *served*…' She drew out the word in full Anglo-Australian. '…if Mike fostered you. There! That's it. I can't put it any better way than that.'

Yikes! He didn't have to go to Australia! Mike had swung it. He was going to stay here at Sharpe End. *Wow!* 'But I guess I can come over and visit?'

'Oh, yes. My goodness, yes. Open arms, open arms. We're just doing what's for the best in terms of your Queen Square treatment; like Mike says, that's the key that fits the door… I don't know that we can match that at the Royal Perth.'

Pax nodded wisely. 'I get you.'

'Do you? Do you really? You don't mind? You're okay about it?'

Was he?! 'Sure, I'm okay. If you reckon that's for the best…'

'I do. Whatever's for the best, that's my thinking. We're always there, of course, we're always family – and all of that will be put in the fostering papers.'

'Oh, good.'

'But, well...' She hesitated, smiled, hiccupped. 'Beg pardon – I wasn't going to give this to you till you were older, but I think now's the right time...'

Pax was genuinely frowning now – no more pretence. *What was she bringing out from behind her back tonight?*

'When I went to your house in Port Elizabeth – which we'll sell for you, by the by, and put the cash in trust with a good rate of interest...'

'Yes?' *Get on with it!*

'...I found your dad's graduation watch. From Cambridge. He wouldn't take it on trips, but he wore it very proudly at home. Here.'

She brought round her hand, and dangled the watch on its bracelet in front of him – and instantly he fell back onto his pillow. He remembered it. *He remembered it!* He had seen this watch on a man's arm, on his father's arm – gold and delicate against the tough tan.

'It needs a new battery, but I think you should have it. Mike can put it in his safe for you. I was going to pass it on when you graduated yourself.'

'Thank you.' Pax took the watch. He could say the name on its face without reading it. *Cyma.* It was slim, smooth, and very special on its gold bracelet – and it was his! Pax and the watch belonged together. First he'd had a stave, then he'd had a knife for carving, and now he had a gold watch that was his very own.

'I remember your grandmother gave it to him – he graduated before the old lady went.'

Pax had long since guessed that this aunt coming from Australia meant he hadn't got any grandparents still living; he had no grandfather like Joseph. Except, he *had* got Mike. *He was going to stay.*

'Look after it, won't you? Treasure it.'

'You bet I will.'

'He never took it to the war zones. He told your Uncle Stephen once, the APLs could have his legs but they weren't having his watch.'

APLs. Pax knew APLs, didn't he? And he must have frowned.

'Anti-personnel landmines – I'm sure they call them APLs. Or ALPs...'

'APLs,' Pax said, quietly. 'I'll look after it.'

It was an APL that had killed Zuri.

'Good boy.' She leaned over and kissed him on the forehead, the way he'd kissed Mary – and he smelled the sweet fragrance of oranges. 'I'll stay till the fostering papers go through – Mike's going to get them put at the top of the Social Services' pile.' She stood up off the bed.

'But we're always there, Peter, we're always there for you. Pax, I mean…'

'I know you are,' he said, as sincerely as he could.

And I'm always here.

Till I get back to Solitaire.

Chapter Twenty-Two

The road east to the coast was long and no more than a track, along which the spindly line limped, following the *Médicins Sans Frontières* jeep. Dark florets of smoke rose into the sky some way behind the refugee column. Were the rebel killers getting nearer, would the wounded make it to the coast? From time to time, a light aircraft throttled back across the column – not the enemy, but not sounding very friendly, either: the jeep radio crackling with impatient messages – 'Go faster! Leave the worst, get to Moebane, just!'

Peter was trying the impossible – to keep in touch with the jeep without sucking in the exhaust fumes that trailed it. The hot sun was diffused in an opaque sky – the fragile line of refugees not even having the substance to cast shadows. He was sweating beneath the burden on his shoulders – which was Zuri's little brother, his hands hugged around his forehead: a position from which he kept telling people, 'Is good. I can see big long way with no feet…'

Leonard Foster, wearing his wide-brimmed hat, was up and down the line, giving water and encouragement; but not a lot of either – enough of one to keep tongues from swelling, enough of the other to keep hearts from shrivelling. 'It's not far. You see those trees – they're near the sea…'

'Uncle – you telling us wishes!'

'No, honestly – on the map, Moebane's there beyond that line of forest.'

'Even I can't see it yet,' the footless boy joined in. 'I shout when I do.'

'You do that!' Leonard Foster encouraged.

For the first kilometre the boy had been light; but as the trudge had gone on he had grown heavier, and heavier – and unlike a burden carried in the hand, there was no way of giving either side of the body a rest. The weight became relentless: the calves and the backs of Peter's knees ached, his spine compacted, his shoulder muscles pained with sharp stabs. He longed for a halt to be called; but the jeep whined on and on as the next ridge revealed not the sea but another wide valley, the column's speed reduced to the pace of the slowest. Now every shift of the energetic child on his shoulders was torture.

His father came up to him, and gave him a short swig from his own water bottle. 'You're a hero, Pete,' he said, 'I'm really proud of you... Here – I'll give you a spell.'

Peter bubbled some reply around a slug of water as the man lifted the burden off his shoulders, a relief of the pain that was a painful stab itself. *But after what had happened to Zuri, what the heck did his father have to be proud about?*

Pax saw all this in the darkness of his room as the truth was underlined for him, the wounding discovery of the other night. His memory loss was no escape from a fear of attacking gunships, it was an escape from his own guilt: guilt over the death of Zuri back in the village, days before the gunship ever attacked the ship. The helicopter on Solitaire had triggered his terrors, like one of Mike's sensor components – but it wasn't the cause of them.

Now, lying there, he stroked his father's watch under his pillow. And he lay and deliberately recalled that time.

'You did nothing wrong, Pete – don't harbour that idea. Your best intentions were to run that girl to safety. You hadn't heard what they shouted from the helicopter, you didn't know they weren't shooting us up. You didn't dive in a ditch on your own and huddle, you ran the quickest course bravely in the open to get that kid away from danger.'

Peter's father was crouching on the quayside, waiting with the wounded while the cruise ship manoeuvred into Moebane harbour to moor up.

'The mines, the APLs, were always there – you ran her away from a new threat. The people responsible for that kid's death – and thousands of others' – were the war criminals who laid the minefields, and the arms traders that made the dirty devices in the first place. You did your best under stress, Pete – and I don't want you ever to forget that.'

The difference in Pax's mind tonight was his father being the clearer of his parents. Probably because it had been her sister who'd come to Mike's, Pax had connected the past with his mother – and Diana getting at him for the swing-ball accident had triggered her coming alive in his head, blaming him for what he'd done. But tonight, with the Cyma watch seeming so familiar in his hand, it was his father he remembered being closer to him in those moments on the quayside, giving him comfort.

But, mother or father in the foreground, one way and another his past was coming back to him. Like Mary's puzzle book where you drew lines between dots to make a picture, some of those lines were creating a clear image in his mind. Parts of his life were revealing themselves, his memory was starting to work the way Dr. Mughal said it would – but not on its own. Things were being triggered; and until they didn't need triggering, could he ever say that he was cured? No, he couldn't. He'd got nothing like a full picture in his head. He still didn't remember the school, he couldn't recall any of those family photographs being taken, he had no idea what the house in South Africa looked like. Those were all things he'd only been told about – they still involved some other boy as far as he was concerned. And as he lay there, in and out of the triggered past, he realized the rightness of that decision he'd made a couple of weeks before. His treatment at Queen Square was his big excuse for staying with Mike, and therefore his only route back to Solitaire – so he was going to continue sitting on what came into his head, at least until after Jenny Lancaster had gone home. Which wasn't pretence, he told himself – he wasn't *doing* something to mislead. It was more...*lying low*.

Lying low with Mike. Learning to fly. Two birds of a feather – Mike had said it. And he turned over in his bed and thought about the man who would soon be his foster parent. Although, what were the words that had slipped out at Cranfield Airport? *My grandson*. And Pax knew it, of course – he wasn't stupid: he was filling a great hole in Mike's life, too, foster-son or stand-in Joseph. He had a part to play, that much he understood. Meanwhile, a lot of the man was still a mystery to Pax. He hadn't had a business dinner at Sharpe End since Pax had been here – and Magda said he used to have them all the time. He had been to visit a castle on army land. He had secret connections with a factory in India – although that was probably only a business secret, not *secret-service* secret. Well, the great thing was, Pax was going to have the time to find out some of those things in the coming months.

Tomorrow, though, he would go to the shops and proudly buy a battery for his father's watch.

Jenny Lancaster was going to visit old friends. Special Delivery brought Pax's new passport on the Saturday morning – but with the fostering processes still having to go through the following week, she told them her plans over breakfast.

'I'm taking myself off to old haunts.'

'Why, are you an old ghost?' Mary cheeked – getting a hard stare from Diana, and a snort into his handkerchief from Mike.

'No, Mary, I'm not – but it's nice to go back to where you once lived. See the streets again, and the shops, and the people. I'll have a few days with my school friend Sheila in Paddock Wood, then pop down to Hastings to the Church Fellowship: but I bet it's "all change" everywhere...'

And Pax couldn't help thinking how Solitaire would *never* change – it would always be his island in his head, till he got back there some day. Even though he now knew that it would have to be without Zuri...

'Well – talking of trips, I've got to go away myself,' Mike suddenly announced, cracking into an egg with, '*Off with his head!*' 'Three days, later next week.'

Diana Lucky didn't seem surprised, so it had to be about work. And with any luck, Pax thought, she might have to go with him. *Good!* He'd have a great time here with Mary, Magda and Pedro...

'And, much as I'd like to take both of you, I can't,' Mike said directly to Mary. 'School...' She put her elbows on the table and her chin in her hands, disappointed. 'But, now that his passport's come, I can take Pax – if it's okay with Jen...'

Everyone turned to Jenny. 'It's okay by me. Why not?'

Now that his passport had come? Were they going to another country, then? Pax's mind raced. No! They'd never get to Solitaire and back in three days – unless Mike had bought a long-haul ex-army helicopter. *Or, could that be why he'd gone to Castlemartin?*

'Monaco! Monte Carlo!' Mike flourished. 'The richest principality in the world!' And, banging time with his spoon, he went into his old party piece, singing 'Money, Money, Money' at the top of his voice.

When he got to the *Ahaaas*, Jenny joined in, swaying in her seat, tapping the rhythm on the table with her fingers.

Diana suddenly turned to Pax. 'Do you know that song?'

Pax frowned; was flummoxed for a second over what to say. Diana stared into his eyes. 'I just wondered how much better your memory might have got, with everything that's happening...'

'Come *on*! They play it on the radio all the time,' Jenny cut in. 'Of course he knows it!' And Pax had the sudden feeling of family sticking together.

*

With just the two of them driving along the M1 to Cranfield, Mike opened up to Pax. 'It's in the diary as a business trip,' he told him, 'but d'you want to guess why we're really going?' Pax hadn't a clue. 'It's the Monaco Yacht Show. Rows and rows of the most beautiful vessels, and enough champagne on tap to fill Walthamstow Reservoir.'

Luxury yachts? Mike had a country mansion, superb cars, a private jet, a Cirrus prop – what didn't he have, or want?

'Flags of all nations a'fluttering at the mast, lads in shorts buffing up the brightwork, waiters serving cocktails to the richest people in the world; and all the yachts parked up next to one another like shoes in a shoe shop. *"Like the look of this one?" "Try that for size."* See the latest gizmos, twirl a ship's wheel or two, watch 'em swapping this boat for that, like I used to swap comics on my front doorstep.'

'Sounds great!' Pax's eyes were alight. He'd seen television pictures of those large, ocean-going yachts; they could go anywhere in the world with the right skippers and crews. *So if Mike decided to buy one, might it one day soon be anchored off Rainbow Cove – on the holiday visit he'd promised?*

'But I'll do a bit of business while we're there, just to

shut the taxman up.' Then Mike took a hand off the wheel and clapped Pax around the shoulders. 'We'll fly out to Monaco in the Lear – but let's leave it to Dame Fortune what we come back in!'

Co-piloted by Ray Powell, Mike flew them to Nice International Airport, with Pax taking it in turns to sit at the controls – but there was no 'hands on' for him this time. He watched and he learned, though, as Mike put the Lear onto the runway with hardly a bump. From there it was an executive car to the hotel in Monte Carlo, the glitzy heart of Monaco, with Ray Powell left behind in France to babysit the aircraft at Nice.

It was early evening when they drove through the upmarket district – expensive cars, fashion-show pedestrians, the world's top shops in the world's most exclusive country; with the Hôtel de Paris sucking out Pax's breath when they walked into the foyer – huge and grand, old-fashioned, but with modern amenities like super-fast lifts. Mike had booked a luxury suite – two rooms each side of a large sitting room – with a view from the balcony of a very blue Mediterranean. And as Pax walked through the glass doors to look at it, instantly his chest filled, and he was lifted with a weird desire to be out there, diving into those warm, gentle waves. The wide horizon before him and the smell of the sea air were so real, so *touchable*. He closed his eyes, the sight of the blue water too much for him.

'How's that for a view! A million dollars a pixel!' Mike took a photograph of Pax and the sea.

And how many dollars for granting this greatest sight Pax had seen since leaving Solitaire? 'Your business must be going great guns to give you all this...'

Mike laughed. 'It puts bread and butter on the table – and a dollop of jam as well... And I'd never have found you, now would I, without something in the old back pocket?'

But right now Pax didn't know how he felt, beyond extremely mixed up. Apart from those times with the terrors, he'd been happy on Solitaire, and then he'd got used to living in that big house at Sharpe End. At night he'd gone into his head, found his memories of Gambellia and the APL minefields, and discovered his guilt. And now he was here in the sun, looking out over a beautiful blue sea that got to his heart; but where he'd been suddenly hit with the gnawing feeling that he didn't belong anywhere any more – because didn't belonging mean not only a place, but *people*? He sighed, inside. Mike, yes – but imagine someone like Zuri: and then it wouldn't have mattered where in the world he was...

'You know what?' Mike was saying. 'You and me, tomorrow – we're going to look for the swankiest, most state-of-the-art, sturdiest, ocean-going yacht, and we're going to see what the owner's asking for her. Why else get up and go to work every day?'

Pax looked away, ashamed of his thoughts; because he knew what the man was saying – even before he said it, Mike was without any doubt confirming the promise he'd made up in the Cirrus. 'We'll berth her in Antsiranana, Madagascar – that's where I hired Maitrait and his *Brume Rouge*.' And Pax's throat choked with the thanks he wanted to mutter. Mike had lost his daughter, his granddaughter, and he'd lost Joe; but instead of feeling bitter about Pax not being the one he'd gone searching for, he'd given him everything he possibly could.

'The world, old lad, is our oyster!' – before Mike turned and went back into the suite. But Pax didn't follow straight away; the man needed a few minutes on his own. While Pax also wanted private time. Delving into the mind and finding memories was one thing; but creating enough space in his brain for the facts, the emotions, and the rapid changes in his life – that was something else. It would take a heck of a time to get a hold on everything that was happening to him. But the hardest, most unbelievable thing in all this, was...how Mike buying a yacht fitted into Pax's dreams like a crucial piece of a jigsaw.

Chapter Twenty-Three

They had a room-service breakfast on their Mediterranean balcony – hot croissants, *pains au chocolat*, fresh fruits, and the best bowl of coffee Pax had ever tasted – the sun shining its privilege on them while a dramatic storm played out at sea. Just like on Solitaire, Pax thought, a storm could suddenly whip itself up, empty the sky down on you, and be steam-drying off the leaves all within a couple of hours.

'I'll get my business done while the sun's out to play – and if that storm's heading our way we'll go to the

Aquarium, world famous for its marine research – then I'll show you how to lose your pocket money in the Casino...'

A slight breeze flapped their clothes as Mike led them down the slope of the Avenue D'Ostende to walk west from the hotel to the Port of Monaco. On one side were the millionaire apartments, on the other side was the sea, a churlish grey further out, but still sparkling blue within the harbour. Mike marched along as if he owned the place, and suddenly put in an army change-of-step. 'Well,' he said to Pax, 'who wouldn't have a skip in their step, two good friends off to buy a yacht.'

They strode along tipping their faces against the breeze, optimists who hadn't bothered with rainwear or umbrellas: Mike in a white linen suit, and Pax in a collarless white shirt, navy shorts, and a pair of expensive deck shoes. And on his wrist, glinting in the sun, was his father's gold watch.

Mike had been right. The Port of Monaco was crammed all the way along the front with the most expensive-looking yachts in the world. And although they were berthed tightly together, and nudged irritably at each other in the breeze, nothing was taken from their elegance or their class.

'Pampered blighters, yachts!' Mike said. 'A car you

service and clean. A plane you check and fuel. But a yacht you fuss over till you're putting a gloss on a perfect polish.' Pax could see what he meant. Ladders and rails were being shone, decks were being mopped, and from waterline to radar-dish, people were touching up the flotilla like artists at their masterpieces.

'So – which one do you fancy?'

Help! Pax blinked his eyes and stared at the gleaming array.

'Think *attributes,*' Mike said. 'She needs a decent draft for stability, but doesn't have to be huge – we're not entertaining the king of Morocco every Saturday night – and just a couple of decent cabins with room to swing a cat...'

Pax could hardly believe he was listening to this, buying a yacht being talked about as if they were just out shopping.

'...And low maintenance. Never mind the spit-and-polish, she's going to be moored up in Antsiranana a lot of the year. We'll see – we won't jump into anything, we won't jump...'

They walked on, each in his own silence, the wind off the sea a background to the dull drone of yacht generators, of motor boats puttering in the port, and the increasing clank of sail lines hitting against masts: but there was no clamour, no police sirens, no stacking aircraft like in London. Just the feel of rich safety, here in the peace that money could buy.

Boom! A clap of thunder rumbled out in the Mediterranean.

'There she is!' Mike said, checking in a leather notebook. 'Just in time, before this lot tips down...' The sky above them had suddenly darkened. 'The *Ocean Drifter.*'

'You knew about this one?'

'No. Sorry, old lad! Not for us. A spot of business first – I told you I had to do a spot of business?'

He had; to shut up the taxman, he'd said. *And Diana!*

Mike hurried his step, off the boulevard and over a small wall towards the quayside. 'This is where the business is. Aboard the jolly old *Ocean Drifter*. A contact I've got to meet. Shan't be long – then you and me are gonna hit the town.'

Pax stopped, astride the wall. 'Do you want me to...?' He waved an arm inland. He could easily lose himself for a while, go off for a walk around the port.

'Be best, old lad. You won't run off with any *mademoiselles*, will you?' Now Mike was looking for his route between a couple of delivery vans to the yacht's gangplank.

'Definitely not!'

'Follow the prom along and round the harbour. See what takes your fancy. Remember what we're looking for…'

'Okay.'

'If it tips down, duck in one of those shelters, it won't last. This is a bit private. You've got your smart gold watch – see me back here at the *Ocean Drifter* in an hour.' Pax checked his Cyma. It was spot on eleven o'clock. '*Knock-knock!*' Mike shouted, as Pax turned to go. 'Ahoy, *Drifter* – any milk today?'

A bald and handsome figure appeared at the rail of the yacht. 'Pramod Advani,' the man said, holding out his hand for a welcoming shake with Mike. 'Come aboard, before you get wet.'

'Mike Symonds, Symonds's Systems,' Mike said.

'And the young man! The heavens are going to open any moment.' Mike looked round at Pax, hesitated. 'You told me he was coming. So what's secret from him? In a torrential downpour?'

The man was right, and Mike had been wrong. The sky was darkening like night, and a wind was whipping up. Strolling round the harbour wall wasn't going to be any holiday jaunt. Mike made his decision. 'He came to see the yachts,' he said, beckoning Pax to the gangplank, 'but if you're sure you don't mind him joining us…'

'Come!' the man hurried.

'Then please meet Pax Foster-Symonds. My heir.'

It was as if a bucket of iced water had been thrown into his face. *Heir! 'My heir'! Had he heard that right? Or was there some foreign word that sounded the same?*

He quickly found himself sitting on a deep-cushioned armchair beneath an awning, sucking Coca-Cola from frosted crystal that could slip through his numbed fingers any second. His brain was numbed, too, and his legs were as weak as the straw in his glass. *Heir!?* That meant owning everything when someone dies: which was for sons, or daughters, or grandchildren – definitely for family. But was Mike, who had no family any more, going to pass everything on to Pax – accounting for the new name he'd just given him, Foster-Symonds? A loud snort said he'd got to the bottom of the Coke. And his wits. *Mike's heir!? With his money, his house, his plane, his cars, his business? With the yacht he was going to buy – and probably an island as well!* Pax could no more take all that in than he could grasp the size of the universe.

Mr. Advani ordered clear plastic curtains to be closed around them to stop the rain coming in, and bossed a boy about, getting Mike's drink sorted to his own liking. 'One cube only, ice; and cold water in jug.' He repeated it fast in another language, which the boy understood. But while all this was going on, Mike sat looking out at the rain sweeping in across the harbour wall – and deliberately not at Pax. This was the way he did things at Sharpe End, and how he'd dropped his sudden surprise about Pax not going to Australia, staring out of the Cirrus as if he *hadn't* just turned the world upside down.

Pramod Advani sat himself on a swinging lounger. 'I'm sorry I didn't lay on good weather, but this will not last too long.' A streak of lightning flashed somewhere out of Pax's sight line, but the thunderclap from beyond the outer harbour wall told how quickly the storm was closing in. 'So...' The man raised his glass and looked across at Pax. 'You must think yourself a very fortunate young man.'

Pax felt the backs of his legs sweating against the cushions, his stomach rolling over. *Heir!* Yes, it *had* been the English word – a concept he still couldn't grasp.

'You knew about my family, didn't you?' Mike confirmed.

'I did. Yes. Very, very sad. According to the news reports, this is the...young fella...you found on the remote island?'

'Solitaire,' Mike said. 'We've got a strong bond, Pax and I. His folks went down with mine, on the *St. George*, and good folks they were, too: doctors fighting poverty and disease in darkest Africa.' He looked across at Pax, soft-eyed. 'But they say it's the good who die young...'

'Well, Symonds's Systems is a big empire,' Pramod Advani told Pax. 'Worldwide. But I'm sure we all want Mike to be its emperor for a very long time to come.'

'Absolutely!' Which sounded crass to Pax as he said it – but how *should* he sound? He just didn't know any more. He'd talked in his own way to the goats on Solitaire; he'd got used to dinner-table chat at Sharpe End; he'd even managed to sound a bit like 'family' to Jenny. Now how long before he sounded like the heir to a fortune – when all he really wanted in the world was to talk the way he'd once talked to Zuri?

'Well, I'm thinking we must let the weather look after itself and discuss our business, eh?' Pramod Advani turned away from Mike, and as if on cue he was handed by his boy a slim, leather-bound folder; while Mike took a smart little iPAQ PDA from his pocket.

Pax got up. He felt he ought to make the offer to go below – but Mike waved him to sit. 'You stay, old lad, now you're here. Look and learn, look and learn...' And Pax had the strong feeling they were words he'd said many times in the past to someone else. He looked at his watch, the sort of businesslike check Diana would have made.

'So...' Pramod Advani began.

He had to be the one doing the selling, Pax thought. The man was sitting forward in his seat, looking a lot more edgy than Mike, who was scratching his cheek with his iPAQ stylus.

'Well, what we have to offer you, sir, is our status. India has not signed the Ottawa Treaty. We are not bound by the impositions on everybody else, so in my city, in Nagpur – with a very skilled workforce, nimble fingers and good brains – we can make the components and assemble them, everything to your total satisfaction...'

Nagpur! That was the name of the place Diana had talked about. *The illegal place that wasn't illegal!*

Mike said nothing; listened.

'...With us you do not have to make this piece here, this item there, you are saving all the transport costs, and you are not having to disguise what you are doing...'

Disguise? Mike still said nothing – but Pax was leaning forward. What was all this about? Why should Mike have to disguise what he was doing? Was it to fool other makers of the same things? Or was it really something illegal? Mike's face gave nothing away, and there was definitely no look of guilt on it, either towards him or the other businessman: the odd blink was at sudden flashes of lightning.

'You have government contracts. Everything in the bigger way of what you make has certificates, is okayed by all the national signatories and the United Nations. Clean and legal, clean and legal. You are whiter than white.' The man smiled, and shook his bald head slightly. 'But with the troubles between my country and Pakistan, and with the Taliban troubles to the north, there is a very big market for APLs. And this we can satisfy for you, and we can deliver from Nagpur without any shipping problems whatsoever...'

Pramod Advani's voice tailed off – but not in reality: there in the stormy air he went on outlining his business proposition to Mike Symonds; but those three initials just uttered had silenced him in Pax's head. *APLs!* The abbreviation had hit the yacht like a thunderbolt, panging Pax's stomach – and he leaped up, demanding: *'APLs? Did you say APLs?'*

'I'm sorry, my young friend. So sorry. Jargon.' Pramod Advani looked upset at his sales flow being stalled. 'Mike will forgive me, but for meetings like this he will have to teach you the jargon...'

'I'll fill you in later, old lad, as we go on. But for now, we're talking about anti-personnel landmines, known as APLs in the trade. Okay? Sorry.' Mike was apologizing to them both, but in a totally unfazed way, crossing his legs and preparing to listen to the rest of Pramod Advani's pitch.

'*You sell landmines?*' A volley of storm raked across the harbour.

'Make and sell. I did – until Britain signed the Ottawa Treaty and put the kibosh on all that. But now, in India, which hasn't signed...' Mike's eyes had opened up with the prospect of a new business opportunity.

'But they...*kill*!'

'And they deter, young friend,' Mr. Advani said. 'In Afghanistan an area is left in such a way that the insurgents cannot ever return.'

Pax's heart was racing, and his head felt as if it were filled with helium – light enough to float away. He stared through blurred eyes at Mike, who came and went.

'Of course, it's only a small part of the business,' Mr. Advani was saying. 'We might, or we might not want to go against the spirit of Ottawa...'

Pax was gripping the back of his seat with both hands. His lungs had run short of oxygen, and his words came out in breathless squeaks and pants as he stared at Mike. 'What...else...do you make? Your...silicone sensors? What did you sell to the army at Castlemartin?'

Mike laughed, stood now as he saw the look on Pax's face. On his own face was reassurance, and explanation.

Pramod Advani dropped his hands to his sides until this interruption had ended. 'You've heard of "tanks"?' Mike asked. Pax could just about nod. 'So why are those lethal and powerful vehicles of war called "tanks"? Not very descriptive, eh? Poor specification, you might say.' He turned to include Pramod Advani, who might not have known, either. 'Because while they were being developed for the First World War, the government wanted to keep these strong, frightening weapons secret. So the factory in Lincoln that developed them code-named them "tanks" – after the water-container shape of the central structure. People outside thought they were making things for lofts. Ha!'

Now Pax knew where this was going, and he tried to take in a deep breath for what was about to come; but instead it was an inward sob, like crying.

'…Therefore to keep the general peace, old lad, we call our overall manufacturing business by the name of our central component – "silicone sensors"…'

'So…what…else…do you make?' Pax got out. And he couldn't believe how he suddenly felt, how he was staring across the deck of this yacht not at Mike, his dear friend, his new family, but at Michael Symonds OBE, for whom suddenly he could hardly hold down his disgust.

Mike was enumerating on his fingers. 'We make sensors

for fuel pumps and the domestic market at Milton Keynes, rocket components in Poland, parts for ballistic missiles in France, bomb fuses in Russia, and the silicone brains for them all are made in Peterborough. If people want a trigger to pull, we make it: which is what we test at Castlemartin,' he finished, proudly.

'You...make...*wars!*' Pax's mouth was dry, but he had the voice for outrage. 'You make sure the killing keeps going on!'

'Oh, come on, Pax, old lad.' Now Mike's face showed surprise, and a piercing directness came into his voice. 'I feed two thousand workers, and pay the Exchequer enough company tax to run a handful of your parents' hospitals...' He no longer sounded like Mike, the granddad; he was making his case as a hard-headed businessman. 'Don't be soft about war, my boy. War's always with us. Look anywhere in the world, read up on any period in the past. What's going on all the time, always has? What's the story of the human race? Eh? We went down Whitehall in the "duck" – and whose were all those statues? Soldiers! We went on the *Belfast*, which is berthed there for ever more. Why? As the nation's pride!' He dropped his voice a tone, like someone knowing where they were hitting. 'You washed up on Solitaire, and what was on your island paradise?'

'A weather station.' Pax got in a loud reply against a sudden downpour of rain.

'For what? For whom? Basically for the French military. NATO. Are the French so *très* kind as to monitor Indian Ocean weather for passing canoes?'

'Not the French,' said Pramod Advani, folding his arms.

'Right! For defence.' Pax injected his passion with some argument. 'To defend ourselves – that's okay. And if you shoot at me, I'll shoot at you back. I was ready to do something to you on Solitaire before you did something to me.' He stared into Mike's eyes: at that moment no one else on earth existed except Mike. 'But if you didn't have a weapon, and I didn't have a weapon, and no one had weapons, there wouldn't be the smallest fraction of the killing that goes on.'

Mike laughed, shaking his head. 'Man will always find a way. And while man is man, and he wants what he wants, someone is going to put food into his own family's belly by servicing those needs.' He opened his palms in a sort of gesture of peace between the two of them. 'So why shouldn't that be me? *Us?*'

'Mike is very correct.' Pramod Advani nodded himself into the dispute again. 'We provide both sides so we cannot lose... Right now in Gambellia, like Congo, like Sudan –

we sell to government and rebels both.' He stamped both his feet at the cleverness of it.

Pax's body was suddenly wrapped in the coldest, clearest anger, like a statue made of ice. He had to wait a long time, heaving for breath, before he could force anything out. 'So some of your parts were in the missiles that sank the *St. George*!'

Mike's head dropped.

'This is very likely, very likely,' Pramod Advani commiserated. 'But it is war. This is an unfortunate by-product – collateral damage...'

'And don't think I'm not so painfully aware of that, old lad,' Mike said, his eyes glistening.

But Pax was delivering hard fact, not giving sympathy to the man: '*Which means...you helped to kill Joseph – your own grandson!*'

'I try to tell myself...not—'

'And...you killed my mother and father.'

'Not directly, sir. Weapons are always in the hands of those who use them,' Pramod Advani said.

But, 'Yes, again – in the same roundabout way,' Mike admitted, his voice way down in his throat, hardly to be heard in the driving rain. 'There's a lot I owe you...'

'And...and...' Pax could barely get it out. For a second he thought he might never say it before his heart exploded.

'And an APL just like you make...killed my Zuri!'

Mike looked affronted. *'Made!'* he corrected. 'I obey Ottawa. Everything is legitimate, everything is sanctioned, everything I make carries export certification at the time of manufacture from the Department of Trade and Industry. Whatever I do – and even if I do business in India it'll be within the Indian law – my whole business is open and above board, and it will be the same for you when you inherit.'

Pax looked at the man he had come to love, who was standing there sweating as the humid downpour battered the plastic sheeting, rocked the yacht. Except, this was not the same person. This was not the kind, kid-like, generous, loveable Mike.

'I wish I'd never set eyes on you! I wish you'd never saved my life on Solitaire. I wish I'd never let you bring me to this filthy world you live in.' He drew a great, invective breath and shouted, *'I hate you, Mike Symonds!'* He had to get away from him – and on a sudden impulse he turned his back on the man, pushed apart the plastic curtain, climbed the rail of the yacht, and dived off through the teeming rain into the waters of Monaco Port. Whatever happened, wherever he was swept, he was not going to stay in the presence of Mike Symonds a second longer.

Chapter Twenty-Four

He hit the harbour water and swam a fast crawl to get away from the yacht, no thought of where he was going, what he was doing, what he was leaving. Nothing counted except getting away from that man who had helped to kill his parents. There might have been shouts behind him, there might have been clamour and a splash as Pramod Advani kicked off his shoes and dived into the harbour after him. But against the sound of the sea and the rumbling storm, Pax heard none of this. He looked ahead and saw the harbour wall, the only pause in his rhythm the waste of two good strokes as he pulled off his deck shoes – his whole intent to get out of sight and away for ever from Mike Symonds's world. He was fit, he was a good swimmer, and he was a survivor! He headed for the port entrance and swam out through it, hit at once by churning waters – a heavy swell pushing him east, to where he wouldn't be followed, any place where he wouldn't be seen.

While back at the *Ocean Drifter* Mike Symonds was pulling the defeated Pramod Advani up the ladder and shouting for the crew to lower the yacht's speedboat.

'Not outside the harbour mouth, Mike, not in such weather!'

'What is it?' Mike demanded as the speedboat was winched into the water.

'"Seafast". But Mike—'

'Keys?'

Pravod Advani threw them to him. 'It is very responsive, but take care, there have been problems with the fuel pipe.'

But Mike could hardly have heard him; he was already swinging himself down the ladder and stepping over into the speedboat. 'Get up some piping hot tea!' he shouted. 'My poor old lad's going to need it!' And after a quick look over the controls, he throttled the outboard Mariner into life, leaving a huge cough of black exhaust sitting on the water as he took off to zigzag across the harbour, marking his course with a resolute wake.

Pax's only thought had been getting away from Mike Symonds; but as he went with the high swell, a mantra was running in his head. *Not me – Mike Symonds! Not me – Mike Symonds! Not me – Mike Symonds!* Exhausted with the swim across the harbour, and buffeted by the angry waves, he could still force out the words that logic put into his head. *'Not me – Mike Symonds!'* Okay, he'd made a mistake. Yes, he'd run Zuri the wrong way – but it wasn't him who'd killed her. It was an APL that had exploded up and into her belly – made by the likes of Mike Symonds. *Hell,* a kid like him should be allowed to run the wrong way without killing someone. Zuri's death *wasn't* down to him – it was down to those APLs planted in the bush.

Which meant... The slap of the sea cleared his head as the sense of it came to him, the ultimate truth of his personal crisis. *Which meant...the guilt he'd felt wasn't his guilt at all.* The guilt he'd taken on was the guilt of people who made their money from war. The terrors in his head weren't his, they were *theirs.* 'Not me – Mike Symonds! Not me – Mike Symonds! Not me – Mike Symonds!' He struck for the shore.

But out beyond the safety of the harbour, getting back to land wasn't so easy: there was serious danger in this suddenly raging sea. He'd been in this peril before, in the storm on Solitaire – and that time he'd been lucky, but could he be that lucky again? The high-running waters were driving him towards the east, towards promenades being pounded by huge waves. How could he land there without being smashed against a concrete wall? Or else, how could he stay afloat offshore long enough for the seas to go down? He trod water, stared around him, and saw how far he'd come. And one thing was dead certain. In his exhausted state, there'd be no fighting the swell and going back to the harbour and Mike Symonds, not even to save his own life.

Pramod Advani stood at the stern of the *Ocean Drifter* and watched as Mike Symonds and the Seafast came back from a search of the harbour. He narrowed his eyes to stare at the sole occupant, and turned to command his boy, 'Leave tea. Bring Cognac.'

But Mike wasn't coming aboard. He stood at the wheel of the speedboat and shouted up through the heavy rain. 'He's not back here?' Pramod Advani shook his head. Mike looked all around him again. 'Well, he's not in the harbour. Little hothead must have swum outside the port.'

'But Mike, he won't survive outside. This sea's a killer. And that Seafast is not so tough, it's been cutting out...' As if to add strength to his words, giant waves were crashing in over the harbour wall, unsettling everything at their moorings. 'Send for coastguard!' Advani shouted to his staff. 'Send for *gendarmes de mer*!'

Mike wasn't listening, though – he was turning the speedboat about. 'I love that boy!' he yelled behind him – and threw himself into the bucket seat to head the Seafast for the harbour entrance.

What was that ahead? There on the brow of a high, lifting wave, Pax saw a yacht, caught out by the speed of the storm. Like him, it was outside the harbour, anchored about halfway to the shore, slewing at its chain fifty metres away. So if he could only make it...! *Could?* He *had* to make it! He had to! Even if it capsized it'd have enough buoyancy to give him something to cling to.

He tried to rest his body for a few more seconds, breathed deeply while he let two giant waves swell and run in beneath him; then on the third he kicked his legs, thrust his arms forward, and started swimming towards the anchored yacht, holding his rhythm, keeping himself across the run of the sea. But it was a bid that was draining everything from him, each throw of his arms ached to be the last, each kick of his legs sank lower in the water. He was still too far from the yacht, each stroke weaker than the one before…he wasn't going to make it…when, *what was that?* He suddenly saw its orange dinghy, still tethered but blown off like a kite by the surface wind. A lifeline. A last chance! He had to make a final mighty effort to get to that dinghy, any way he could. Sapped out, he was suddenly caught by a chop in the face from a maverick wave. He swallowed water, coughed, rasped, choked, went under and came up. In his exhaustion he could have let go of this terrible world; but in a weird flash of *I-have-been-here-before*, his mind overruled his body and found some last dregs of strength to swim for that dinghy – a last, desperate effort to get to something to hold him up.

And he made it. With arms like lead and cramp killing his right leg, he somehow got himself close enough to clutch at the dinghy and cling to a loop of lanyard – when another freak wave leaped sideways in and beneath him, and for a split second he was lifted level with the dipping rim. A last and lucky kick. He slid over the side to land face down in the half-filled dinghy, where he lay and let himself be tossed into the air and thrown sideways, clinging for sweet life to the lanyard, determined to hold on while the storm blew itself out. *Not me – Mike Symonds! Not me – Mike Symonds!*

*

Mike gripped hard at the wheel as the force of the sea tried to wrench it from his hands. He pushed the speedboat to its limit as he sped out from the shelter of the harbour to hit the tempestuous Mediterranean. His head shone wet, his linen trousers clung, his shoes were soggy, soaked by the spume off the waves. He tried to take on the heavy seas diagonally, running across them – because to head directly into a wave would send the boat somersaulting nose over stern, while to get smacked sideways would roll it over and over, and under. He couldn't sit for this – he stood at the pitching wheel, his eyes searching the water for a sign of the boy: for Pax, his adopted grandson and his heir. High on a crest, low in a trough, he dodged the full force of the waves and somehow kept the speedboat afloat. The boy hadn't been inside the harbour – and no one could swim outside it very far, not so quickly. So as he searched he shouted, steering east across the run of the waves – no way on earth could Pax not have come in this direction.

'Pax! Pax, old lad! My Pax!'

But the words were rammed back down his throat by gusts of wind – when he suddenly saw what he'd been looking for: a head, still afloat, the head of someone swimming.

'Pax! Thank God! I'm sorry! I'm sorry – and I'm coming!'

The sight held his eye for a crucial second too long and a surge came under the speedboat to lift it high on a crest, and send it skittering down its far side. But the boat stayed afloat – and there was the boy again, also cresting, also dropping into the next trough. With all his strength, Mike spun the wheel and steered for him – for Pax, for his boy.

'Hold on, old son! I'm here! Reach out!'

He took a stinging slap from a slice off the top of a whitecap, but he held on, he stayed afloat, and skilfully he brought the boat to where he could leave the wheel for a second and grab at Pax.

'Give us your hand! Here I am – *here*!'

But as a scud of current raced the boat fast – too fast – towards his boy, he suddenly saw what it was. No boy at all. No Pax – but a bobbing shipping lane marker. Mike groaned, swore, went to put the boat about to go on with his frantic search; but in his haste he had stalled the outboard motor, and all at once he had no power. Wet, slippery-fingered, he twisted the ignition key and the engine coughed – as a huge wave drenched over him. But he was holding the boat into it and he came out to twist and twist at the ignition key again. And nothing but *cough,*

cough, cough. There was fuel, he could see there was fuel – but no matter what he did, however hard he tried, it wasn't getting through to the motor.

Another wave lifted and twisted the dead speedboat – wallowing in the scudding trough before the next, inevitable wave came down on it, Mike cursing at the system's failure to give him power. And a lightning flash froze him there, a man standing soldierly at the helm – shouting out into the storm.

'*Pax! Pax! Come back to me!*'

All strength drained, just alive, Pax looked around at the calming sea. Between him and the harbour wall the debris of a white boat shone in the scattered sun – something less buoyant than his dinghy hadn't been so lucky. But he dismissed all that, because the sloshing water and the smell of rubber here in the dinghy was bringing things back to him – being in that other dinghy with the swirl and the suck as the ship went down, the crying out, the bodies – and suddenly in his head he could hear again the voice of his mother who hadn't made it, crying up from the water.

'*Pax Dieu. Pax Dieu.* The peace of God...'

He lifted himself, well aware in Mediterranean daylight that she wouldn't be here at the Port of Monaco, but he looked into the water all the same, just as he had that night, when he had grabbed at her, but seen her slip beneath the waves. His mother had gone. Now, as the storm slowly moved away and the sun began to reclaim the sky, the reality of his mother's tragic fate hit him again – and fixed itself into his mind. She had lived trying to help the crippled and the wounded, and she had died at the hands of people like Mike Symonds who had done the crippling. And wasn't that a more precious piece of life's jigsaw to hold in one's hand than strolling along the front at Monte Carlo on the lookout for an ocean-going yacht to buy?

Pax was in shock. Lying there in the dinghy, holding tight to the lanyard with both hands, he stared at the sky. Mike had been good to him, and kind, and – for whatever reason – he had loved him. With a tight throat, Pax remembered the adventure park as if it had happened in some other life – and the 'duck', and the Cirrus prop, and all the meals and silly games and shared videos and fast drives. He thought of the clothes he'd been bought, the pocket money he'd been given – and how very special he'd felt at Sharpe End. But the businessman who changed after dinner from his London suit into slacks and sweatshirt so he could feed the goats with Pax and Mary, and balloon a football over the house – that lovely man had been someone else all the time. Pax had loved a monster – with whom he wanted nothing more to do, not the Mike Symonds who was on that yacht. It was a wrenching loss to bear; but now he could mourn someone else, someone who had come back to him, and who had drowned again before his eyes. His mother's last words came into his head once more: *Pax Dieu* – God's peace. And now he heard the voice of his father, who had gone God-knew-where: *You did nothing wrong, Pete – it was the war criminals who laid the minefields, and the arms makers who made the dirty devices...* Now Pax could mourn him, too. And, giving the sea ten minutes to calm some more before he swam to land, he lay and thought of Solitaire. He pictured his island before Mike had come: the discoveries he'd made, the skills he'd learned, the friendship with the female goats, the swims in Rainbow Cove, the cool fresh water of the spring, the darting flame birds in the trees. Well, with the terrors gone, he would have all that on Solitaire – one day. He made himself that promise – however long it might take to keep. Once he was on his own again, he would go back.

And with those resolute thoughts he slipped over the dinghy's side and, in the relative calm after the storm, he swam for the shore.

*

No one took much notice of a barefoot boy in dripping wet shirt and shorts walking along the Boulevard Louis II, heading west towards the border and France. There was purpose in his stride, and determination in his heart – to get away from this place. And the sooner he did this now the better, before a search of the sea and the coastline was carried out on Mike Symonds's orders. He walked away from the sounds of the ocean and strode inland up the Rue du Portier, understanding better with each step just what he was going to do. Okay, Solitaire again one day – but flying south to land at Nice airport he had seen how big France was, how vast the open spaces, and how easy it would be for a guy like him to live a life of his own. Which he was good at. Solitaire had proved that. So – as he walked he came to a decision, an adventurous choice, but firming up with every step. In the summer he would live rough in the open countryside of the south of France, the way he was used to living. There were fruits and plants to eat, streams to drink from, beaches to sleep on, and when he got himself out into the woods and fields of France there'd be grapes and olives, and villages where he could chop wood: a drink of water and a piece of bread wouldn't be a fortune to pay him, would it? And when winter came he would hop a ship, and get himself across the Mediterranean to North Africa. And from what he'd seen on television, who would go looking for a missing boy there? He would be free, himself, his own man. He could do jobs in the markets and the ports, and, if need be, he could beg. But never more would he trust anyone who showed great love for his own family, and cared nothing for the rest of mankind.

He walked on, not hungry yet but on the lookout for fresh water. He had nothing on him; no money, no ID – his passport was back at the Hôtel de Paris. But he'd lived without one before and he'd do so again – super-confident of how well he'd get on.

Above all, he would force everything about Mike Symonds out of his mind – like going into a new dissociative fugue.

In that mood, as he strode the road that led to his freedom, two people in colourful robes came towards him from the opposite direction, heading for the sea. They swung along looking like father and son, the way Mike and Pax had swung along themselves, walking in step, talking together. One was a tall black man in a robe, carrying a felt-covered board on which hung bangles and watches, and over his arm was more colourful cloth. Beach traders.

But – *watches!* Pax took a quick look at his Cyma, stared at it hard. His father never took it on rugged trips, but Pax had just swum with it in the waters of the Mediterranean. And his chest lifted as he saw that it was waterproof and still working; showing the time as twelve o'clock.

The boy gave Pax a smile as he passed. He was small, eager eyed, carrying his own heavy leather satchel of things to sell. And Pax's stomach twinged as some spark in the boy's eyes reminded him of Zuri's little brother – which suddenly stopped him in a new confusion. Why did that have to happen? He was set, he knew where he was going – why did he have to be brought down by a flash of memory? It had hit him hard – and it sank him there to the pavement, crouching and holding his head in his hands as the pair walked silently by: the man and the boy each on two firm legs. He looked between his fingers at the smart apartment blocks across the road, the marble and glass still glistening from the storm, but his mind was filled with Gambellian memories of poverty and mutilation. Sky-high millionaires here, and ground-shuffling victims there. He gave a loud groan at the harshness of the world. Them, and us. Oh God, this was definitely a world to get away from.

Except – hang on! He straightened his back. He couldn't just shut out the past like that – not on purpose. That boy's face, that memory, they'd told him that his mind couldn't simply blank everything from before, the way his illness had. Just looking down at his drying, expensive clothes bore that out: and as an apartment window opened opposite, a reflection of the sun suddenly shone at Pax a crucial clarity, gave him a glimpse of a different answer, or part of one. Yes! He shuffled as he crouched, there on the pavement. An hour ago, the Monaco millionaires who lived in these apartments hadn't been *them,* they'd been *us* – Mike Symonds was no different from these other rich people; and he and Mike had then been good friends. It was weird, it was confusing, it was disloyal and it made no sense – but crouching in that uncomfortable position, a strong yearning for some other plan started hollowing into him; an ache in the stomach and in the throat. A huge wish filled him: to have Mike back as the person he'd seemed before that nightmare discovery on the *Ocean Drifter.* Which Pax knew he should kick out of his head – except, *as an heir to a fortune, couldn't he make some difference himself?*

Hell! It was totally muddled. He sat back against a low wall and sucked at his knees like a street kid having a rest; and as the sun steamed the wet from the Monte Carlo roofs, some glimmer of this other plan began to grow in his head. It was crazy, it wouldn't work – and he'd have to keep telling himself why he was doing it, apologize to his dead mum and dad and Zuri, but keep in front of him his overriding reason. *That this was for the greater good.* And, yes – it had to be worth a try! *He would go to Mike and tell him that if he loved him, if he wanted to stay friends with him, if he truly wanted Pax to be his heir, he had a choice to make. He either carried on as he was, making and selling weapons systems, or he had to close his arms factories around the world and turn his production lines to something good for mankind: things that would make a difference to the lives of the Zuris and their grandmothers and their little brothers in poor countries.* As well as pumping petrol to engines, surely there were digital devices for pumping fresh water to clean tanks, *real* tanks. There had to be all sorts of life-saving things Mike's silicone sensors could trigger.

And for a start, instead of buying an ocean-going yacht and an island, Mike could pay for the removal of all the APLs in Gambellia.

Blackmail? Yes! *Bad?* No!

'*Casse-toi!*' A jangly-braceleted woman was leaning over a balcony and shouting across the road at him, waving her arms, clearing him from her privileged view. '*Vagabond!*'

Pax looked up at her, got to his feet, and with a strong sense of doing absolutely the right thing, he turned to face the way he'd come and headed back towards the Port of Monaco. Okay, Mike could say 'no': a hundred to one he would; but Pax must at least give him the chance to be a decent man – and his friend again…

The activity at the harbour had drawn a small crowd. The blue flashing police van and the French *SAMU* ambulance were parked at the nearest access to the *Ocean Drifter* as Pax came to it, filtering his way through the onlookers, ready with his apology for causing so much concern by diving into the sea. But this would be his only apology. He would definitely not apologize for shouting at Mike the way he had, nor for seeing the world the same way as his mother and father had. He would thank Mike Symonds for the love he'd shown him, he'd tell him how grateful he would always be to have shared the good times they'd had together – and, most of all, he would thank him for saving his life on Solitaire. Then he would lay down his conditions for being an heir. *Pax Dieu!* Mike would have to take the path of peace.

He swallowed as he made his way through to the yacht, which was frantically busy. The plastic curtains had been pulled aside and Pramod Advani was on the deck talking to a gendarme, while pushing through the crowd were two ambulance men carrying an empty stretcher towards the *Ocean Drifter*. Overhead a small helicopter flew in from the west and began circling the harbour.

Pax stopped when he heard Mr. Advani giving some sort of statement to the gendarme. He crept nearer to the gangplank to find out what was going on.

'*La vedette* – speedboat, yes?' Pramod Advani was saying. The gendarme was staring into his face. 'Empty. *Vide! Chavirée!* Capsized. Broken. Upside down.' The arms dealer showed what he meant with his rolling arms. 'Faulty fuel pump – I tried to tell him.'

'*Et le pilote?* Driver?' the gendarme was asking. '*L'Anglais…*'

'Dead. A body is seen. The helicopter searches.' Pramod Advani waved at the sky.

'*Le garçon – ou l'homme?*'

Advani shrugged his shoulders.

Pax stopped, stunned. Mike was dead. Died trying to find him! He tasted the dryness of his open mouth as he backed off the gangplank into the crowd, bent his knees to be out of anyone's eyeline. *Mike had been killed in the rough sea when his power failed. When a fuel pump – and a sensor – had let him down!*

Like some foraging creature, the cruel grab of loss suddenly burrowed deep inside him: that final shock that someone you had loved will never be with you again, the voice never heard, the behaviour never needing to be excused, or changed, or enjoyed. Mike Symonds was dead: a single-minded arms manufacturer who would not be missed by the world. And a loving grandfather who would: a brave man who had died trying again to save him.

Pax backed further away, once more unable to unthread from his tangled thinking just how he felt. Until he looked down at the watch on his wrist, as if to fix the time of death. And suddenly he put his hand on it, stroked it, thinking of whose wrist had once worn it – this Cyma that through everything was ticking on, ticking on, like his father's and his mother's spirit, working on and on and on through all sorts of dangers and adversity.

And now that spirit was surging inside him, too. Pax, with options closed to left and right, was looking at the only other option in the world. He wouldn't be Mike Symonds's heir any more – he was sure no will had been changed, Mike had come out with it on the yacht as if the idea had only just firmed up in his mind. Which meant that Pax Foster would never have the chance to do the things he'd like to do with those 'silicone sensors'. He also knew that Solitaire had always really been a dream, a fantasy that could never come true again – especially now he knew who he was. But there was this something else that was right for him, wasn't there? *Going back to his own real family's business!* Yes, there was another dream to live – which he would start living right here and now – by going back to the hotel and telephoning Diana Lucky, and telling her what had happened. He would arrange to get taken home – to Sharpe End – but for only as long as it took to sort himself with Aunt Jen. He had money; he had a house in South Africa, and his parents would have left him their savings. And he was coming up to an age when he could stand on his own two feet as a man – so there were tons of ways of doing what he wanted.

Which, whatever happened for a year or so in between, wherever he had to live, would be to keep his carving on his shelf, and work hard at his books, and train to be a medic like his parents.

He was going to give his life to the same people to which they had given theirs: people like his precious Zuri…

And with his mind now very clear he turned away from the sea. 'That's it, then!' he said aloud.

Author's Note

A matter of fact: The Îles Éparses (Scattered Islands) are situated around Madagascar in the Indian Ocean, and form part of the French Southern Territories. There are three individual coral islands, Europa, Juan de Nova and Tromelin; an archipelago known as the Glorioso Islands (consisting of two smaller coral islands, Île Glorieuse and Île du Lys, and a handful of rock islets); and finally, Bassas da India, an atoll, or ring-shaped reef formed of coral.

Bassas da India rests on top of a long-extinct, submerged volcano and has a shallow lagoon. The Glorioso Islands are lush in vegetation and are also surrounded by an extensive reef system. Europa, Juan de Nova and Tromelin are all important wildlife sanctuaries for seabirds and sea turtles. Juan de Nova is also famous for its guano, an accumulation of seabird droppings that serves as an extremely effective and lucrative fertilizer or gunpowder ingredient. The famous eighteenth-century Indian Ocean pirate, Olivier Levasseur, is also said to have used Juan de Nova as a treasure store.

All of the islands lie in the path of tropical cyclones and Bassas da India and Juan de Nova have been the site of numerous shipwrecks. The wreck of the British ship SS *Tottenham* can still be found on the southern reef of Juan de Nova, where it ran aground in 1911. Bassas da India is uninhabitable, as it becomes totally submerged during high tide for up to three hours, thereby also making it a significant hazard for passing ships.

In fact, nobody lives permanently on these islands. They are only visited by researchers and scientists studying the local nature and weather, and by the military. Except for Bassas da India, the islands each have their own airstrip, and all support weather stations, which are overseen by French troops from Réunion, garrisoned on Europa, Île Glorieuse and Juan de Nova. The climate of Tromelin makes it especially important for forecasting local cyclones in the western Indian Ocean.

In the 1860s, French colonists attempted to settle in Europa. Although they later disappeared, the goats they brought with them have survived, with approximately three hundred still living on the island to this day. In the early part of the twentieth century, another small colony was also established on Europa and the tombs of these settlers can still be found there.

The granite island of Solitaire is an imaginary addition to the Îles Éparses.

B.A.

BERNARD ASHLEY spent time in the RAF before training to be a teacher, specializing in drama. He went on to work as a head teacher for thirty years and now writes full time. His first novel, *The Trouble with Donovan Croft*, won the 'Other' Award. Since then he has been shortlisted for the Carnegie Medal three times, as well as the Guardian Children's Fiction Prize.

Bernard loves the theatre and has also written for the stage and for television. The children's TV series *Dodgem*, which he adapted from his own novel, won the Royal Television Society Award for best children's entertainment programme in 1993.

Bernard is married with three sons and four grandchildren and lives in Charlton, south-east London.

Also by Bernard Ashley

SMOKE SCREEN

Ellie hates leaving behind her friends, but the worst thing about moving to a pub by the canal is that the dark, swirling waters bring back traumatic memories. And Ellie's troubles only grow when she discovers the shady dealings that take place in the Regent's Arms on Friday nights.

There is somebody who could expose the truth – if only she could escape the evil gang that holds her captive.

Smokescreen is an electrifying thriller that twists and turns through the shadowy underworld of a dangerous trade.

ISBN 9780746067918

Praise for Smokescreen

"An extraordinarily powerful story; Bernard Ashley at his commanding best."   *The Guardian*

"A powerful and thought-provoking read which pulls no punches."   *Books for Keeps*

"Insightful and topical... Gripping stuff."

Publishing News

"A tense and gripping novel, skilfully plotted and convincing."   *School Librarian*

"An electrifying thriller."   *Lovereading4kids.co.uk*

"An extremely good read."   *Write Away*

"A thought-provoking read."   *Bookfest Ireland*

Tim Wynne-Jones

THE BOY IN THE BURNING HOUSE

Ruth Rose is the wild and troubled stepdaughter of the local preacher, Father Fisher. She thinks she knows the truth behind the sudden disappearance of Jim Hawkins's father, but Jim doesn't want to believe her crazy theories – he'd rather carry on rebuilding his life in peace. Eventually, Ruth Rose's burning conviction sparks in Jim an equally fierce determination to root out the truth, no matter how painful. And when they start to uncover a web of guilt and deceit, he realizes just how dangerous Father Fisher is.

"This classy teenage thriller really gets the heart pumping... Phew – it's hot!" *The Funday Times*

Shortlisted for the Guardian Children's Fiction Prize

ISBN 9780746064818

For more gripping reads
log on to
www.fiction.usborne.com

Tim Wynne-Jones

THE SURVIVAL GAME

Burl can't take any more bruises from his bullying father, so one day he runs away with just a penknife and a fishing lure in his pocket. Despite his survival skills, Burl knows he won't last long in the frozen Canadian wilderness, so he is filled with hope when he stumbles across Ghost Lake, and a secret that could save him.

But his father is after him and Burl is dragged back into his dangerous games...

"Gripping – gut-churningly exciting in fact." *Time Out*

Winner of the Canada Council Governor General's Literary Award

ISBN 9780746068410

Tim Wynne-Jones

Dec hasn't seen his mother for six years. His memories of her lie shrouded in dust, preserved in their old family home which now stands empty. Dec senses that his father is harbouring a secret, but he can't prove anything. Then he makes a horrific discovery, and suddenly the house is alive with ghosts of the past.

Could Dec now learn the elusive truth about his family?

"So intriguing you'll want to read it all at once."

Book Club

**Shortlisted for the Grampian Children's Book Award
and the Guardian Children's Fiction Prize**

ISBN 9780746078785